LARYSA DENYSENKO

THE SARABANDE OF SARA'S BAND

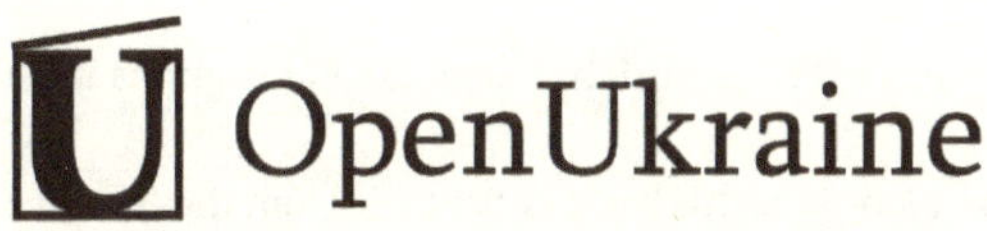

OpenUkraine

Arseniy Yatsenyuk Foundation

SARABANDE OF SARA'S BAND

by Larysa Denysenko

The translation was made possible thanks
to the financial assistance of
Arseniy Yatseniuk "Open Ukraine" Foundation

First published in Ukrainian as
"Сарабанда банди Сари" in 2008 by Nora Druk

Translated by Michael M. Naydan
and Svitlana Bednazh

LARYSA DENYSENKO

THE SARABANDE OF SARA'S BAND

TRANSLATED FROM THE UKRAINIAN
BY MICHAEL M. NAYDAN AND SVITLANA BEDNAZH

GLAGOSLAV PUBLICATIONS

CONTENTS

A NOTE ON LARYSA DENYSENKO

Of Lithuanian and Greek extraction, Larysa Denysenko was born in Kyiv, Ukraine in 1973. Denysenko wears a number of hats among her professions, including those of lawyer, novelist, literary and art critic, telejournalist, screenwriter, model and writer for glossy women's magazines, and columnist. Originally Russian speaking, she mastered the Ukrainian language at the age of 23 when she began to work in the Ukrainian Ministry of Justice. She holds a degree in law from the Taras Shevchenko Kyiv National University and has studied at The Central European University in Prague and in the Ministry of Justice in The Netherlands. She currently lives in Kyiv and practices law, dealing largely with issues of corruption, the death penalty, and children's rights. She also was one of the authors and hosts of the culturological television program Document+ on the Studio 1+1 channel and well as on the 1+1 International channel from 2006-2010. Her novels include *Toys Made of Flesh and Blood (2003)*, *The Coffee Taste of Cinnamon (2005)*, *A Corporation of Idiots (2005)*, *Dances in Masks (2006)*, *24:33:42 (2007)*, *Mistaken Imitations or Life according to the Timetable of Murderers (2007)*, and *The Sarabande of Sara's Band (2008)*. She also has published three children's books and five other collections on cultural and literary topics. Her first novel won the 2002 Coronation of the Word Grand Prize.

Denysenko's *Sarabande of Sara's Band* is largely a dialogic novel with a polyphony of voices that conveys most of the action through the rapidfire interactions of the characters in one-on-one situations or in small groups of family, extended family, and friends. Most of that interaction revolves around the novel's male protagonist Pavlo Dudnyk, from whose point of view (but from varying perspectives) the entire story unfolds. After a divorce, Pavlo moves in with his schoolhood friend Sara Polonska, who used to mock him in school with the nickname "Underbutt." What he doesn't realize at first when he moves in with her is that he has also "married" into her extended family, Sara's band of Polonskys, with their myriad quirks and peculiar behavior. Pavlo, too, has his own band of mildly dysfunctional friends with their own issues. The novel presents a number of small slices of Pavlo's life, lively repartee, and, sometimes, silly situations, such as when Pavlo and his best friend's wife Eva discuss their first sexual encounters as teenagers. The novel is also filled with a great amount of word play and humor, which make it a challenge to translate. It gives the reader a good deal of insight into aspects of the everyday lives, loves and mores of the current generation of urban intellectual Ukrainians.

We have decided to maintain Denysenko's punctuation for the most part in the translation. She tends to use periods instead of commas after quoted speech, and her choice to do that at times creates a rapid pace in the text.

I am most grateful to my co-translator Svitlana Bednazh for her expert emendations and thoroughness in editing my drafts of the translation. It is significantly better as a result of her efforts. Many thanks also to translation studies specialist Alla Perminova for assisting me in resolving many sticky wickets in the translation, particularly in the areas of current slang and surzhyk expressions, the latter of which is a street idiom and a mishmash of

Ukrainian and Russian. I, of course, am responsible for any errors.

> – Michael M. Naydan
> *Woskob Family Professor of*
> *Ukrainian Studies*
> *The Pennsyvlania State University*

CHAPTER I

At the very least about a perfect morning, imperfect marriages, former classmates, and a family crypt.

When I look at my coffee maker in the morning, it seems like I'm an oil tycoon. There it is – my black gold, at first slowly, and then very quickly, it fills the glass pot. It would be interesting to know if the freshly baked tycoons taste their oil? Or whether it tastes good for them if you weigh its value? It tastes good to me.

Every morning I do things precisely this way. At first I breathe in the coffee aroma, then I take my first sip and place the cup on the table. I open up the immense window that goes from the floor to the ceiling a little bit, I light up a cigarette, and then I return to the coffee. It's not as hot. Only after that can I make myself a few bite-size sandwiches. When my morning starts in a different way, that means just one thing: I have serious life changes going on or problems.

I spend about an hour in my kitchen every morning, sometimes even more. At that time I manage to drink up several cups of coffee, read the newspaper or a chapter of a book, drink a glass of juice, if I haven't forgotten to buy it, eat several bite -size cheese sandwiches, and if I have inspiration – make and eat an omelet.

I often turn on the television with the intention of hearing something interesting or useful, but something like that happens quite rarely. That is, I turn on the TV nearly every morning, but I heard something interesting or useful just three months ago – that was marked on a sticky on my refrigerator. I note everything that strikes me. That day on the morning news they were talking about people feeding a small whale. I like whales. I like them so much that I'm sure I wouldn't be opposed to keeping a small whale at home, but in as much as that's impossible, I don't have any pets at home. It's likely I like them so much because they're like fountains, and I really like fountains. Once I even used to collect pictures of them, but then something happened and I stopped collecting them.

My kitchen isn't a kitchen – that's what my mother thinks, taking into consideration the kitchen of that apartment, in which my childhood flashed past and in which right now the old age of my parents live. In my kitchen you can easily have a party for ten people, it's a large dining area. Besides the usual kitchen furniture, there's a couch here, two comfortable wide armchairs, a table, and even an old German upright "R. Yors & Kallmann" piano. It's black, shiny, and adorned with two candelabras.

It reminds me of a family crypt. You get the impression that his honor Judge R. Yors and the well-known author of the operetta Kallmann found their eternal repose right here.

On this crypt there is even a family coat of arms, which looks like: an elephant, an Indian Raja gazing at the sky, a UFO, or a Soviet satellite. The upright piano is an inheritance of my former wife. Neither I nor she knows how to play it. Usually, one of our mutual friends played it (most often a canine waltz). But nearly everyone still argued over why this upright piano had a third pedal. I never took part in these arguments, in as much as I didn't know why the piano had a first or second pedal, not to speak already about the third one.

My wife's father, in fact, handed down this piano to me personally. He used to treat my wife less carefully, perhaps because she was younger than the piano and not as expensive. When we got divorced, my wife asked if I wouldn't object to the piano for the time being staying at my place. I categorically objected, but it remained here anyway. My wife was a lawyer, and as it's well known, it's impossible to frighten lawyers with objections.

I just had turned twenty-one when we got married. My wife and I were the same age and former classmates. Between the time that you're sitting at the same desk, and the time you fall a sleep in the same bed, it's not a big difference. That's how it seemed to me. I think I simply just didn't really think about it, but gave preference to a person, whose hand I felt warmly all ten years of school. Physical warmth is closer for a child than the spiritual. The need for the spiritual is formed later.

In school I was a cleverer student than she. I can't name a subject I couldn't handle. She was a satisfactory student, but she was very active. Already in the seventh grade they entrusted her to be in charge of the lessons on peaceful Soviet society,[*] to participate in all the school and extracurricular representative activities, and to be the taskmaster for the others. I see her on stage – purposeful, sure of herself, a blonde with smoothly coiffed hair, not a kilo of excess weight, and without any hesitation. A straight, gray skirt, a cream-colored blouse, skin-colored tights, black pumps, fresh water pearls on her neck.

It's interesting that even back in school I understood that Inna, that's her name, could completely be the helmsman of my life. The question of choice for me has always been the most complicated. I couldn't calmly decide even simple things – I wavered, exhausted myself with doubts. I often

....

[*] These were propaganda lessons conducted on September 1 on the first day of the school term about the "peace-loving democratic peoples of the USSR" vs. the bourgeois decadent warmongering west.

　　　　　　　　　　　　　　　　　　　LARYSA DENYSENKO

fell asleep and woke up with one and the same brain signal, from which my stomach, hands and eyes became moist: "And if suddenly nothing turns out?" Inna knew what needed to be done and in which order. To every one of my questions "And if suddenly nothing turns out?", she answered so sincerely "why shouldn't it?" that I instantly calmed down. With her knack, she even charmed my parents, who are quite solitary and childish people.

Of course, after completing school, my life without Inna began. Not because I wished for that. It's just that she was no longer sitting next to me. She went to study law, and I – geography– at the university. It turned out that we ended up waking up in the same bed – she wanted that. But this differed little from the process of copying homework. The same kind of help at school. I – would give, and she – accepted, as was fitting. Later one of my friends would say, that in this way "your typical women's psychology was formed." However, then it seemed to me that my post-school life was without Inna. In truth, all my important life situations were not resolved without consultations with her. But somehow she asked, why don't we get married, since we understand one another so well and have been with each other for so long? I accepted this question of hers as an inevitable decision.

Our marriage was childless. Inna wanted one, but just couldn't get pregnant. Before we received the results of tests, she blamed me for everything. "Active spermatozoa rush to meet ovules, like joyous dogs that flap their tails! But your spermatozoa are somnambulist dogs, who don't flap their tails, they're ill."

After this observation of hers, for a long time I couldn't come. I couldn't externally release an insatiable flock of feeble dogs. Then it turned out it was not me who was at fault for us being childless. This certainly became the beginning of the extinction of our marriage. She wasn't able to forgive me for my joyous dogs that flap their tails.

"You would have gotten divorced anyway, because you finally began to long for independence," one of my friends said. He was right. I became a successful correspondent and analyst. Then I was working for a well-known travel agency. I prepared materials for their site, pamphlets, analytical notes regarding places for vacations and active tourism. All the leading publications that needed articles on travel trips, the customs of faraway lands, and the behavior of animals, began to publish me. I was able to write about all of that brilliantly.

Despite my school and university successes, which did not augment any of my confidence, my career and creative victories added a certain unknown ingredient to my dough. A different person began to be kneaded out of me. Unaware of this myself, I learned to make decisions. I sold my one-room apartment in the center of town that I had received from my grandmother, took out credit, and acquired a contemporary three-room apartment. With this, certainly, I really surprised Inna's father. He looked at me as though I were Achilles, who had made a shield and a sword from his heel, or stepped on the throat of my enemy with it. This irritated Inna. Probably, this is the way a person feels, who, her entire life, has driven a horse, until later a lord jumps out of the carriage, who has been pampering himself on pillows, and takes the reins in his hands. Such treachery! I understood everything, but I couldn't do anything – her persistent activity and excessive pressure also began to irritate me. "Weigh the fact that the double letters of a name add a sense of purpose from birth to a person. This is like the pecking of a beak – until it nails the unfortunate bug, it will keep pecking. You had very few chances for success with her." That's what my friend Tymofiy said about Inna. He wasn't a psychologist, but always expressed himself with a knowledge of the matter.

Seven years of marriage. I can't believe we lived so many years together. How many times I said "hello" to her, how many times she wished me good night, and how many times there was "thank you, please, I don't understand you, sorry, I also had that in mind, stop that, wait, that's disgusting, don't get worked up over such little things, where's my charger, what should I do with this, that's not my fault, and who's supposed to take care of this, for the third day we don't have freshener in the bathroom, shut your beak, where are we going on vacation, who's going to finish the borsht, did you invite Tanya, it's your fault for everything, and I warned you, you should have listened to your parents, why did you need that, you'll never understand this, you're at home, tea or coffee, an omelet or salad" — thousands, tens of thousands, or maybe hundreds? And how many kisses there were, spermatozoa – those that flapped their tails and those that didn't? How many vowels and consonants of our married interactions? Thou-sands! But we weren't there. Maybe, because, we had never lived together. It's painful to part at the time when "she" and "you" have managed to turn into "we," at least in part. That was not our case. It seemed to me that our marriage – was "she." When "I" was born, just like for any child growing up, I wanted independence. And I got it. Right now I'm thirty-two. I got used to living like "me," and I really liked that – living like "me!" Despite that, from time to time in my life a "she" appeared, but my life hasn't turned into a "we."

Until I Met Sara

I went to the wardrobe, opened it, and for a long time looked at a sundress. I grabbed the hem of it and put it next to my face. A piece of tiny-petaled azure silk. This was Sara. Sara was in the kitchen. In the kitchen she was a teacup with the image of a rainbow on it, and also with four brown coffee cups, an orange plate with claret red chrysanthemums, and an open bottle of Martini & Rossi. There she was a ceramic tray with dry fruits. There she was a carton of milk and a box of "Start" oat and fruit cereal. Sara smiled while I was champing on the "Start," like pastry, washing it down with coffee. She never did it that way.

Sara was in the bathroom. There she was a means for caring for curly hair. A toothbrush. Almond oil. A comb and a hair dryer. I opened up the almond oil, sullied my nose with it, began to smile. That is the scent of my happiness now. In my bedroom Sara was a silk nightshirt, left on a chair by the bed; a silver frame with a family picture on the windowsill in the accompaniment of azaleas, similar to a medley of southern American girls in multi-colored hats; a straw basket, where from now on, my and her clean socks lived, our running shorts, her stockings, her nylon underwear; a thin hair band with small gold stones, which turned Sara into an Eastern princess, and which today like a golden-toothed smile lay on a bedside table. Sara's heart lived in my stomach, I sensed it every moment.

When I caught sight of Sara (and this happened during a group tour of travel agency managers and travel writers to Prague), I didn't recognize her. It's true, I haven't at all managed to think anything about a slender woman with beautiful hair and a splendid bust, but here Sara Polonska recognized me. "Hi, Underbutt," she greeted me. And she laughed her awful laugh. "I never thought I'd be meeting you at nearly all the geo-tour sites. You spoiled, delicate butt, you've somehow managed to sit down on several chairs! Hi, old man, how long since we've seen each other!?"

Just the word "Underbutt" helped me figure out who this stranger was. Because only one insidious being ever called me "Underbutt" – Sara Polonska, my former classmate. Fat, curly-haired Sara, who looked like a dirty, disheveled ewe. And she called me that because during our studies at the university I used to swim and often tucked a towel under my rear end during class. I was thin, and it was more comfortable for me that way: it's painful to have bones leaning propped against the wood, if, of course they're living bones. Sara, who sat next to me on the left across from the aisle, was the first to notice my habit. She took an interest, what I was stuffing in there? I don't know why I told the truth back then. After that I became several nicknames richer: "spoiled butt, "Underbutt," and "not-on -that-towel."

I couldn't stand Sara Polonska. Even in the pre-Underbutt period she used to annoy me. That happened to me from time to time. For example, I hated my mother's curling iron. Two times I even tried to get rid of it. Even though I didn't use it and should have been indifferent to it or at least more tolerant. But – no.

I wanted it to disappear, my mood was ruined each time I saw it in the bathroom where it hung on a common wire hook. One time I said to the curling iron: "I'll fix you, you devil's plague." I remember that till this day.

I didn't use Sara Polonska either, but I wanted her to disappear. Those eternal wide velvet slacks of hers. Always brightly colored, from which her rump seemed even bigger. And those shaggy strands. Her wide face, and on it a small nose, as though she had stolen it from someone. Her eyelashes were so thick, as though someone had cut paper to make a beard for a paper man. Add to that she was extremely stacked. One time in the women's bathroom she tried to put two glasses of water on her breasts and hold them up, but they spilled. Ha-ha-ha! In school I was also interested in knowing if you can hold up a cup on your erect member. But I didn't actually try to check if that were possible, till now I don't know if you can or can't. Let someone else do that. If Polonska was a guy, maybe she would have checked it out then. It seemed, a grown-up woman, almost a qualified professional, but a dipshit is still a dipshit.

I personally was convinced that this was just an unsuccessful attempt, because Sara Polonska with her huge breasts could hold up two glasses of water on each one, and on her butt she'd be able to balance a two-liter jug. I still remember her black coat-mantle. We called it "the bat." Under that coat you could easily hide about ten or so Chinese from the firm arm of the law. Add to that the fact that she laughed so harshly, that it seemed like she would squash you with that laugh, the way a boot crushes a worm in the rain. And at one party, celebrating the Day of the Department, I saw Sara Polonska puke out bits of pizza and salad at her feet, after which she calmly continued to dance in that puke. Just as I became conscious of what was flying out from under her energetic, powerful feet, I ran to the bathroom to do what she had done, without interrupting the dancing.

And I still remember that she was married, and her husband was a military guy. I recall one time he was waiting for her by the university – a harsh figure in a uniform next to a red-colored Moskvich car. Maybe, because of the color of his car and the uniform, we called him "Fireman." In general I remembered quite a lot about that Sara Polonska.

From that Sara Polonska the Sara of today took just her bust (this time it didn't frighten me with its expressiveness and size, and quite the opposite, drew my gaze) and her manner of laughing, but right now it seemed to me, as though with that harsh laugh, not a boot worm-crusher, but a friend with a gift in her arms was approaching me. In general I've never liked it when someone constantly and harshly laughs, and Sara Polonska was doing it just like that. She was laughing. For me a laugh meant clinical idiocy or derision, but not in any way a nice mood, success, and a friendly attitude. I presume that I lived for so long with Inna because she never laughed behind my back. But I'll return to Sara Polonska – she had slimmed down ten kilograms. She said she didn't want to talk about it. And laughed. She also didn't like to talk about her former husband. She just made the observation that she would definitely introduce us. I can't say I was particularly happy about that prospect.

Her hair remained incredibly curly, but it wasn't black, but chestnut-colored now. It glistened, it flowed in the sun and beguiled. She was wearing a simple white sundress and white leather shoes. For reasons unknown to me I fell madly in love with this Sara Polonska.

Sara was also surprised by our feelings. "Underbutt, how the heck could this have happened? Could you even have thought about something like this?" To that I answered, that if she continues to call me "Underbutt," I'll call her "Underboobs," because she was barely visible from under her tits. We laughed loudly, but a wonderful couple was established: Underboobs and Underbutt. The heroes of Czech cartoons: either mushrooms, or birds.

Our colleagues traipsed around Prague, and we with each other. "It seems to me when we were in school, you couldn't stand the sight of me, isn't that so?" She asked. That was a serious question. Sara posed it while she was lying down in bed, playing with her hair, pulling up and kissing her rounded knees toward her head – she loved to kiss her knees – and I looked in the hotel information directory for the number to call to order breakfast. I was naked and happy. I didn't know what I was supposed to answer: the truth, a half-truth, or a half-lie. Or simply lie, to tell her that I found her attractive, but not enough for me to admit it. It was hard for me to tell a woman, with whom it was so good in bed, that I thought she was monstrous. "I was married then," I heard my voice. Fine, like a mosquito's stinger, that's striving to find a hole in a mosquito net. I really was married then. Sara wanted to ask something else, but got distracted by a phone call – it was her mother. She didn't return to that topic later.

About the fact that Sara Polonska will move in to my place, a real sailor told us, who was similar to a fake sailor. Similar to an out of work actor, who for some reason chose the image of a sailor for his life outside the theater. He was wearing a red sweater, an earring hanging from his right ear in the form of a tiny anchor on a golden rope. He was drinking beer. Strange, crumpled wrinkles plowed through his face, which was the color of oak bark. It seemed that each time he crumpled them differently. "I'm a sailor, lovey dovies," he greeted us. "I'm a sailor, and I have to see foam." "If you wish, you can treat him to beer. He's a real sailor," the bartender said. I also thought he didn't notice anything other than that TV series about desperate housewives. We treated the real sailor to beer – at that time our hearts were filled with love for our fellow man. "If you order more for him – he'll also tell your fortune," the bartender informed us. The pair worked in concert. I admired the way the bartender shook out the money from us. We ordered the beer. The old guy slapped a little of the beer foam on our left palms, began to mutter something, and then said: "She's going to move in with you. Soon. Now you have to lick off that foam- then the prophecy will come true." I don't know why we did that. At least I was quite squeamish, but we licked off the beer from each other's palms. Who first started to do that: me or Sara? I don't remember. Sometimes it seems I should remember that without fail.

I made acquaintance with Sara's parents in a movie theater. We were watching *Match Point*, part of that was also about getting acquainted with the parents. I said to Sara that I had seen that flick and, in my view, it wasn't the best movie for meeting parents after watching it. The main character was a mercenary killer son-in-law. Who, additionally, got away with the killing of a woman, with whom he had cheated on his wife. Do I need that? She laughed. She said that her father has a wonderful sense of humor. "He'll like that, you'll see!" I didn't feel very confident. I thought for a long time before that meeting, which tactic to take – to be chatty or reserved? I didn't have any experience in meeting the parents of a girlfriend. Because I met the parents of my former wife in childhood, they for me were just ordinary adults. When I told Sara about this, she just started to laugh: "Well then, just take them for ordinary adults, if that works."

Sara's father reminded me of the joyful characters of an Emir Kusturica movie. From time to time he would sing something (even while watching a movie. People would hiss at him, and he would politely apologize and start singing again), and his fingers either danced in the air or on some surface. A cigarette that he twirled between his pointing and middle fingers looked like the hypertrophically large penis of Indian gods. I imagined the face of Sara's father and face of my own father with two portraits with one and the same signature: "Father." My father looked more convincingly like a father. Under the portrait of Sara's father one would want to write: "vagabond," "honored artist of Moldova, Viorel Nega," or even "Bartok." I would have believed it. On the backdrop of Sara's lively father, Sara's mother looked like a girl on a swing: they were swinging her so fast, that it was impossible to determine what she looked like. This was very strange, because Sara's mother was a large woman. But I managed to perceive her only fragmentarily. A large, puffy mouth. The voice of an opera tenor. In profile her hairdo recalled a black moon. I noticed that her skirt was too short for such shapes and such an age. And her gaze – captivating. She loved dahlias and family holidays. In any case, it was easier for me with Sara's parents than with my own. It seemed, as if they were completely satisfied with me. But, more certainly, they were completely satisfied with one another and with life.

When Sara asked when I would introduce her to my parents, I shriveled: "Listen, do you really feel like doing that?" I asked her then. She said that it's the least interesting for her what they're like, but if it's a problem for me or for my parents, she's not planning on being insistent. I thanked her. I can't say that it was a problem, besides, in our family no one ever introduced anyone to anyone. I understand this can seem strange, but that's the way it was. I didn't know, for example, my father's or mother's friends. It's possible my memory kept their names on long reins, but they were unfilled names. Like movies that didn't interest you: you understand by their title you once saw them, but what they're about or who's playing in them – it's impossible to remember. His parents, of course, were acquainted with Inna and her parents, and also with Tymofiy and his mother – the parent conferences at school helped that – they didn't keep up relations either with Inna, or with Tim, and all the more with their parents.

"If you can imagine a family for yourself, for example, as a dinner service, then our family service consists of accidental objects. Maybe, a similar pattern or color links us, but that's all." "And all that's normal! I realize that everyone has their own traditions. Not all families are like ours. We're quite like a circus dynasty! Each passes along something to another. If we trained lions, then the lions would hang out in our living room! We always show one another something new and interesting." Sara laughed and winked. I was surprised that this didn't anger me, although I realized: her family will take me for entertainment.

It was really easy with Sara generally speaking. First of all, I was constantly waiting: here right now she utters the wrong thing, then I right now insult her, here right now she does something, and we argue. She did and said a lot. For example, she constantly dumped the filters with leftover coffee grinds into the washbasin, which I couldn't tolerate. "Sara, is it hard to toss this out in the garbage can or in the bathroom?" "Take note that I can put this on your azaleas and grow fruit flies, or spread this fabulous mixture on your socks, or even make three piles, and in one of them hide your idiotic little ring. Then you'd start running!

Instead I just clog up the washbasin with wet coffee grounds. Big deal – you can always clean it." We didn't argue. When I did something wrong, she just laughed and said "Ehhh, Underbutt." When she did something wrong, I kissed her or feigned that I'd strangle her on the spot. In a week after returning from Prague, we began living together. She moved to my place. The prophecy on the beer foam of the Czech sailor came true.

On the third day of her trip to Mexico, where she went to check out several tours, I got depressed. Rasarasarasara! She was supposed to return in two weeks. A standard tour, I often was on those kinds. I could have gone with her, but because of urgent orders I was forced to stay at home. I immediately finished my usual lengthy breakfast of five cups of coffee and began to get ready – I needed to get going to the city for a meeting. I dialed her number. "The subscriber is temporarily unavailable." "Sara, go away." I said out loud. She was hiding among the dried apricots, prunes and cashews. Sara's sweets, so as not to eat cookies and get fat. I smiled and bit into a nut.

I returned home in an elevated mood, in spite of the fact that the subscriber Sara further was inaccessible. They ordered a big writing project from me on whales. And I adored whales and dolphins, dolphins and whales. Though in truth, dolphins are whales! "What a beautiful day, what a beautiful day," the record spun in my head. I already had pulled out my key when I heard music echoing from my apartment. The key fell. I really heard music, and it wasn't just simply music – music from the TV that had been left on, or a CD. No. Someone in my apartment was playing on the "R. Yors & Kallmann" family crypt. They were making mistakes and playing it over again.

They say when you meet a ghost, you grow cold. I didn't grow cold – I had the kind of impression that someone was beginning to fry my guts. It was stuffy and hot. That's how I felt. I felt just like that when I was given anesthesia. I once laughed at Inna for her account about the ghost of Mayakovsky.* In her girlhood Inna divined fortunes with her friends, summoning the spirit of the dead poet, in order to pose several questions regarding their future. Girls love doing that. However, they summoned the spirit of the poet Vladimir Mayakovsky. And he came, said a lot of crudities, and then for a long time didn't want to fly out of the window vent, as they politely asked him to do. Instead, he grabbed and made the chair under one of Inna's girlfriends break, and her girlfriend fell. In answer to my observation, that that chair had long been broken and haphazardly glued together by Inna's father, Inna directed a wicked look at me. "Don't intrude on this, you don't know anything about this," she said. "After that, at night I heard someone pressing on one or two of the piano keys. And one time someone played a small piece. That was him. Mayakovsky. Our piano reminded him of something. Maybe, it somehow was connected with Lilya Brik."

I didn't believe it. Besides that, when the piano ended up with me, no one from the other side played on it. "Mayakovsky, Inna," I declared, beforehand looking over all the relevant information on the Internet, "didn't know how to play the piano." "He knew how," she stubbornly asserted. "How do you know that he didn't know how to play?" "Because it's not discussed anywhere." "But why talk about this separately? Back then all educated people knew how to play musical instruments," Inna argued confidently. "Almost all his wives knew how to play the piano, and he learned! He

....

* The great Russian Futurist poet Vladimir Mayakovsky, known for his bombastic writings, who committed suicide in 1930. He was involved in a love triangle with Lilya Brik, the wife of his good friend Osip Brik.

played for Lilya Brik." "Nonsense," I responded uncertainly, beginning to doubt myself. I always doubted myself.

"No, this is not nonsense!" Inna the Doubtless insisted.

How do you learn such self-assuredness? If I were a country, then, for sure, my own feuds would tear me to pieces. Inna was an absolute monarchy. One thing was left for her under those kinds of conditions: to be wary of insidious kin, who every minute make efforts to toss poison into your apple juice or into a roasted duck, not to forget about young terrorists, who make explosive charges in cellars. Of herself, of her crown, and of monarchic rules, she was completely sure.

And here now I'm standing outside my door, and he, Vladimir Mayakovsky, the poet and ardent tribune, is playing in my apartment on the "R. Yors & Kallmann" family crypt. Why today of all days? Although, thank God, it's good that it's not at night. I didn't know what to do. I silently stood in front of the door and burned with all my innards. But the door opened. It seemed to me that I began to creak. A sturdy man with curly hair gazed at me lost. I immediately recognized him – it was Sara's uncle, her father's brother. He was among those whose portrait right then was living in a silver frame on my windowsill. What's his name?"

"Oh, is that you? So you've already returned." "Yes. I've returned. Already," I said. "Sorry, I'm in a rush, but Emile is there, he'll explain everything to you. All the best, Pavlo!" "All the best, Gestapo." He looked at me with reproach. "You know, I don't know if using my family nickname will help us build family relations, Pavlo." I also didn't think that way, but I couldn't remember his name, though the fact that he's "Gestapo," I remembered beautifully. "Sorry. I didn't do it on purpose," I said. He academically shook my head. And when I entered the house, I remembered. Gennadiy Stanislavovych Polonsky. That's his name. Ge. Sta. Po. Sara's favorite uncle. As much as I understood, Sara's cousin Emile was playing on the crypt. Good. But it would be interesting to know, why is this cousin playing in my kitchen, and his father, who's leaving my apartment, saying to me that he's in a rush and disappearing without any explanation?

I went to the kitchen. Like a rat – to the awful sounds that the unknown-to-me Emile was squeezing out of the "R. Yors & Kallmann" family crypt.

CHAPTER II

At the very least about someone else's child, someone else's husband, someone else's dog, and the Sarabande for string orchestra and piano by G.F. Handel

I thought I'd calmly enter and make my way to the kitchen, but a growling from beneath the floor got in the way of me getting there. "Maybe Mayakovsky, did play the piano, who knows, but growling, that's a bit much even for him." I tried to calm myself down. If you think hard, you can arrive at the believable thought that for Mayakovsky it's more natural to groan than to play music. I was stupefied. But I managed to lower my eyes. A slobbery, hairy, tongue-wagging mug was looking at me. It was a dog. He was wagging his tail and growling. "Emile?" I inquired of him just in case. He began to bark. In the meanwhile no one stopped playing. It was abominable playing. As though Kallmann, who had violated the harmony of that piece, savoring individual notes, had regained consciousness in a crypt. For example, "C" or "G." It seemed to me that those notes could be tasty for Kallmann. I heard a "Grrrrrrr." The dog wouldn't let me move.

But I tried to move anyway; after all, it was my home. But it was for nothing. "Uweeeeesssipppiiii," I heard. "Good Lord!" I had the impression that I had crushed an infant or a piglet, or something more tender, warm, and soft. The dog began to bark crazily. He blocked my path and wouldn't stop barking. But I became a bit relieved and I understood that I had stepped on an ugly rubber thing with a squeaky contraption inside it. "Emile!!!" I began to bellow. "Why raise such a ruckus? Come here!" I heard the answer: "I can't!" I noticed. "There's a strange dog here." "Terry, stop that, Terry, he's one of us." The little wretch didn't stop making his music. "He's one of us – stop that. A stranger – that's yum-yum," I explained to the dog. He wagged his tail and went off into the kitchen, scraping his claws along my tiled floor. In its maw the animal was holding the ugly rubber thing. The ugly thing was even fearful of squeaking. And I understood it.

I entered and saw him. Emile. True, at first I saw Sara's headband with stones on his head. "That's already too much," I thought. The little dude continued to play. Sure of himself, he sat like a fairytale prince and ran his feelers along the keys. "Hey," I said. "Hey," he answered. "Emile, as far as I understand?" "You don't understand this, my father talked to you about this, I heard it." "Good. Maybe you'll stop playing and we can talk?" "I can't, I have fifteen minutes more. I have it all calculated. In a week there's an academic school concert, I need to be in good form." "What kind of abomination are you performing? That's not even music, but God knows what. And, by the way, be so kind as to remove Sara's headband. I don't like it when someone takes her things." That really annoyed me. No, I understand, the twenty-first century is the twenty-first century, you won't hide anywhere from that if you haven't died in good time. And David Beckham has taught these kinds of little dudes to drag girlie trinkets on their heads. Though if in my class someone imagined to drag such a thing on his head, he'd have problems. But, on the other hand, did David teach them to take other people's things?

"You talking about the headband? It's mine." He had dark and wavy hair. It was quite long. A little prince. I looked closely – the little dude wasn't lying: the glass of the stones was a different color. "Good, it's yours – so it's yours. Sorry

I didn't realize that right away. I'm not an expert on headbands. So you're not going to stop playing?" "I told you already, I have an academic school concert, I have a schedule. Would you stop playing under such conditions? Sara, by the way, didn't say that you're such a drag. You always have to learn through your own experience. It's absolutely impossible not to rely on anyone." I really was itching to smack him on the back of the head and barely restrained myself. Instead I scrounged in the cabinet and pulled out a bottle of comrade Varadero Anejo – a dark amber Cuban Rum – and started to really go at it without futile words or any aesthetics.

"Goodness! You should be more careful with that!" I heard. And I nearly choked. "Uncle Alik was at our place. His real name was Oleh, but everyone called him Alik, because he was a drunkard. That's right. He also began drinking right in the middle of a hard day. Not even from the bottle like you, but in a refined way – from a goblet or a glass. And then he had drunk himself blue. Everybody without fail drinks themselves blue! When the alcohol detox guys were called, they put him to sleep, and also gave him all kinds of injections and drips. And they set out pills in fistfuls on the table like in a button store so that he'd take them in the morning. After they had squeezed some cash from Uncle Alik's family for the house visit, Uncle Alik would sleep more than twenty four hours and not bother anyone. But he could have died – choking on his own saliva. That's why he needed to be constantly looked after. Of course Aunt Iraida, not to speak of Stelka (that was her daughter with Uncle Alik; she knew how to scratch between her legs with her heel), didn't feel like spending their time that way. Do you know what they did? They stuck a staple remover into Uncle Alik's mouth and tied a little bell to it "Made in 1998" (Stelka at that time had just graduated), and when he would stir, the bell would start to tinkle, and one of them would get up and check if Uncle was choking or not. Well, approximately, like on a night fishing trip, when everyone was drunk out of his gourd, they put on an elastic string, lay themselves down wherever God made them a bed, until a bream pecked! Tinkle!!" Here Emile stopped playing. During his sermon I could swallow the beneficial liquid just once.

"Here! I've finished playing," the little dude announced to me. "Let's have dinner now." "What were you playing?" This happens to me. I'm like that dog, who till now was still fidgeting with that idiotic rubber thing: when some kind of question keeps nagging at me, I can never get rid of it until I figure out what and how. "You don't want to have dinner?" "I do. And I will. But I'm asking you what dreadful vile thing were you playing?" "It wasn't a dreadful vile thing I was performing. I see that you're not an expert either on headbands, or on music. This is the Sarabande for String Orchestra and Piano by G. F. Handel. It sounds a little strange to an ear not trained by high-quality music. It's because I'm performing just the piano part; there's no one to perform all the other parts. There are no strings. Do you happen to be a string player?"

By the way, the score for piano was composed later! Handel didn't write it. Maybe he did write it. But secretly. No one knows that precisely. It's the same story as with the words. Take the word "chocolate." Try to say it. It's very juicy: choc-o-late. But what would it sound like if it only had a "ch," "c" and "t?" Chct. It doesn't sound good! And o-o doesn't sound good. But take "l-a" – that sounds good. But this sooner is an exception than a rule. Just when you combine these letters in a single word – it plays to its full strength, do you understand? You know, I have a fantastic recording of that work. I can put it on and play it for you right now! When you play it with an orchestra, you perceive it totally differently." "Thanks. Maybe another time," I answered quickly, because the entire time I was thinking about how kids of today are hell. Who taught him to babble like that? Who taught him that his thoughts can be of interest to another person in this world? I'm a great sinner, but at those moments I used to begin to think that when I have a child, it will be mute. Forgive me, Lord, I myself don't know what I'm saying.

"Now can we have dinner?" "Yes we can. But for that I need to return to the hallway." I remained silent. The little dude too. The little dude knows how to be silent when he himself wants to. He made himself comfortable on my favorite armchair. "But why aren't you going? Do I need to escort you or something?" "A dog" "The dog?" "Yes, the dog. Yours. He doesn't allow me to peacefully move around the house." "Drop it. I already told him that you're one of us. That's enough for him. He won't bother you. Terry isn't some kind of drag here." Making fun of me, you little monster. "And why'd you have to go into the hallway?" "There's a bag with food, I've bought something. There's nothing to eat." "Well, don't worry yourself over that. Momma passed along food with us. We aren't some kind of horde. We know how to be thankful for hospitality. Besides that, Sara told me what you usually eat. That's not normal. Dad and I need different food that's balanced and nourishing!" It'd be interesting to know what else Sara told him?

In the meantime I opened up the refrigerator and nearly passed out. For good reason. In the morning in the refrigerator I would've noticed a box of milk, a box of juice, a pale sliced cheese wrapped in cling wrap, a can of sprouts, a block of *Pâté* de fois gras, a plastic pack with cherry tomatoes, dill that looked like the tail of a tired foal, and two green apples, because I don't eat apples of any other color. That's all. Right then there were two mysterious containers standing there, two small pans, a jar, and some kind of pyramids, wrapped in white napkins. "So what did you buy?" The little glutton Emile took an interest. "In fact, nothing special," I said. I had bought hot dogs. 200 grams.

The little dude rustled in the kitchen. "You'll soon be trying mom's fantastic baby carp, braised with carrots, plums and walnuts. Delicious, you've never dreamt of anything like that." He pulled out the little jar. "Sweet fish? I, thank God, don't dream of sweet fish." "No, it's spicy!" I couldn't eat anything like that. Emile enjoyed it. He scarfed down my juice. I won't have juice in the morning if I don't go to the store for it. "You have a bad appetite. You're a weak person!" The little dude announced. "My appetite – that's a secondary thing. Listen, can I hear, what in general are you doing here? Because when I met Gestapo by my door… that is…." "You said it to him like that? Gestapo? Oho. Did you think long about that?" It's interesting whether this generation has at least a drop of respect for grown-up people? "That's what I said. I couldn't remember the name of your father. I'm not even acquainted with him," I growled out harshly. The dog tore itself away from the eyes of my carp and looked into my eyes. The dog didn't approve of me. He kept dropping his saliva on my bare foot. If you constantly press your fingernails into the palm of your hand, torn, dotted lines will decorate your palms.

"Well, I could do without any kind of impersonal forms of address." Of that sort. From where do they get such words? "I forgot impersonal forms of address. Besides that, it's impolite." "It's more polite than to use certain personal ones. I can imagine how overjoyed his father was. Gestapo! How can you?. And a person living with Sara is telling him this. And a person is telling him this who you can call – an ass!!!" "If you utter just one more vile thing in my direction – you're out of here. I don't give a damn that you're Sara's cousin," I pointed out. "Her favorite cousin! She really loves me, because something will become of me, as all those whose opinion I listen to observe. And why are you angry? I used your method of communication.

Your name is Pavlo Dudnyk, right?" I was forced to agree with this because my name really was Pavlo Dudnyk. "Pavlo Dudnyk. There we have it. Du-Pa.* Dudnyk Pavlo. Pa-du-pa! Nice. The same kind of play on words like Gestapo, even better!" The little dude burst into laughter, a piece of carrot in the form of a star flew onto my tiled walls. "You always first have to measure it on yourself, and then mock others." He was incredibly pleased with his sharp wit.

"Don't they sometimes call you Amelie in school?" I asked gently. "What are you saying? I go to a special mathematics school. The majority of my classmates are Jewish, understand?" "No. What kind of explanation is that? You want to say that young Jewish mathematicians don't watch French comedies? And can't tease a boy by the name of Emile with the girl's name Amelie?" "Jewish mathematicians watch a lot and see a lot; they also know how to tease. But they don't want to waste their valuable time and don't use their highly developed brain on such idiocies." I want to kill Emile Genadiyovych Polonsky. I definitely need to write that on my refrigerator. I pulled out my cell phone to get in touch with Sara. "Are you dialing Sara? She won't answer till tomorrow. They went to a place where there's no phone connection. She alerted us so we wouldn't worry." She didn't alert me.

"You are so strange." "A very accurate conclusion. Is that because I'm not eating the sweet carp?" "No. It's because you're not asking what I'm doing here. What I'm doing here and Terry, and what my father will be doing here when he comes back from work! You need to ask about that. That is any normal person definitely would ask." "And he's also

....

*   "Dupa" means "ass."

going to be doing something here, your father?" I took an interest. "Of course. You understand, the problem is that we have remodeling going on." I remained silent. "That's why mother concocted that she's going to work on the remodeling, and we have to wait it out somewhere. Because my dad absolutely needs to think and work in peaceful surroundings. And I have to study and practice. I already told you about the academic school concert. Do you understand? And Terry is with us, because he's a quiet dog, although he doesn't like the remodeling guys. Besides, it's harmful for a dog to breathe in various lacquer fumes."

"And isn't it harmful for mother to breathe in lacquer fumes?" "It's harmful. That's why she'll live at Nastya and Romko's place." "Who are they?" "They're Sara's parents." Damn it, it totally slipped my mind! "I know. I was checking if you were talking specifically about them. And why all three of you won't live there?" "What a bore you are. I've told you already about my academic concert at school, about peace and quiet. Didn't I say that? There. I have to have a piano and my dad needs peace and quiet. That's why it's better for us to stay in an apartment where there's a piano and relative peace and quiet. Sara said you have a piano. And Terry is always at dad's side." "Just not right now." "What not right now?" "Right now dad isn't here, but Terry is!" I tried to burst into laughter. It came out unconvincingly. "Very funny," Emile noted. "If you want Terry to listen to you, you're better off calling him Butterfly, that's his full name." "You've given the dog the name of a Japanese prostitute?"

"Knowledge of the classics ruins certain people." That's what Emile said. "But if it's really of interest for you, we named him Butterfly in honor of a *metelyk*. Butterfly in English is a *metelyk* in Ukrainian. And he's a butterfly because he has enormous ears: when he runs it's as though they're flying. That happens with thoroughbred springer spaniels. The large ears are a mark of the breed." I sensed the time had come for us to one more time to treat ourselves to the Varadero Anejo. This time I prepared my special rum glass and pulled out an apple from the refrigerator. "And where did you get the keys from?" "Sara gave them to us. What's wrong? You have a problem with that? We practically are one family. Listen, you can't eat cold apples, it's harmful for your teeth. You need to warm them in hot water…."

I openly pumped the Varadero Anejo, to which I added a little of Sara's Martini & Rossi. In order to sense her support. It turned out not so bad. I remembered giving Sara the keys to my apartment. From Saintes-Maries-de-la-Mer I had brought home a gypsy doll. Sara la Cali. Black Sara, the sacred protectress of all gypsies. I really believe in the fact that nothing happens to us accidentally; every incident is assiduously calculated by God, and that's why it loses its accidental essence. When Sara and I decided we were going to live together, I got an assignment from one of the tourist sites and set off on an interesting tour through France, one of the stops of which was the Provence town of Saintes-Maries-de-la-Mer. Twice a year in that town the holiday of St. Mary and her servant takes place – St. Sara. Twice a year – on the 24th of May and the 22nd of October, because right on that day Sara Polonska was born. Can that possibly be a fluke?

In the cathedral of Saintes-Maries-de-la-Mer, which is more like a fortress than a temple, in the murky underground crypt stands a statue of Sara the gypsy. She has a black face and is dressed elegantly: a multi-layered gypsy costume, several skirts, lace, silk; on her neck strings of a necklace that jingled from a heavy breath. Each time for the holiday they dress the statue of St. Sara in bright new skirts, new necklaces, earrings, bracelets with tiny tassels, and they carry her on a special palanquin to the banks of the seashore. They plunge the statue into the sea, and each time the waves return the swarthy Sara to the Provence shore….

I gave Sara the doll and asked her to undress. Then I dressed her in silk scarves that I had picked up in Aigues-Mort, hung necklaces on her neck, and bracelets on her wrists, grabbed her in my arms and dragged her into the bathroom. And the ordinary tap water returned Sara to me, and me – to Sara. St. Sara isn't canonized by the Catholic church, but this doesn't get in the way of being a real saint for all the gypsies and wanderers. And I canonized my Sara for myself. "From now on you are my saint." We laughed in the nearly dark bathroom. Sara got up and looked like a statue; her large breasts seemingly were holding up a necklace in the air. The moons, the stars, the little suns, and other trinkets on her bracelets jingled from my heavy breathing. Then we made love, drank French Muscat wines, and then I told Sara to look closely at the doll. I fastened my key onto the doll's necklace. "It's yours," I said and entered into her. My juicy, my saint Sara.

And now that key was in the possession of the little dork. While I was diving into recollections, he continued to speak, scarfing down pastries with cream. His mother had taken the trouble to make desert. "Of course, a musical education is necessary if you want to be a developed individual, and my parents have striven for that regarding me. And I have no objections. Because they have always taken into consideration my opinion. At first they wanted me to learn to play the violin. But I said that I won't play the violin because it looks like the female embryo, and to move a bow along an embryo – that for me is disgusting. I never go to string concerts; I can't watch all those bows rhythmically moving… But I do like to listen. Momma's afraid I'm going to look at sex the same way." I grew numb. "In what sense?" I asked, hopelessly striving to seek out remnants of the liquid of the Varadero Anejo. I needed to think up something so the Varadero Anejo would multiply in droplets like amoebas. "The droplets look like amoebas!" I said. And then I decided to finish off the Martini & Rossi. "Take the pastry! You need to eat something, because you're dreaming of something." The little dude offered it to me. He followed my actions. I took it. "About sex," I said.

Emile looked at me seriously. "Momma had in mind that I'll also perceive sex just with my ears. That is, I'll listen, and not look or be engaged in it. In that sense." I shouldn't have reacted to that at all, but I couldn't restrain myself and asked: "So how will you?" Emile rebuffed me. "I'm twelve years old. I'm capable of resolving all my sexual issues without anyone else's help, with my own hands." After that this sniveler winked at me. I was shocked.

In fact I didn't have any experience communicating with kids. When I had the opportunity to converse with them, I didn't feel very good. I had to force tiresome questions out of myself: how are things in school, what do you want to be, what's your favorite color, who do you look more like – your dad or mom. By the way, certain acquaintances of my parents till this day readily ask me such things! Work replaces school, instead of whod oyou want to be – how do you want to live, where do you want to work, and are you-planning to get married — those are all the changes. It was even worse with Emile. I didn't need to ask-interrogate him about anything. He babbled an awful lot about everything. Next to him I felt like a pool table pocket. How does a pocket react to a billiard ball? I don't know. It waits, but understands: as much as they miss, someone definitely will hit! "A certain association with women appeared," I thought. "Tymofiy would have liked this; he loves to analyze." Something splashed and I jerked. Terry-Butterfly was drinking water from a little red bowl. Thanks to the fact that my gaze was concentrated on the floor, I noticed one more bowl with water and another empty one. The second bowl of water stood next to the "R. Yors & Kallmann" family crypt. The little dude followed me with his eyes.

"While you were out – Ilya Rasvetovych* came over." I tried to concentrate on that name with the intention of comprehending what that might mean in children's slang, because I didn't have any acquaintances with that kind of fairytale name. I pulled out a cigarette. "Do you drink and smoke?" "Uhuh. Besides that I can do it simultaneously. You'll see in a second. I'll show you. Like Gai Juli Ceasar. I think you are aware of who that is. And here's there's this… Ilya Ra… ra… how do you say it?" Ilya Rasvetovych is a genius piano tuner." "Who?" I couldn't hold back and asked again. "A piano tuner. It's completely understandable that you don't know who that is. These are specially trained people, musical veterinarians, who look after the health of a piano." "A pianologist! A pianotrician! A pianolinist!" I uttered. Emile didn't answer anything, though he stopped talking about Ilya Rasvetovych. He crawled to the refrigerator, took out a small pan from there, cheese and cold pork. "I'll heat up some chicken bullion right now, make some sandwiches, and you'll eat all this because you've gotten drunk, and my father will arrive soon. And he doesn't like it when someone is over the limit." "Well what of it?" "Yes. And let's not ruin the first day for him in a new place." A sagacious child. I drank up the bullion. It turned out to be tasty. Though I'm not particularly fond of bullion and wouldn't buy it for anything.

"Ilya Rasvetovych said that the piano is in horrible shape. He's seen something similar only at the Saranskys when a hamster crawled into their piano. They didn't know anything about it and thought that their hamster disappeared or the cat had wolfed him down. The Saranskys are very inattentive. They're already really old. And Yelka – their granddaughter – never communicates with them (just hello, old people, and good-bye, old people), and never helps them. She brings

....

* The name literally means "son of the dawn."

them medicine and cheese from the market (and they wiped her butt till the third grade, steamed a roll in milk with sugar for her, sang for Silva and Edwin, pretended to be Chukchi,* so she wouldn't cry and wouldn't feel like an abandoned child. But children are ungrateful little animals, whom as they get old, you feel like spoiling more and more; that's how the Saranskys put it).

They failed to observe the hamster, and Yelka paid no attention to that at all – the hamster is much smaller than the old Saranskys. Though they're old, they're both as heavy as two bulls, how could they reach the hamster! Yelka didn't even know that the hamster was living at the Saranskys. And the hamster didn't die and didn't disappear – he kept living in the piano. And he gnawed on the thick felt of the hammers, and then the hammers began to ruin the sound. And Ilya Rasvetovych at first thought that it was moths, and he instructed the Saranskys to sprinkle lavender mixture there, until he later discovered the hamster because the lavender didn't help." "Hamsters don't and never have lived at my place. But when they appear, I'm not going to do battle with them with the aid of lavender," I informed the little dude. "You have a different situation. I've shown you an example of an irresponsible attitude toward your instrument. You simply have not given water to your piano, and here it's started to dry up, and you also have not very often played it. I'm softening everything that Ilya Rasvetovych noted regarding your attitude toward your piano. But right now the sound is just as it should be. And we put out a bowl with water. There it is. So be careful, especially when you wake up in the middle of the night." "Thanks for the warning, but I rarely go to the kitchen at night. I'm not the kind of guy who gobbles food at

....

* A native tribe in the far northeast of Russia, who were the brunt of ethnic jokes in Soviet times.

night," I said. "Well, now you'll visit it more often. Because you're sleeping here." "I'm going to sleep in the kitchen?" "Where else would you? You don't have a very big apartment. I dragged my things to your bedroom. And dad will be living in the study. He often works at night. There's one place left to sleep – this couch. In the kitchen. It's yours." "And why is it mine and not yours? I can let the study be at the disposal of your father. I have a laptop. It doesn't matter where I work on it. And I respect his age and… what does he do?" "He's a professor. He does research in meteorology." "Is that farting or the weather? I'm confused. I don't understand why he needs to work at night to talk nonsense about God knows what regarding the weather or farting. Anyone can do that. Anyway, it's not important, let him stay in my study, work, do whatever he wants, even fart or say sooth by the rain! Of course, several of my books and disks are there, but I can take everything I need. But why will you be sleeping in my bed, and I have to spend the night in the kitchen, eh?"

"First. If I come down to your level of knowledge – dad works on the weather. Farting, as you expressed it (in principle, among cultured people it's called meteorism), is worked on by doctors who specialize in chronic colitis, constipation, acute digestive tract maladies, and dysbacteriosis. And I surmise that if you continue to further feed yourself the way you are doing, you definitely will intersect with the experts mentioned. Second. In general, meteorology – is the study of the Earth's atmosphere. My father specializes in physical meteorology. This is the development of radar and extraterrestrial methods of studying atmospheric phenomena. And synoptic meteorology: as it is well known, is the study of the system of weather changes. You don't have to work like that with your head, you don't have to remember, but for a geographer with a diploma and a person with higher education, your knowledge is lacking.

Third. Momma says that a child shouldn't sleep where he works. Ideally grown-up people also shouldn't do that, but if that already happens to be the case, it harms them less than a child. If you extrapolate the given fact on our situation, it means that I shouldn't sleep where I practice my piano playing. I practice in the kitchen, therefore I need to sleep in a different place. It's all very simple." While I was thinking of a worthy answer, the doorbell rang, and Terry, adroitly overcoming the barrier – my leg – flew out into the corridor. "My dad! We'll have dinner right away. I forgot to tell you that when we sit down at the table, don't begin any conversations with my father about work. Talk exclusively about other topics!" "For example, like the weather?" "Well, you're a drag," Emile responded. He ran to open the door.

Usually, children are baffled by obvious idiocies that they hear from grown-ups, but my trick with farting and the weather failed to succeed. My supper consisted of three cigarettes, a single cup of tea, one pear pastry, and two glasses of champagne. Gestapo had brought the "To Our Acquaintance" bottle of champagne. I don't know why I drank it up. Maybe to our acquaintance, and maybe so I could sleep better in a new spot. In the kitchen.

The son and father ate up the chicken, the sweet carp and a lot of pear pastries. Terry ate up the two-hundred grams of hot dogs and oatmeal kasha. I noticed that they had placed a different box next to Sara's box of "Start." "Hills." That was Terry's "Start." Just so I don't mix them up!

I just one time had gotten interested in the weather. That was entirely sufficient for Gennadiy Stanislavovych to give me an incredibly long lecture about adequate and inadequate behavior during meals. Emile gifted me with an expressive look of "Iwarnedyoudork." In the time that the lecture was going on, any person could have made it to Boryspil Airport. It's too bad that person was not me. I don't remember how and when I fell asleep.

CHAPTER III

At the very least about a non-ideal morning, and also about the fact of what your ideal apartment and your quite pleasant life can turn into in just 24 hours.

I dreamt that my head had ended up in some reeking maws of a beast, for sure, a tiger's, and I, accordingly, was a courageous trainer. I wasn't fearful, but the odor was excessively bothersome; the saliva of that beast made my face wet. Suddenly my leg jerked, and I felt my knee touching something slimy, maybe it was my intestines. I shuddered and woke up. And I saw the mug of the beast right above me. It wasn't a dream. It was Terry, who had put his front paws on my collarbones. He shamelessly thrust out his tongue. Never in my life was such a disgusting object next to my face. He stank of digested hotdogs. Terry dripped saliva onto my face. "Ah," I said to him. He pressed me even more strongly with his paws and whispered: "Woof!" I didn't know what to do to get him to leave me in peace. It seemed to me right then and there, that the dog would bite my nose or piss on the bed. I didn't know his intentions.

As much as I could, I looked over the bed. That which my knee had come across turned out not to be my intestines, but a rubber duckie. I dreamt of waking up in bed together with Sara instead of with this hirsute beast Terry and a rubber duckie. Horror!

In the meantime, Terry wearied of silently trampling on my collarbones, so he began to get more active: he barked right into my face, jumped along various parts of my body, like a tiger along pedestals, and finally grabbed the rubber duckie and put it right on my mug. "He died from asphyxiation caused by a rubber duckie." As if I had read it in the *Fakty* [Facts] newspaper. Lord, how shameful it was! I felt like a paralyzed old granddad, ridiculed by a disgusting grandson. And then I started to shout. Terry began to bark madly. "Shut your puss! Right away!" Could be heard from somewhere. Terry calmed down and laid down on my chest, growing silent. However I decided not to give in and began to bellow: "Take your dog!"

Suddenly something unbelievable was heard. It sounded like this: "Wake up, slut! Get up, be a human being! Why are you lying down, you slut? Lift up your stinking ass and get out to make something of yourself, damn it! Take your legs and arms and wake up, you slut! When will you wake up, slut? Come on, wake up, you slut!" I memorized those lines because I listened to them three times. After the last "slut" my apartment began to stir. Gestapo floated into my kitchen. In a T-shirt and military green shorts. "Good morning," he said. He pet Terry on his head. Terry's head turned into a brace for Gestapo's hand. I was holding the disgusting rubber duckie in my hands – I wanted to nail the slutshouter. Gestapo ardently stared at me. "Did you go for a walk?" "With the rubber duckie?" I asked with surprise. I grabbed the rubber duckie by the neck and flung it. And in as much as Gestapo silently was staring at me, and Terry was barking animatedly, I continued: "No. I didn't go for a walk with him. This is Terry's toy. He put it in my bed, and I wanted to beat the slut down with it. That is, not a slut, but this thing that kept calling her this entire time." "Naturally. That thing, as you unsuccessfully allowed yourself to express it, is called an alarm clock," Gestapo said. "I'm little interested with whom or with what you're playing in your own bed. Play with a duck, that's no skin off my back. I asked if you took Terry for a walk? As a matter of fact, couldn't you get up and get dressed? Emile will be coming soon and we'll have breakfast, and it's not very convenient when you're still tossing around in bed."

"You mean I have to walk your dog?" I wrapped a bed sheet around me. "Listen, that bed sheet somehow looks inappropriate, you're not in a bathhouse and you're not a Roman emperor, don't you have any morning clothes?" With his forefinger Gestapo pointed at his military shorts. "No. I don't have any morning clothes. Evening-yes. A tuxedo. Should I put it on? I generally walk around naked in the morning." Something rattled in my head. "At least in front of me and the child, you're not going to walk around naked. You need to put on something." "All my clothes are in the bedroom," I said. "And Emile is sleeping there." Gestapo very elegantly, as though he were getting ready to cover his own hand with kisses, lifted it up and looked at his watch. "Emile will get up in a few minutes. Where exactly are your clothes? I'll bring them."

And here I heard piano music. I recognized it, how could I not, because this was that very same work of art that the little dude tormented me with yesterday. "The Sarabande for String Orchestra and Piano by G. F. Handel," I uttered. In the eyes of Gestapo, something similar to respect, flashed past like a short tail. "Yes, you're entirely right. This really is "The Sarabande for String Orchestra and Piano by G. F. Handel. My and Sonya's technique. A child should live by means of a music piece, which he studies; that is over the course of an entire hour of being in an active state. So where's your clothing?" "In a straw basket. Short pants and a T-shirt, will that work?" "You're asking me if that works for you? Aren't they your clothes? You what, you buy clothing of different sizes?" How do people communicate with him? I don't understand. "My clothing is there and Sara's." I've squeaked instead. Gestapo floated out of the kitchen, and literally in a minute Terry and Emile burst into the kitchen. "Hello!!!" Emile began shrieking. He ran to the bed and kissed the crown of my head. This was so unexpected that I again took the disgusting rubber duckie into my hands. Terry immediately began to try to tear it from me. "Where's the tea? Have you taken Terry for a walk?"

"I haven't taken a walk with Terry," I answered, striving to put on my shorts and T-shirt on under the bed sheet. At that time Gestapo was looking through the window. Maybe he was checking on the weather. "Why do I have to take a walk with Terry?" "Because you don't have go to work in the morning!" The little dude answered candidly. "That is?" I asked again. Emile gave a sigh. "I'll explain it to you right now. We have no one in our family who would have such a hard time of getting it, but already, maybe, there is." I got angry. "Better tell me where the tea is. We must have breakfast." "The green tea in bags is in the wooden box. And the black is in a tin with dragons on it." "Is the green in bags?" The little dude and his father decided to demonstrate for me how the Polonsky male choir sounds. It's the same thing as eating a burnt corpse in a crematory. Have you been in a crematory? I was in one last week. We buried uncle Heorhiy. He had cheated on Neonila. Neonila – his wife – therefore is now a widow. Old lady Saransky (do you remember the story about her piano hamster, I told it to you yesterday?), it was like this, old lady Saransky won from old man Saransky fifty bucks on the death. She bet on the fact that Neonilka, at any rate, would outlive her sweetheart Zhorka! It was like this, Heorhiy cheated on his wife; that's why she didn't put on his favorite music – a Jewish chanson, but instead put on beating drums. Everyone was really surprised, especially auntie, who puttered about the crematory and bawled about who should carry the wreaths, and also how my teacher Tetyana Mykolayivna (she teaches us history) indicated to everyone where to stand. But she didn't live with uncle Heorhiy and didn't know what kind of a rascal he was, may the earth for him be down from Chinese down coats," Emile observed. After those words I ran to the bathroom because I was feeling nauseous. "You're like pregnant Yelka! She used to vomit every morning on an empty stomach when Misha got her pregnant. Then the daughter of the old Saranskys even stopped cooking chicken!" I managed to hear Emile's voice.

In the bathroom it calmed down a bit. This was my little world. On the shelves there were figurines of little play toilets that I had brought from various countries of the world. A funny drawing was hanging on the wall: two hands opening up theater curtains, behind which a little round butt is peeping through. A short reading stand also stood there-a stand for magazines. There were magazines containing my articles, yesterday's sports paper (when I had constipation I have the habit of reading sports paper and shouting to myself "goal, goal" or "puck, puck" – depending on the season), a coloring book about the adventures of a tiny mouse, and Arabian fairy tales. I grabbed the book and found salvation among the benevolent evil spirits – ghouls, djinns, and Marids. "Emile – is an evil Marid, shoot to Madrid…" I was itching to rhyme the word "Jew," but suddenly found that to be embarrassing. " Emile is a child. Emile is Sara's cousin. Sara – is my saint." I began to curse myself. And here I saw that opposite my bathroom drawing of the backstage butt there was something amusing hanging.

It was a standard piece of paper, and at first glance, there was nothing strange, if you didn't read what was written on it. What was written there reminded you of a schedule. A red marker noted dates, a blue one – names, and in ballpoint pen-addresses, names, and commentaries. It was like this: "From October 28 – Karina, abbrev. poodle, a little boy Kostya (quasi-normal), mother Hanna (a wicked aunt), bldg. th. apt. 34; from November 1– Cleopatra, Eng.

spaniel (red, not very purebred) Yevheniya Petrivna (loves cream cakes), bldg. th, apt. 4; from November 6 – Wazuka, an akita-inu (a very rare Jap. breed!!!), uncle sim. to MM, bldg. th., apt. 22; from November 6 also – Pancake, spot. Fr. bulldog, Nona (unknown age, ver. nice!), neighbor. bldg., 2nd floor; from November 12– Tsunami (Tsuna, Tsuni-Mooni), German, Tamara Antonivna, senior investigator of the city procurator's office, bldg. th., apt. 76. – to be expl.).

My finger, that till now obediently skated along the paper, got stuck on Tamara Antonivna. The fact of the matter was that I figured out who Tamara Antonivna was. Everything converged: apt. 76-that was the apartment next to mine, and Tsuna-was Tamara Antonivna's German Shepherd. I just didn't know that her patronymic was Antonivna. Usually everyone called her "Tamara the cop." That is she's a detective, ehe. Small, snout-faced and disheveled Tamara. If you could cover Tamara with a fence in a way that you'd only see her hairdo-the red top part of her hair, and below – her legs in solid brown pantyhose, wearing black shoes-hooves, no one would have doubted the fact that behind the fence was a pony, whose other pair of legs had disappeared. Tsuna was a trained German Shepherd. I can't say that she particularly liked me, but I could peacefully ride up in the elevator with her and not defend myself with the well-known soccer method.

"Th. bldg. – judging by everything means this building. Yes-yes. A grannie lives with Klopochka in our building. And I knew that Klopochka was a female spaniel. I wasn't very good at breeds of dogs, but I know what spaniels look like. The grannie once came up to my apartment to explicate relations. It seemed to her that I specially was tossing cigarette butts in a way so as to strike her balcony. "I'm never able to sweep it clean! How much can one keep mocking? When will that nicotine flatten you, you pedaled horse. It's an outrage!" When I pointed out to her that it was impossible because she lives on the first floor, and I – on the tenth, she snipped back that it was even worse, because I, you see, am throwing my butts onto her balcony as I'm walking past it. This Ms. Paranoid Butt's real name was Yevheniya Petrivna. Nice to meet you. And those who were Karina, Kostya, Hanna, Pancake, Nona, Uncle MM, and Wazuka – I didn't have any idea.

"Suka-wazuka.[*] Wazuka-suka," I whispered when I heard: "Are you stuck? You need to eat more, your ass is falling into the toilet already! Wake up, slut! Lift up your stinking ass and get out to make something of yourself, damn it! You need to take Terry for a walk!" "Who the hell is Wazuka?" I asked. Emile, who was dressed as though he were getting ready for a meeting of a cigar smoking club; instead of an answer gave me a leash, on the other end of which the irrepressible Terry was jumping. "Put on a sweater and jeans, go for a walk right now, because Terry might not be able to hold out!" "And where is your father?" "He already left. He passed along that he's expecting Valentyn Yuriyovych over, so he asked that you mostly keep quiet during supper." "Valentyn Yuriyovych is coming over to our place?" "That's right. Go, take Terry for a walk! We'll all be late because of you. Go already, go. I'll wait till you get back. You're lucky that I emphasized that my first class is phys ed and I convinced my father that you need my help; he also needs to write a note that I felt nauseous in the morning, so I couldn't go to phys ed. Though it was you who was nauseous."

"Who is the bitch Wazuka and Valentyn Yuriyovych? I won't go anywhere until you tell me." I began to threateningly wind Terry's leash around my hand. Terry let out a safety

....

[*]   "Suka" means bitch in Ukrainian. We've opted to keep the rhyme here.

device "woof." "Wazuka is actually a bitch. Though, we, dog people, don't accept that word; we say – little girl. Though when Karl Petrovych was alive, he was a neighbor of the Saranskys, he always used the word 'bitch' for his Motya, because she was always getting pregnant, and Karl Petrovych used to repeat: 'Your mother, this bitch is getting pregnant not by me, but it's my problem, and not those sires.' And Valentyn Yuriyovych is my father's friend. He's a violoncellist. Nobody's gotten pregnant from him yet. Though he tried to seduce Sara. But how could a man, whose shape resembles a violoncello, seduce a girl like Sara? You'll see yourself how too narrow his upper shoulders are and how too wide his lower shoulders! It's momma who calls the ass 'the lower shoulders!' Momma says it's not natural for a man to be a violoncellist, but that's how it's worked out for Valentyn Yuriyovych since childhood. Momma calls him a musical pervert. But I didn't say that to you. Go. When you get back – I'll tell you more. And I'll make you breakfast." "Thank you," I said, for the umpteenth time complaining about the fact that I ventured to demand explanations from the little dude. So, I put on a sweater and jeans, running shoes without socks, and went for a walk with Butterfly.

The weather was beautiful outside. I just began thinking about the weather – at the same time I remembered the professor of meteorology, his son, and Valentyn Yuriovych the violoncellist, who tried to court my Sara. "A musical pervert was in love with his wife, Sara Polonska. This was a man so similar to a violoncello, that if not for his head, no one would be able to guess who was playing on what," I managed to think when suddenly Terry tore into the bushes, and a painful branch of acacias gave me several slaps in the face. It was enough to dream and speculate, I could have been left without an eye. And I really loved to speculate and dream. One of my dream-speculations was: I was putting together books for my unknown biographer. I imagined myself to be a well-known deceased person, whose biography is being researched, so I was putting together book narratives … "Uuuu." I kicked a brick with my foot.

"Terry – fu!" "Don't worry, I have a girl, and she doesn't play around! We can calmly talk!" I heard a gentle voice. A nice girl was looking at me, who was holding on a leash a comic big-eared creature. Azure blue eyes can be so sunny! "Spottie, look who've we met! Ay, such a handsome one, how dignified we are, such a sniffer, a real man!" Dog people are crazy. No, I'm saying it precisely, they're crazy. Terry continued to sniff the comic big-eared creature. "They're greeting each other! Well, enough already, enough. I'll let you loose right away, Pancake! Will you let loose yours? Maybe let them run a bit?" The girl beamed kindness. "Yesterday I chatted with your son. Such a smart boy!" Judging by those words, she was in a state of infatuation from Emile. She couldn't think that my son was – Gestapo. That would have been too much. "Then will you let Terry loose? Or has he not yet done his poopers and you need to step aside so that nothing distracts him?"

I grew stiff. This was someone else's and not my life. I never came across people in my life who were worried whether dogs were pooping, at least until the time that their shoe ends up in dog poop. I didn't know how to let Terry loose, though with pleasure I would have loved to let him go to hell! "A carbine," the nice smiling girl said to me. The little flop-eared creature sat down on my running shoes. "Oy, Spottie likes you!" I didn't know what she had in mind. Carbine. As a name – it's very strange. Though they name striplings Emile. "Pavlo," I said in any case. "Oy, very nice to meet you. Nona. Let me help you; there's no way you'll unleash him; maybe your son takes him for a walk more often, is that so?" She went over. Size 2. I thought. The collar on her jumper was winning for her. I don't know what she fumbled with there, but Terry released himself; the dogs began to run around us. "Nona and Pancake." I remembered the writing on the bathroom schedule. "Nona, do you happen to know who is some old guy who looks like MM?" "Excuse me?" "Don't pay any attention."

She began to tell me about Pancake's allergy. And I thought about how my life had changed. At least, my languid coffee morning. "Lord, I still haven't had a single cup of coffee!" I said out loud. "Oh," Nona answered. Her sunny eyes seemingly grew overcast. She knew how to sympathize. "Look, yours pooped! Now you can run home, I expect, you'll manage to have your coffee. You, maybe, also have to go to work? And my little parasite still isn't pooping. We'll have to walk to the park. Be well. Pass along our greetings to sweet Emile."

"Why did you let him go loose? How will I wipe off his paws now?" Terry stretched out on my bed with a very satisfied look. "I couldn't hook him up to the leash. You'll have to show me how to do that," I grumbled. "And why did you unleash him? You didn't have anything to do?" "So he could run around a bit with Pancake," I explained. "She says "hello" to you. And Nona does too." "From Nona? Super! Tell me, she's a Goddess, isn't she?" I didn't have anything against the fact that Nona is a Goddess. "All the same you let him loose for nothing. It's good that everything worked out and that Terry didn't run away with the bitch." "Terry runs after bitches?" "Of course he does. He hasn't been neutered. Though it was suggested to Momma that he be neutered. Auntie Genya. That's Momma's friend. Her name is Henrietta, but everyone calls her Genya. She said it like this: "Sonya, you have three sires in the house, neuter at least one of them – do you understand how satisfying that would be!" But she said that because she had a hard time going through menopause. Right now it's over, and auntie Genya doesn't want to neuter anyone, at least, I haven't heard that."

"Let's return to our pre-walk conversation. What did you hang in my bathroom?" "Do you mean the paper card?" From his words I understood that he had hung something else in the bathroom. I went toward there. The paper card with notes was in place. Next to it was a glued plastic hook. And on it – a lilac-colored stone on a red silk thread. "What kind of shamanism is this?" "That's an amethyst. Do you know anything about the healing abilities of precious and semiprecious stones? Amethyst is able to cure any kind of stomach ailments, that's why it's here." "I understand the stone." "Well, thank God! That's good, you're quick this time!" "But what's this? A list of dogs and neighbors?" "It's not so banal. This is a schedule of bitches' periods." "What?" "Well, bitches' menstrual periods, what don't you understand? In heat! Terry's very passionate. If a bitch is in heat – there's a lot of trouble with him. He runs away. One time he nearly raped a male dog, who recently had been mated with a bitch. He smelled like a bitch, so Terry ran after him. And then for a week he thought he had become gay. He hid behind the couch and sighed, but it passed." I kept silent. "At home we have an enormous placard hanging on the door to the pantry. It's hard for me here, because I still don't know all the bitches, just having walked past the building, and yesterday I met Nona and found out when Pancake goes for a walk; she's from a neighboring building."

"That is, from 28 October if I correctly grasp it, a poodle from our building is in heat?" How sweet that is that a schedule is hanging in my bathroom of bitches' periods; a obvious proof of the fact that a maniac zoophile is living in this house! "I grasped it. An apricot-colored poodle-woodle. Karina." "Naturally. And who is Wazuka and uncle, sim. to MM?" It's written here. Wazuka – that's a dog, of the akita-inu breed, a really rare Japanese breed of dogs, they're similar to huskies. Do you know what huskies look like?" "Approximately. Aren't they shaggy, big, and red?" "Maybe, just like that, I don't know what you were just thinking about. Because to fathom you – it would be easier to chop off half a grove. That's how old man Saransky says it. He sat in prison for his convictions." "For which convictions?" "Political. He was opposed to the fifth paragraph.* During the times of Joseph Dzhugashvilli." "Oh, Lord." "The Lord too was opposed to that column by the way. What else interests you?" "Old guy, sim. to MM. Wait, let me guess, this is an old guy similar to… to whom is this old guy similar? It's as if he's not similar to anyone. Maybe, he's disposed? But disposed to, but not similar to. Or maybe this guy is crazy over?… What can he be crazy over?… M&M candies? What idiocy."

"Better if you sit down, let your brain rest a bit. Help yourself. I made breakfast for you like I promised." I put on the coffee. "When do you need to go to school?" "I'm out of here right now. But don't worry, I'll be back in four hours." "What's this?" I looked at the plate that was sitting in front of me. It smelled of something sweet. A white chocolate paste. At the center of this composition "white and black are friends forever" Emile had embedded a teaspoon. It reminded me of a monument-pylon. "What's this?" I repeated. Sweet curd in chocolate, what else?! I crush them so they look more homemade." "Thank you, but I'm not going to eat this. If you want – stuff it down yourself. I vomit from sweet curds!" I poured myself my first cup of coffee. "You know, to constantly gnaw on hard cheese, you'll ruin your stomach and blood vessels with fried eggs – it won't come to anything good. An example for you is uncle Taras…" "Whose uncle is he?" Oleksa's." I began to growl. Terry too. "In a second,

....

* The fifth paragraph or fifth line was instituted by Joseph Stalin (Dzhugashvilli) in 1932 in the USSR. It indicated ethnicity in the Soviet passport and was used by the government to discriminate against Jews and other ethnicities and nationalities.

Terry, I'll give you little balls!" Emile poured out for the dog some dry food from the Hills carton, thought for a bit and added a little bit from the Start carton. "And what about uncle Taras?"

I didn't notice gulping down the coffee. It was too fast. I poured some more. I really hankered to drink it up. I clambered to the cabinet. "If you've clambered for the rum, I have to warn you that there's one bottle missing." There was no bottle. In place of where it was standing I noticed a scrap of paper. "Pavlo, because of force majeure circumstances, because of all this disorder, I forgot about the birthday of Viktor Leonidovych, that's why I permitted myself to borrow the packaged bottle of rum from you. It looked very presentable. I couldn't find anything more appropriate in the apartment. Besides the strange sculpture, in which it's as though a father is tossing his children. But in as much as Viktor Leonidovych is a father with many children, I decided that it was too risky to give him such a composition as a gift; it could insult him. Thank you for your understanding. I'll return the bottle to you in the nearest future when I make my way to an appropriate store. With respect, Ge. Sta. Po.

"Don't pull out that one either, because Valentyn Yuriovych is coming over, whom we also need to treat. And he loves exotic drinks." The fourth cup of coffee. "Do you want some cheesecake with raisins? Made of vanilla-flavored cheese, it's really tasty." I didn't notice myself taking the cheesecake, since I was already slugging down my sixth cup of coffee. The Turkish pot was empty. I poured into the coffee pot another portion of coffee. "Wash your hands, after cheesecake they're always greasy! You'll smudge everything up. Here, will you have one more little one? Momma makes them well, but Sara makes something vile and it's not cheesecake. It's good that I stayed home to feed you. Because you're ruining your stomach with that coffee. And uncle

Taras also constantly used to drink coffee and cognac, and used to eat pork cutlets and mutton on an empty stomach, then someone suggested to him that before he eats-drinks all of that, he should at first drink up a tablespoon of olive oil, but since uncle Taras was very greedy, he used to buy sprats and used to pour sprat oil onto a tablespoon. Sprats, because they were cheaper! But that was profanation, and not a preventative measure. And then, they found an ulcer in uncle Taras. And he couldn't eat anything at all, or drink coffee or cognac.

He, of course, didn't give in right away. At first he was too clever by half and took a Baralgin tablet before eating, and then one more after eating, but the ulcer progressed. Then they made him a mixture of squeezed flaxseeds, honey, and aloe juice, and he was forced to use that vile mixture for an entire year six times a day before taking food. And he ate cooked meet, fish and oatmeal kasha; he barely survived. So are you thirsting to do that?"

I wasn't thirsting. I was drinking my eighth cup of coffee. And obediently chewed on the cheesecake. "That's all, I have to go to class. It's good that my school is closer to your building than to mine. Oh! I nearly forgot. The old guy, sim. to MM. That's Wazuka's owner, he's similar to Marilyn Monroe. White hair, with a birthmark in the corner of his mouth and manicured skin! A giant, nearly two meters tall. Have you seen his fingernails? Fake! Old lady Saransky calls those kind "beef cutlets" and says they should be thrown into a mine, because it's repulsive to look at them. I'd seen that kind in Thailand. One of them, in raspberry-colored lace, feathers and glitter rested against my father's lap. You should've heard what momma said… but that's trivial! Be well, don't despair, you don't have to take Terry out because I walk him during the day!"

When the little dude had left, I uncorked the bottle of rum (in the end, go to hell Valentyn Yuriovych!), poured myself a glass a good four fingers high, cut up an apple, threw on several of Sara's nuts, and I went to my bedroom – to take a rest. Terry ran after me. I opened the door and stopped. The appearance of my bedroom struck me.

CHAPTER IV

*At the very least about children's rebuses, programming
of the future, a metal flask, and Tymofiy.*

My bedroom had the look of the back of a person sick
with bronchitis, whom a caring mommie covered with
mustard plasters. Along the walls, on the floor and even
on the ceiling someone (I'm saying "someone," in truth
I really understood, that the little monster Emile had
done this) had glued, at first glance, clean, white sheets of
paper. But when I approached the first of them, then I saw
that something had been scribbled on the sheets. On the
one that impudently paved my wall opposite the bed was
written: "Nona. Goddess of Nocturnal Emissions."

I filled up my glass and my plate with the sliced apple,
which already had managed to rust, and began to look
over everything all around. On yet one other sheet was
noted: "I. Repin. Portrait of a boy. A gift of the Taganrog
Museum of Art to the eminent Ukrainian personage Emile
Polonsky. You – are the soul of our people." Along four
attached sheets Emile traced out: "Book shelf, my favorite
books and books given to me by authors," and along four
other sheets: "Disks. Movies. Music. My favorite. And giv-
en as gifts."

Several other sheets attested to the fact that "the eminent Ukrainian personage Emile Polonsky" was the first
Ukrainian Jewish cosmonaut, who didn't hide the fact that
he was Jewish;

"the eminent Ukrainian personage Emile Polonsky"– is the laureate (first prize) of the Buzzoni International Piano Competition (Bolzano, 2008), the laureate (second prize after breaking his wrist) of the Rubinstein International Piano Competition (Israel, 2009); laureate (first prize) of the Biotti International Piano Competition (Epinale, 2001); laureate of the P.I. Chaikovsky International Competition (Moscow 2012), laureate (first prize, the mastery of the hand of the genius has been renewed!) of the Maria Callas International Piano Competition (Athens, 2014), laureate (Grand Prix!) of the Van Cliburn International Piano Competition (Ft. Worth, USA, 2015);

"the eminent Ukrainian personage Emile Polonsky is awarded special distinction by the President of the United States Hilary Clinton – to the best pianist in the World (2015, Washington, USA);

at Sotheby's, for the first time in the history of this auction house, the opera score (written in pencil) "Do Well-known Bees Buzz?" by the eminent Ukrainian personage Emile Polonsky was sold for three million pounds (2020, London);

"the eminent Ukrainian personage Emile Polonsky" - laureate of the Nobel Prize in physiology and medicine for decoding the code of a one-hundred per cent sports winner (2021, Geneva).

While I was reading all this I grew perspired. My hands were so moist that when I leaned with them onto the official certificate of the Nobel laureate Emile Polonsky, it was nearly washed off by the flood invoked by me. My ears were burning so much as if all the Chinese on the Planet were saying my name. Altogether. I looked back in search of the rum. The glass was sitting on a night table. Thank God that there is something that serves as a compass for us in this life. I fell on the bed, grabbed the glass, but – too soon, because something really heavy tumbled on the bed that I spilled half the glass. On myself and on the cover. It was Terry. "What's with you?" I asked. Terry barked that he could eat an apple. Of course, if it's of no use to me. He slobbered all over my feet. I tossed the apples onto the floor. I didn't need to. Terry jumped up in a way that the rum literally remained on the bottom. "What the heck is this?" I got indignant. Terry in an instant finished the apples and blinked at me with his devoted eyes. "Terry, slaves are not us, we're not slaves!" I say to him. Terry's tail is saying to me: "No-no-no, guy." Or "Well-well-well." I strive to understand the dog's tail. My God… I stretched out on the bed and fixed the pillow. My hand felt yet one more sheet of paper. I pulled it out.

"Hey, butthead! I thought you'd rummage around in my room. I'm not hiding anything, relax. No naked babes! It's easy to pull off the sheets of paper from the walls and floor; they're attached with special thingies. So don't work yourself up. You'd be better to remember what '2515' is? Emile."

I stared at the floor. Terry lay across the white sheet in such a way that I couldn't read anything. Maybe that's for the better. I looked at the ceiling. To read the notes on the sheets attached to the ceiling, I had to rise up and stand on the bed. Terry was overjoyed and instantly joined me. A dog needs little for joy; any kind of your movement makes him happy. On the ceiling sheet was marked: "The ceiling is adorned with the kisses of women, under glass, in transparent frames, all of this is illuminated with halogen lamps. These are the kisses of those women who have been in love with me." Now Terry was next to me, and I could take a look at what was written on that sheet that Emile tacked on to the floor, but I was afraid to read it. I needed to go to the kitchen for a shot of rum. Before I did that, I sent a text message to the little scoundrel. "Emile, during your break, call me right away. Pavlo."

Sara's telephone didn't answer.

"Sueno que me suenas en color

Viviendo y desviviendote por mi
Para ti todo mi amor
Todo mi amor…"[*]

I though that next time it will be well worth it to buy a really large amount of alcohol and put it in all the rooms. "I'll go and take a look what's there in the study." I said it to Terry because he so heatedly followed after me that I simply couldn't help but share my nearest future plans with him. In the study everything was more or less as it was in my time there. However, certain changes didn't pass over it: the desk looked more in order and the floor cleaner. Gestapo was surprisingly neat. As though there were no innovations in the study. Just a postcard in a frame appeared on the desk. On it in an armchair, a guy I didn't know in either a bath-robe or a coat, was sprawled out. For sure, it was a coat, because few people would wear a robe and a hat at the same time (and the guy was in a hat). The face of the man was succulent, and his mouth as if after making the photograph, he had gotten ready to get drunk on the lips of a beautiful woman weakened from making love or on a roast duck.

Maybe it was a bathrobe. I took the postcard into my hands. A black and white brown-haired guy in Turkish slip-pers. Slippers and a hat. A hat and slippers. "What does this testify to?" I asked Terry. He didn't answer, but comfortably stretched out on the couch. The atmosphere of the study was calming.

Maybe I should also nap a bit? I didn't feel particularly well. It seems, the gobbled up cheesecake of the production of Emile's mother, didn't particularly enjoy a visit by that Varadero Anejo. "Ola, dear, no one is as joyful for you as I

[*]   I dream that you dream about me in color/Living and totally de-voted to me /For you all my love/All my love. Lyrics to a Paulina Rubio song. Many thanks to Cynthia Ramirez for assistance with the translation from Spanish.

am. Value, do value my friendship. You need to lie down so that everything is put into order," I thought. And I just got ready to imitate Terry as I saw this. It stood in the cabinet's frame. There where earlier there had been a sculpture that I had brought from Oslo. A copy of one of Gustav Viherland's sculptures that symbolized health and family values. A father playing with his children. The sculpture looked really strange: if you don't grasp that it holds the meaning of the family values and wellbeing, you might entirely presume that the father is being a monster to his own children, hurling them for the sake of his own satisfaction. I bought this to spite Inna. Right then she was aggressively accusing me of letting my fatherly feelings atrophy.

Now instead of a caring athlete-dad in the frame there stood something that looked like a not very big thermos. A metal flask. I heard my heavy breathing. Never. Ne-ver has my own apartment so frightened me as on this day. What could have been there? Rosehip compote? Ideal weather? Explosives? The unborn little brother of Emile, forgive me Lord? Or maybe – real flesh? Jews do that, right? Circumcision….

"Hey, well, have you guessed? 2515? I swear, no!" Emile called. "Have they circumcised you?" "If I'm honest, I don't think that concerns you. But in as much as you have the voice of a madman, I can say that I wasn't circumcised, though old lady Saransky used to say that men with a circumcised membe…" Emile, don't yap. Don't. Not circumcised. Good. Then what is in your father's flask? Is he circumcised?" "You're obsessed. If I'm not going to yap, you won't hear my answers! Sacred air is in the flask. Don't open it, because I did that one time already, you can't imagine what happened to me for that. Better not to experiment." "Sacred air?" "Listen, did you want something? My five-minute break is already ending. My advice to you is: formulate things more precisely and don't be enthralled with repetitions, our mathematician Moses Lazarevych always says that, and he's right, because…" "Moses? Good. First. What kind of sacred air? Second. What have you done with my room? Third. When will you be home?"

"First. The sacred air of Jerusalem. Dad specially gathered it into a flask, he's very protective of it. Of course you can open the flask, let out the air, and let in some different air, but I wouldn't recommend you do that. Second. Out of your bedroom I've made my ideal room of the future. Momma says that if you model your life, making use of all possibilities and things, it will be like that way. Third. In half an hour. Ta-ta."

I felt lonely. I most itched to open the flask and let out the sacred air of Jerusalem to hell, but I realized that this won't help me. Will it help? I rose up. Terry sensed my hesitation and also jumped down from the couch. Judging by the wagging of his tail, the flask also intrigued him. 2515. 2515 – is a swear word. If it's a primitive number and these – letters, then this is… beae. Beae – is the spirit of the sacred flask. Sometimes technology, that is invented for bringing people together, just deepens your loneliness.

Tymofiy was also outside the zone of reach. Maybe somewhere there, in this unknown zone, together with Sara they are dancing a tarantella. I went into the kitchen, opened my laptop. Not a single letter. Even Hercules Ivanovych Kozhevnikov hadn't sent me an offer to buy the latest piece of crap, Oleksa Vatutin didn't share his recipe for renting land, Jane Smeelly and the rest of the morons didn't suggest I buy Viagra, rubber tops for the penis in the shape of hearts and Rolex compasses, and no one of the staff workers of three offices, with which I collaborated, sent me the Chinese god of money and other guides to prosperous happiness. When spam doesn't reach you – you don't exist. Terry indulgently looked at me now already from the kitchen sofa. He sweetly sighed – he didn't doubt his existence.

Write a letter. "Sara, if you can read Cyrillic where you are – let me know. Beae." I wrote you. Sent it off. "I love you!" After that I wrote one more. "Tim, hey. Where are you? Beae" To that letter I received a quick answer, a polite automatic response informed me that Tymofiy Topolyuk is out of the office, and they're expecting him back no earlier than in three days. And if I need something urgent, I can contact Hanna Minko. That information surprised me a little. I can't say that Tymofiy and I are in touch every day, but when he travels somewhere, then at least he asks me if he should bring me something from there. So I called. But not Hanna Minko, but Tymofiy's mother.

"Hi, Pavlyk. Fiyka's not here," she said. All the same we forgive the mothers of our friends for a lot of things. Especially for these awful nicknames like Pavlyk, Fiyka, Katyusya Olehunchyk, Kolyasyk, Loryk, Svitlanka, Dryusik, Nyusik… Characters of an insect-parrot world. "Do you happen to know where he is?" "At a chess tournament." "At a chess tournament? So why did he nudge his way into a chess tournament, he doesn't play chess?" "Did I say to you that he went to play? No, he went there for vacation. The Society of Psychologist Amateurs organized the competition for social interaction." "Of course." I remained silent, but for some reason didn't put down the handset.

Certainly Tymofiy's mother understood that she needed to ask me about something. "And how are things with you?" Well, of course, how are things. "Not bad. You could say everything's okeedokie, pretty normal. It's just this morning that Gestapo took my Comrade Varadero Anejo." "I, of course, understand, Pavlyk, that you're a grown up man, a little bit shaky after your divorce; even more so from such a smart girl like Nyusik, and right now you're too weak. Of course you can build relations with anyone. And I don't feel like meddling in your life, but in as much as you already called, and in as much as you're not a stranger to me, then I want to tell you that I simply can't understand what the Gestapo was doing in your house, and why you're living with a Latin American? Pavlyk, do you take drugs?" It was difficult for me to find the right words, so I politely thanked her for her trouble, and told her that I don't take drugs, apologized for troubling her and said goodbye.

I've already talked a bit about Tymofiy. He wasn't a psychologist, but he really loved to express himself like a psychologist, to analyze actions of people and their words. Tymofiy, just like Inna, was my classmate. She couldn't stand him. When Inna saw him, her eyebrows crushed her eyes, pressing down on them. "A real dumb shit and latent homosexual," Inna used to say about Tymofiy. I asked Tymofiy out of curiosity why he actually chatted and conducted himself with Inna like an idiot. He had a special manner of "winding-up-Inna," as he used to put it. When he talked to her, he constantly asked things again, stammered, blinked his eyes, and had a lost languorous look. Besides that, he made gestures – with his right hand, as if he were offering something: the heart of Danko, takeanappleorange, or something similar. "You understand, that if I allowed myself to speak with her in the way I speak personally with everyone, she would expose me and would forbid us from speaking. She doesn't need you to chum around with anyone who's smarter than she is. And, sorry, you wouldn't do anything. I'm not a self-sown seedling, so that all kinds of people similar to me appear spontaneously all around me. I value friends, old man. I value you. It's simpler for me to pretend I'm a simpleton."

"Why do you rage over Tymofiy, what's it that he does?" I asked Inna. "And you consider that a normal person who talks to tripods?" Tymofiy really talked to tripods – he was fascinated by physics and chemistry. "You consider that a normal person will call tripods 'little giraffes'? And the fact that he pets them, you also consider that normal? I don't think so." I didn't care what Tymofiy said to tripods and how he pets them, he didn't call me a giraffe and didn't stroke my neck with his hand. That's why I answered that, in my view, every person is disposed to establish relations with anything, including tripods. I noticed the way Inna touches the holes between her teeth with her tongue – she very recently had one tooth extracted and she does that every time she tries to restrain herself.

"Good. Tell me, do you personally collect silver roosters, do you wear lilac-colored sweaters? Do you imitate Vertynsky singing?" I didn't wear that, didn't imitate, didn't collect. The single thing that Inna knew how to do better than me from the school program was drawing. Especially triangles. Maybe, it was exactly that ability that helped push a person into a corner. "Listen, I don't think that all this collecting-wearing-imitating attests to the fact that he's gay. In any case, he never put the moves on me." Inna shrugged her shoulders. "Time will tell! She prophesized. For sure, I also was under Inna's suspicion. For certain, she already imagined how this may happen between me and Tymofiy for the first time, if it hasn't happened already. "Why do you wear lilac-colored sweaters?" I once asked Tymofiy. "I look good in them. What of it?" He answered. "And why don't you want to collect little dogs or fish instead of roosters?" "Because I like silver roosters. What of it?" I didn't ask about Vertynsky.

Tymofiy right then was working as the main specialist in the citizen complaints department of a government agency. He and I called this "the head of flying saucers division" because a significant percentage of those who appealed to Tymofiy (of course, not to Tymofiy himself, but to the director of the agency), were people who knew about UFOs, visitors, influence of the cosmos on the presence of hot water in the tap, the victory of one or another candidate in elections, the stylish hair of a neighbor woman, and also that "the neighbor's dog bends its back like a cat, he's not a dog." From all of this I would have gone crazy, but Tymofiy got satisfaction from it. I know precisely that he offhandedly answered several of the respondents, gave them advice, met with them, thought up things to occupy them. He kept an index file: all the individuals of the region whose screws were loose ended up on Tymofiy's special cards. Inna wouldn't have been able to sleep if she had found out about the card file. That's why I never told her about it.

"You already know that I finally became a chemist. They say I'll be a second Mendeleev, and I just wanted one thing: to create a medicine for loneliness, a kind of potion for happiness," once Tymofiy began. To that I answered that it was Mendeleev who found that potion for happiness, and that potion is called "vodka." Tymofiy silently looked at me, and then he asked: "You really think so?" I said that sometimes I think precisely just like that.

"My searching ended up with the fact that I received a diploma with the highest grades, defended my dissertation, got a job with a pharmaceutical company and discovered a formula for pills to keep from getting fat, from which only your head gets thin. Because your hair falls out. Yes, right from childhood I wanted to be a sorcerer, but is this an excuse to turn into scoundrel? I knew everything about Tymofiy's first job. About his first job, his first wife, his first cat, and his first pills.

I also knew how he found those "magical pills" on the night table of his lover. She believed more in those pills than in Tymofiy's words about the fact that they're a profanation, and using them was harmful. That didn't stop her from considering him a liar.

My friend's next job was at a winemaking factory. One of the pillmaking managers invited him there. I told him right away that, in my opinion, there was not a single reason to expect that it will be a normal job. To that he sang to me, softly burring in Russian:

"Time, making the rounds of chance,
goes forward,
But your confused flight isn't hopeless,
To the strong are given the wings of height,
Someone needs to believe, to believe
in order to win,
We'll patiently await the first ray of hope."

Maybe time slips past chances, but that's what chances are! And not rules. Tymofiy made fresh wine at the factory. Strawberry. It was supposed to be called "Sister Strawberry." I asked Inna if she'd buy a wine with that name. Inna said she didn't buy wines at all from that producer where Tymofiy was working.

"Bias doesn't play a role," she got angry in answer to my accusation. "It's just they're rogues." Tymofiy also left there. He didn't stay too long.

At that time he got married to Eva. Eva made clothing for cats, dogs, rats, and other domestic animals. "Eva, listen, well you just tell him (he never listens to me), that he's doing idiotic crap. Is anybody going to buy that idiotic strawberry wine? It's a substitute! Why is he wasting his abilities?" I got indignant into the telephone receiver. "Listen, I don't think it's a bigger idiocy than making an itty bitty jacket for a white rat, embroidering dead cats on it." I had nothing to hide.

"Will you now affirm that Tymofiy is a latent homosexual?" I asked Inna with interest. "Sure. And what has changed?" "If you haven't noticed, I'm informing you: he got married." "So he got married, what of it? A few get married. Wilde was also a married man. This is what I want to say to you. Only an idiot or a latent gay will marry a woman who has the name of a well-known seductress with apples and sews hats for mice and gophers.

When Tymofiy with enthusiasm announced that the pill- strawberry wine manager suggested that he works in the antique business, I expressed myself more categorically than the previous time. "This guy's a swindler. And you'll end up behind bars. You won't agree to that job," I said. Tymofiy had a lost look – he had never scrutinized his friend and employer from that point of view. After that Tymofiy worked for a fair amount of time in a shoe store specializing in creams for cleaning suede. To this day he never uses pills and treats himself exclusively with herbs and just drinks vodka. Well, of course, he knows everything about crèmes for footwear!

Till the moment that Tymofiy started to work in the bureau of citizen complaints (and this happened accidentally – he had saved the life of the head of the department, who had a heart attack on the street, pouring into the gentleman half a bottle of valerian), Tymofiy used to put together tests and horoscopes for a stylish women's magazine. Inna stopped buying that magazine. I hmmmed but kept quiet. At that moment I understood that Inna and I had nothing to talk about with each other. Eva went to her mother's in Ternopil and hasn't returned since. The only thing we found out was the fact that Eva's mother had never been in Ternopil.

One time Tymofiy got the idea to declare Eva dead. That happened when he was about to fall in love with Mariana. And he didn't just fall in love, but wanted to marry her. Tymofiy informed his love of his intentions. The next day she went to Ternopil on business and to this day hasn't returned. "She went to look for Eva." That's what Tymofiy's conjecture sounded like. I remained silent. "Ternopil – that's like Twin Peaks," Tymofiy added. "I think I need to go there too." I made him promise not to go to Ternopil without me. For the time being he's keeping it, but it's unclear whether he went to observe chess players. Or maybe, he couldn't bear it and took off for the lovely city of Ternopil to search for Eva's mother, Eva and Mariana.

The feeling of my loneliness grew stronger. This was similar to when your skin gradually acquires the color of dusk. I'm abandoned unnecessarily, a stuffed rabbit without a paw, left on a bench. Next to me is a flask with someone else's air named Bdad, the awful room of a crazy child, someone else's dog, and a zone of inaccessibility. But there are the whales!! Whales, killer whales, and dolphins! Mine, not really such little friends.

I remembered the whales and decided to try to work a bit. An open file reminded me more of a white sheet on which someone was planning to lay down to sleep. I thought that this someone maybe will be me, because I didn't feel like working. "I won't give in so easily. I won't give in with a baaat-tle!" I announced. Terry tore his snout from the couch. He looked at me. And just in case barked. "My friend, you probably know what it means not to give in. What it means to fight for a couch, the right to an obligatory scrap from the table, the right to take your duck to your bed and the rest, right?" Terry wagged his tail and barked twice. It's much simpler to mend things with dogs than with people.

And I began to write. "Orcinus orca. The Latin names of creatures and plants always romanticize their images and make them mysterious. Orcinus orca – how is this not the name of a fairytale giant of the seas? A killer whale is a true cosmopolitan. This dolphin swims all the oceans from the Arctic to Antarctica. With its great tail is shakes an iceberg, as if it were shaking a giant cocktail. In general, the killer whale ignores just the Black Sea and the Laptev Sea; instead you will notice it in seas such as Karsk Sea and the East Siberian. Chillier whales are more to its liking, you find it in the tropics less often. Evidently, in the chillier waters its delicacies are better maintained: the tongues of killed whales…."

I stopped at this spot. I couldn't imagine what the tongue of a killed whale looked like. In order to understand, why killer whales have those damn tongues, I needed to clearly imagine the tongues. The name of a story by Rudyard Kipling wandered through my brain "How the Whale Got His Throat." But I couldn't remember – how? Maybe to fit its tongue? So I quickly wrote a letter to the editor of the magazine for which I was writing about whales. "Talliy, what does the tongue of whale look like?" Vitaliy Markin was person, who, if he didn't know everything, he would manage to successfully hide his lack of knowledge. He worked quicker than Google. If Sergei Bryn had found out about Vitaliy Markin at the same time when he began working out his world-famous Google search engine, he would have named it Taalliy. Vitaliy was a glistening brown-haired guy. In the office the girls from time to time argued over what glistened more – his hair or his shoes. With his external appearance and manner of speaking Vitaliy Markin, whom everyone generally called Talliy, reminded me of a sunflower seed. Not anything special, small, swarthy, but you couldn't tear yourself away from him. And he glistened!

In three minutes I received an email from him. Talliy always communicated with people as though he were speaking from a TV screen. "You'll be interested to know the fact that the tongue of a whale (the length of which is close to 30 meters, and the weight close to 20 tons (I have in mind the weight of the whale itself!), weighs 400 kilograms." I grew numb. I mechanically clicked on the window "you've got mail." One more letter. "It's worth adding, that the tongue of the blue whale (that's the largest of the whales!) has a sack-like form, and its weight can be up to three tons. In order to imagine that better, that's the weight of a fully grown African elephant." I got lost in thought. A fully grown African elephant in the maws of a whale. A whale moves an elephant… Does a whale have a maw or not? Ah! A whale has a gullet. That's what Kipling said. An African elephant in the maws of a whale, as though in ambush. It would be interesting to know, who would fit into Emile's maw?

Beae. Would a gopher fit? Or is it too heavy? A small heap of flies? A little rat? Has anyone ever weighed a person's tongue? I need to look up the memoirs of Hannibal Lecter. He couldn't ignore it.

I read somewhere that the ceremonial red carpet at the Oscars weighs five tons, and its length reaches 150 meters. Maybe a whale's tongue served as the prototype? It takes them two days to lay down that carpet. The procedure takes the efforts of twenty-one people. Do they set out the tongues of whales? Maybe, whale killer maniacs walk on them?

But do whales French kiss? Or is that possible with those kind of tongues? "French Kiss." That's what we called kisses with your tongue sticking into somebody else's mouth. Inna taught me that.

I remember that at first I felt like a birdie that the mother-birdie feeds with a blend of worms. With a single distinction – I didn't want to eat them.

The indefatigable Talliy sent me one more letter. There was an announcement that American scientists have determined five languages, the speakers of which aliens have entered into contact. In fifth place was the English, in fourth – the language of Mayan tribes, in third – Russian, in second – Chinese, and in first – the language of whales!

The inquiring Talliy. Maybe they already are conversing with whales, these beings from the other side. Fully grown African elephants stir in the throats of whales, giant whales with the help of giant elephants slowly and sober-mindedly talk about the fact that people are destroying their planet…

Terry tore away from the sofa and ran in the direction of the hallway. The picture "The Return of Emile." I guessed. It really was him. "Hey, what about 2515? Have you figured it out?" "I haven't. But I wanted to have a chat with you." "And we'll have a chat, I'm not moving out today . I'm off to walk Terry. Heat up the diet soup for me!" Heat up the diet soup? Where will I get it? I'm working on being heated up by a little braveheart.

I didn't find the darn soup. I got lost in my refrigerator. Pans depressed me. There were way too many of them; besides that they were overly pompous. Instead I found cold baked pork that I ate. "Did you heat it up?" "I couldn't find it." "Where did you look?" "In the refrigerator, of course. What, do you have a special flask with soup? I'm not surprised. Your father has a flask, and his son also has one. With sacred soup."

"Maybe you've already got to the alcohol. Well, that's your business. I'm not going to wipe the drool after your children-oligophrenics." I clenched my teeth. "It wasn't worth looking in the refrigerator. I never eat old soup. It's unhealthy. Momma specially visited me to guarantee we had fresh soup. And the main dish in honor of the visit of Violoncello. You haven't forgotten?" With those words Emile ran up to the cabinet where there were already no bottles. "I knew that! You need to push your way to the supermarket for alcohol. Expensive and unusual, because Violoncello is like that. You'll see yourself. Not that I've liked to treat that riffraff with fine drinks, but believe me, we'll manage more cheaply than listening through everything that he usually squeaks, when the drinks don't satisfy him. So it's better to go. And I'll eat right away and will play." "I'm dreaming of that," I said. "I'm seeing it in dreams."

"Once Mumi (yet one more acquaintance of my father) constantly saw a fire in dreams. Imagine, he just shut his eyes, and saw right away a small child frightened by the fire begging for help. Sometimes he smelled the stench of something burning. He began to collect newspaper clippings about fires. He bought himself a fire extinguisher, and what happened?" "What happened?" "It happened that his neighbor was executing female cockroaches every day on the balcony – he was burning them. He called them "Jean d'Arcs." After that momma's called cockroaches that way. Like – you need to buy poison for the Jean d'Arcs! Can you imagine?" "I can. Mumi from what? Mukaltin Mikaelovych or something?" "He's Mumi because he's Mumi."

I turned on the TV. The little dude set out a bowl with soup in the microwave. "A millionaire from Berdychiv intends to create his own political party," a blonde girl with a flat face announced. "It'd be better for him to create a new Berdychiv. Nowhere to waste his money," Emile thundered with the pot lids. Now he was generously spreading out butter on the multigrain bread. 'He's spreading it with a little mountain,' my mother used to say. "So what is 2515?" Why has he been pestering me?

"In principle,I didn't volunteer to guess idiotic riddles, understand? But if you're so itching to find out, then I've decided that 2515 is beae." "No, that's not 'beae.' Well think, just think. Old man Saransky once worked as a criminologist…" "For some reason I don't remember that," tore out of me. "Of course you don't remember, because you don't know and for the time being can't know! But you will. So, old Saransky, when he wasn't quite as old, worked as a criminologist. He always used to say to me that you can always uncover a crime just thanks to the fact that you pick open an individual, who committed this crime, and you'll set him out in handfuls in pots, and only that way! Well, this still could happen – if the criminal forgotten something, returned to get it, all the way here – an entire brigade… and you nail him!

You go to steal something or kill someone-don't attach objects onto yourself that can slide off, and don't take anything valuable." "Well and what of that?"

The little dude sighed. "Look, 2515. Don't think about a riddle – think about me, I'm your decoder." "I don't want to think about you. I went to buy an expensive libation for your Violoncello." "No, wait! Let's finish playing! Then I'll

play Handel, we won't be able to play this at the table..."
He's a child all the same, this chatty Emile! "Good. Judging
from what I saw in my, pardon me, now your room, you can
consider yourself a genius." I swear, the little dude blushed!
"I'll tell you honestly. Accepting this fact won't make my
life easier. It just adds obligations and responsibilities." He
sighed deeply. Terry too. There was nothing left for me other
than to sigh after them.

"We can be late at this rate, think more actively, well!" "I
don't know. My brain isn't set up to accept similar things.
Look here, for example, at the television. It transmits certain
channels, and others – not. I'm set up the same way." "So I
understand this. Too bad that the situation with you can't
be fixed with the help of an antenna and a cable package."
"That's it. I'm tired of your prattling. I'm out of here," I announced. "Wait. Look, I do music. I do mathematics, what
does that indicate?" "And what does it?" "Oh. 2 – is "para";
5 – is "sol", the fifth note in a scale; 15 – is the letter "k," which
is fifteenth in the alphabet. So it comes out "para-solka"
(little parasol). Have you understood now? A simple riddle."

I ran out of the apartment. The elevator stopped at the
fifth floor; I saw two snouts. An apricot one and a bronze
one. "Karina. Abbrev. poodle. Furious auntie Hanna," my
memory obliged me. "Are you without yours?" I heard. "Interesting, without your what?" She squeezed herself into the
elevator. These are strange people – it's as if there's enough
room, but they anyway act like they can barely squeeze in.
"Have you already done your walk?" I decided that to those
questions an unconstrained swing of my head would be the
most successful answer. "We're just going out!" How much
enthusiasm she has! I've never spoken to her, why should
I know where she's going? What's with her? "You know,
Kostik really wanted just a spaniel, but they told me that
poodles don't leave hair all over an apartment. That's the
way it is – Karisha never sheds. How about yours? Maybe,

you vacuum every day – it's so much hair, maybe a vacuum cleaner barely copes with it, do you change your filters a lot?" Finally – the first!

But to how many questions do you need to answer at least something. "I don't do that," I answered. "I don't have time." Furious Hanna laughed. For sure she thought: here's a dirty scum, his wife breaks her back for him. "How is Kostik feeling?" "Good, just he doesn't want to go to school." I made a facial expression "kidsarekids." She answered me "so what can you do with him." And we parted, satisfied with one another. At least it seemed to be like that to me.

The next to our building supermarket contains very strange types of drinks. Some of them I'm afraid to take in my hands, and not to my mouth; Tymofiy informed me about some of them in detail. After not very lengthy ruminations I decided: if Violoncello is already such a demanding absorber of drinks, I could make an original home drink. So, I bought a box of strawberry juice, two bottles of domestic vermouth, an enormous bottle of nut-flavored liqueur, made by our brother Slovaks, and a small box of mint tea. I also bought candy, bananas, several bunches of grapes, a kilo of apples, and ground chocolate. Next to the checkout (not being conscious of what I'm doing), I bought several "Milka" chocolate bars with almonds. And just when I was paying, I realized that I had taken them especially for Emile. And I was stup-i-fie-d by that.

I heard this, of course, on the stairwell landing. Of course, the "Sarabande for String Orchestra and Piano by G.F. Handel." The unrelenting little dude. Suddenly something creaked. I nearly dropped the packages with the components for the libations for Violoncelli. Violoncelli sounds like the last name of a Georgian aristocrat. It turned out, the door of apartment number 76 had creaked. She stood in the doorway. Small, shaggy and angry. Next to her was her black German Shepherd. It seemed to me that both of them were almost the same height. Tamara the Cop. "Good day, Tamara Anonivna!" Politeness in conversation with investigative authorities; may even these authorities stand in crazy slippers in the form of fish faces (and you need that!). "And you too." The authorities answered in their slipperfish. I sensed that my face was radiating joy from meeting with Tamara Antonivna, and also the readiness to oblige. It would be better for me never to have known where she works and what her job is, then I would have felt more confident.

"I've just gotten back from the night shift," she began. That was my chance! I understood that quickly. "We're putting a stop to this. Just don't you worry. Get yourself ready for bed, rest up. And we – promptly! This is my…" "And I know. I know. We've already been introduced. You tell him – quieter. Tomorrow – as much as he wants. I won't be home. And more – I don't object."

"What?" The plan for the liquidation of the "Sarabande for String Orchestra and Piano by G.F. Handel" was ruined. "He'll understand what. Tell him and that's all. Keep it." She placed something in my palm. Something cold. A case with the initials T.A. for a memento? "This is a key." And she closed the door.

Terry tried hard to tear the little package with his snout. "You'll get black eyes, you stupid doggie, there are bottles in there," I warned him. But Terry didn't listen. "Emile, call him, he'll make a pate out of the bananas for Violoncelli." Terry – no." I dragged the packages to the kitchen. The tinkling of the bottles harmoniously harmonized with the wailing of the "Sarabande for String Orchestra and Piano by G.F. Handel." By the way, the table was already set. Napkins, dishes, a salad bowl, and two buckets that served as a stand for the bottles. "The buckets are free to go." "You didn't buy them?" The little dude diligently moved his fingers. "I bought them, but for this drink we need a glass or porcelain carafe. Your father's flask would fit, but there's sacred air in there." The little dude didn't react. "They've given you a key here. And said that they don't object." Emile was amazingly silent. His reaction to my words was a barely noticeable wagging of his head. An actor, dammit!

However, I had much more interesting matters than to explain what kind of key that was. On an agenda – a drink for Violoncelli. "We have forty-five minutes left for all this about everything." Hmm, could esteemed Tamara Antonivna have decided to divest Emile of his virginity? Could she have? I – am a person, corrupted by youthful romanticism. The key and "I don't object" – aren't these the eternal companions of romanticism? I cast a glance at Emile. But he didn't get distracted from his concerns. However, he first pulled out a carafe. It aroused Terry. Damn it. I had forgotten that my porcelain carafe is a duck. And ducks for Terry – that's exclusively his own, male dog thing. Regarding this carafe, I was fortunate enough to acquire it during a trip through the Golden Ring of Russia. The Leningrad porcelain factory, the war years, a duck of blockaded Leningrad! And here right now mad Terry is jumping in front of the table.

"Never mind, never mind," I say. "Terry, no!" Dog incantations don't work the first time. "Terry, you can't have this duck! It's an antique!" I tried hard to evoke a response from the dog. He grows still, turns to me with his butt, and disappears under the table. I was insulted. I toss a not quite eaten bit of cold baked pork under the table. I listen. He doesn't champ. He's stubborn.

But that's already his business. I pour out the box of strawberry juice into the duck carafe, then I add nearly the entire bottle of vermouth, a half glass of nut-flavored liqueur, and there I pour in a small cup of strongly brewed mint tea. It's good that the carafe is big, a liter and a half. I put everything into the refrigerator, prior to that moving out of there one of the pots. I glanced under the table – Terry licked my nose. He forgave me!

"If you want to apologize – wag your tongue!" That was Emile. He proved his point. He managed even to place at the center of the table something yellow. "This – is chicken curry." "How do you wag a tongue?" Emile shows me. He sticks out his tongue, then thrashes it right to left, then left to right. I don't notice as I begin to repeat. "Let's add some panting?" Emile suggests. And the three of us begin to pant. Terry goes mad from our tongue exercises and smiles. The smile of Saint Terry. "Do you, happen to know how much a human tongue weighs?" I'll ask the little dude. But he doesn't manage to answer me, because we hear the front door open. It's Violoncello!

CHAPTER V

In the very least about violoncellists and special drinks.

In principle, what image may it evoke when they tell you that a grown-up person is coming to your place for dinner, a classical musician, and also a former (and maybe even current) suitor of your beloved? I imagined Violoncello to be morose, stout, and a sufficiently ordinary fellow. We all make mistakes. When we entered the hallway, I met a person-leopard. In a moment in my apartment a carnival will begin… Violoncello was a tall guy, dressed in a leopard skin coat, that invitingly dropped on his really overly wide for a man thighs. He had a hat-donut. This head attire looked as if someone had sat on him and groaned. Even now. Party functionaries wore this kind of donuts, in particular, and Tymofiy's father had a hat like that.

I remember when in the winter, drunk, in old slippers (Tymofiy and I called them worn cats, because for months the slippers became frayed, and several threads stuck out like cat whiskers); in the coat and donut of Tymofiy's father I ran out to see off the guests. When I had seen them off to the metro station and stopped next to the building to breathe the icy winds, a homeless guy stepped up to me and asked for help. I turned the inside out of my pocket, from which a white kerchief dropped out. The homeless guy bent over to lift it up, and he saw my feet in frayed slippers. "O, are you one of ours? And I assumed – if that pyramid of Cheops is on your head, then you're some kind of big shot, and you're the very same misery as I am. Sorry, old man."

I muttered, "Greetings to you," but I couldn't tear my gaze away from Violoncello, though Emile had latched on to my arm and dragged me to the kitchen. Violoncello decided that greeting me with his eyes in my direction entirely was sufficient. In answer he winked at me. As though he were giving me to understand that he heard me, and in principle approvingly is disposed to my greeting. A leopard-skin winter coat. I thought that only Salvador Dali was embolden to dress in such a thing – I once was preparing an article about him and marvelously remember his enthusiasm for eccentric clothing. In nearly the very same coat in a not very peaceful area of New York, I once saw an enormous black man with a walking stick. I figured he's a well-known rapper, and nearly threw myself at him for an autograph (I didn't even presume that I can throw myself at someone for an autograph shouting "Oh man," but his look was dazzling!). I was held back in time from an outburst, because it turned out that he was a local pimp, and heightened attention might appear superfluous to him.

"Well, boys, I expect that everything's already ready and we can have supper?" Gestapo said. In as much as I silently watched Violoncello placing his leopard on my coat hanger, Emile answered for both of us. "Yes! According to a special recipe, Pavlo prepared a unique drink for you. I haven't tasted it, but I think that it's something incredible!" "Really? Very obliging," Gestapo spurred me on. It's good that he didn't stroke me on my head, because I don't know how I would have tolerated that. "Valentyn, I already told you that Pavlo is constantly traveling, and for sure he brought back that recipe from somewhere." Violoncello didn't react – he placed his hat on the shelf. "So what's it called, this drink, what's in it? Who created it?" In my view, Gestapo was overly playful. "Ah! After the little party, maybe, he successfully pumped out my rum."

"The drink is Spanish," I said. But for Gestapo that information was too little. He continued to searchingly look at me. It seems that the all dog owners command the art of this look. "The most expensive chef in the world Ferran Adria, the owner of the El Bulli restaurant informed me about this recipe. He said that he made up this drink for special occasions. In particular, it is precisely this drink that's made when the Spanish are celebrating dates of creation of fantastic buildings by the genius Gaudi." (I think my discourse would have satisfied Talliy. I learned this from him. Talliy called this style "deceitful eloquence with the use of foreign names"). It seemed that this should have been enough for Gestapo, but for him it didn't, and he asked: "And what's his name?" "Ferran Gauda." The more often you communicate with people, the easier it is for you to lie. However, is this a lie? In truth I made up this damned drink, why shouldn't I make up a name for it?

The entire time Violoncello unhurriedly was engaged with his outer clothing. Finally all his things were hung up and laid out as he wanted. Without his overcoat he also had a totally pimpish look. A shiny mocha-colored turtleneck, slacks the color of wet sand, a belt with a shiny buckle shaped like kissing lips. On the collar of the turtleneck (this was unbelievable!) a golden rooster bent over obediently. "I'll steal that," the sinful idea settled in my head, instantly letting itself be known. "Tymofiy collects roosters," the sinful idea explained its stealing motive. It's just interesting to figure out how to do this? Maybe, grab it by the throat in a fit of jealousy over Sara and grab the rooster?

"So, it turns out that you're Sara's freshly-baked fiancé?" Such was the first phrase of Violoncello after the fact that he downed half the portion of the chicken-curry and drank up four tall goblets of "Ferran Gauda." I affirmed that it was. "And you do, if I'm not mistaken, geography? Milik, pour me one more glass of that liquid, friend!" Milik – you need to take it for a weapon. Some kind of vile stuff. In my view, such conduct with an overly alcoholic strawberry juice is imprudent. "Valentyn, I already said to you that Pavlo writes travel articles. His main education is in geography, but he doesn't work very closely with it." "Why is that so?" It seemed to me that my voice here is superfluous, and I wasn't mistaken. "Valentyn, you're like a child. Can you make money in our time with geography in its pure form?" "Right now you can make money on vodka in its pure form," I dove in. "And, yes it turns out that you have experience?" Violoncello inquired scornfully . He provoked irritation in me, I itched in my head, my hands and legs itched too. Violoncello instead cut a small marinated zucchini. The marinated zucchini and strawberry juice are a happy combination! Violoncello, maybe, has a strong stomach.

I said that I have certain experience, but once I wanted to be wine steward. A poem came out of it, about which Emile enthusiastically informed us. But Valentyn wasn't enthralled with my rhymed creative work. He said: "And why the vodka here? What link is there between a wine steward, it turns out yes, and vodka?" "I'm sorry, but I need to step out – to pray." "Pray to whom?" "To God, of course. God or to the flask. Do you know about the flask? Do you pray to someone else?" "To the flask? Is this something Indian? I don't pray at all. I'm a creative person. I've gotten used to people worship me. And they worship! Thousands! No, several thousand fans! Young girls dedicate poems to me. Just listen: "O, your music, o, your fingers that pass along the body of the violoncello, we are bewitched – to part, only without you, I'll jump off a cliff." "Don't worry about me. No cliffs. You can bet your last *hryvnya* – I'm not going to worship you. And you, either, I'm not planning to." I escaped to the bathroom. Sara didn't answer. And this is called a civilized country. Where is the network? I felt like taking an interest in it. With whom is she meeting? With narcotics dealers?

I sat in the bathroom with my cell phone in my palms and heard the distant mumbling of practically unknown people to me and didn't understand anything about my life.

I grabbed a coloring book about the adventures of an itty-bitty mouse and began to make its ears turn red. It didn't help. You need to take the initiative in your hands! From the very beginning it was understood that this evening will not be enchanting, but a little more – and I'll vomit. Or it will become something irreparable. In the end, I didn't feel like adjusting myself toward the vile suitor of Sara in the eyes of her uncle and "Milik" (especially Milik!). We'll get him wound up. So, what do I know about him? He's a violoncellist. The operation will be called: "The hunting of the violoncellist by violoncellists." Because I won't manage with him on my own.

It's good. That I know about violoncellists and violoncellos? Not a lot. Better whales, but what can you do, you work with what there is. A guitar with a bow. A violin-overage child. Well of course: Gagarin violoncello – Mstislav Leopoldovich Rostropovich. It's strange that Violoncello wasn't named Leopold or Mstislav. In face, you can work with this material… Yes, then. "The Violoncellist." Amadeo Modigliani, oil, yellow-ultramarine colors.

A violoncellist more than anything reminds you of a Decembrist, who hides in a remote settlement. An ascetic with a beard. This is not similar to the well-fed mug of Valentyn Yuriyovych, but one can talk a bit… How could I forget! When I had a romance with a girl from Greater Novgorod, we often met in Moscow. And we didn't just make love, but culturally were enriched. For example, we went to the theater. It was right in the Mayakovsky Theater that I saw this performance. What was its name? Something classical with a contemporary addition. O! The play was called: *The Lady with the Pet Dog and Other Fowl.* One of the main characters there was a lonely violoncellist by the name of Arkady, who kept a baby rabbit named Filip; and the quality of his play he checked by the intensity of carrot crunching by Filip. This is already closer to the point! Several irritating things could come out of this.

"You, of course, can object to it. I'm used to polemical discussions, but it seems to me that the liberal ravings don't fit this historically agrarian land. Yes, it turns out that you have to take this country by tangibility! Winter wheat, spring wheat. Spring wheat, winter wheat, strict consistency! And not here-there, there-here, and then, it turns out that it's entirely in a different direction." In as much as I understood, Violoncello thrust his political view on everyone present. When he saw me, I grabbed my favorite carafe and began to wave it.

"Are you organizing?" He laughed first. Well, onward, Pavlo. "Do you have a baby rabbit?" I asked Violoncello, carefully snatching away from his hands the porcelain duck-carafe. As I calculated, Violoncello wavered with his answer. "What do I have?" "It turns out so – a baby rabbit. Because a little rabbit is the favorite creature of violoncellists." I intentionally spoke in a kind of voice as if I were preparing to show little boys and girls a cheery magic trick with a balloon! "Who told you, it turns out yes, such a stupid thing?" I decided this time to add not one, but two glasses of Slovak nut-flavored liqueur to the "Spanish" mixture. "I read it in Yo Yo Ma's memoirs." It's interesting to know, what will he yak right now? "Where? And how do you know about Yo Yo Ma?" I remembered about Yo Yo Ma accidentally. When I first heard these sounds – "yoyoma" – I thought it meant a Chinese toy, or hip hop songs. Yo Yo Ma – as it was explained later – was a well-known violoncellist of Chinese extraction. However I wasn't mistaken about his Chinese extraction. "You'd be interested in finding out that geography is the kind of science that includes extraordinarily different spheres of life and development of all the countries of the world, and also society." He was silent. "It turns out so!" I added.

"Boys, let's take a look at what we have for dessert!" "And let's call Snihuronka," I added mentally. Gestapo decided to step forward into the role of a peacemaker. Well-well. "What kind of dessert? So, are we finished with main dishes then? But I'm hungry! I didn't have the opportunity to eat well. The day before yesterday there was a rehearsal. Yesterday we were partying at Karl's birthday, and he didn't think of feeding us. In general, he stole my name given score from me. I would have never begun to eat from his hands! I just keep quiet about how he got the esteemed position! So, can't I now eat as I should? In the house of my best friend?" "I think that a little bit of homemade sausage with jelly apple won't stand in the way. Emile will warm it up right now." Gestapo didn't want to argue with Valentyn Yuriyovych. Here's one thing I couldn't understand, that is how he could be friends with such a… fellow."

"Valentyn, let's step out. I'll show you what I'm working on. Pavlo was so kind to assign me his study…" Emile, in the meanwhile, noted something in a mourning notebook. "What's that you have?" "It's a special notebook. I note dead hours, evenings and days there." "What, are you unhappy?" "It turns out so." I smiled at the little dude. The little dude, when he's not playing and not mentioning the elderly Saran-skys, and isn't issuing his own diplomas about his genius, is quite not a bad little dude.

"We need to heat up the sausages. Tasty food, of course, won't save a ruined evening, but you won't go to sleep hungry. The stomach else will be calm and won't drink bile juice. Old lady Saranska always used to say: if you're waiting for a bad guest – focus more on serving food, because when you're not already lucky with your guest, then with regard to food, you, glory be to the Creator, are able to take care of it yourself." Emile returned to me and winked: "There's also a Japanese cartoon about a violoncellist named Hosyu. He was friends with all kinds of creatures and played Beethoven!" "Hosyu… Emile, listen, was there really nothing between him and Sara?"

"One time Heracles Petrovych, this dishonest philatelist (he once told old man Saransky that he can spit really far, because his teeth have such a disposition that his spit flies really far. Then for a long time they stood on the balcony and argued who could spit further. They spit. And though Saransky won without the dispositions, Heracles Petrovych, all the same, lied to everyone that he won, so they called him Heracles Petrovych Brekhunets [the Liar], though his name was Berkhshvili). He asked old lady Saranska if she was in love with the hairdresser Yuras? It's like this, old lady Saranska answered him that he's either looking at Yuras through others' and not her eyes, through a small magical glass, where Yuras appears as a splendid brown-haired person with a white-toothed smile, and not a little chip, who the entire time has moist hands and skimps on shaving cream for his clients and toothpaste for himself, or Heracles Petrovych Brekhunets offends her. Make your own conclusions, but I'm going to heat up the sausages!"

Just as Emile had set out the sausages on a tray, Violoncello dropped in. In the hour of Violoncello's absence I didn't manage to do anything; I didn't even finish smoking a cigarette. "Do you, it turns out so are having serious intentions about Sara?" "Approximately the same as Hosyu." I answered insolently. We'll see how he swallows this. "Hosyu?" Gestapo was the first to react. I totally forgot about his presence. "I understand it like this, it turns out so, that we are having a natural conversation, so to answer in that kind of way as You are doing, to me seems unacceptable. Isn't that so, Gennadiy?" Gestapo yessed him. "Did you give Sara baskets of lilies of the valley?" I asked.

In reality I was thinking about how to swipe the rooster from him without him noticing, because the "Ferrana Gauda" was nearly gone, and there was no better partner to find in this matter. "Sara isn't a slovenly wench from an English novel, if it turns out so, I would give her lilies of the valley. Even more in baskets. Don't you understand that this is rude? What do they teach you… where there… it turns out so, in the geography department?" I thought for a bit that I wasn't risking anything, and slapped him in the face. From surprise Gestapo started to hiccup; his face became so red, as though he had received the slap himself. I offered Gestapo a goblet of the rest of the "Ferrana Gauda," and with hugs crawled over to Violoncelli to beg forgiveness. While I was talking to him about the fact that when I defend my higher geographical education, I sometimes conduct myself inadequately, which I regret, and about the fact that I recalled the lilies of the valley from a story about Rostropovich's acquaintance with Vyshnevska, I managed to unlatch the desired rooster. "Ha." I heard. It was Emile. He saw everything.

I thought that after my slap Valentyn Yuriyovych would go. Eh, no. I was mistaken. He didn't even go after he drank three cups of coffee, two cups of tea, and ate a box of candies. "A fire in your mouth – make a freshly squeezed juice from apples, chaps!" To go with the home-made round candies of Emile's mother (a nut mixture, raisins, dried apricots, a little honey, coconut shavings), he requested that "Milik" play the Sarabande. In honor of Sara, of course. I didn't support this idea. And he then said that that wasn't very friendly. And I noted that we aren't friends, it turns out so. "That's why we need "to drink brotherhood,"* or be-

⋯⋯⋯⋯⋯⋯⋯⋯⋯⋯⋯⋯⋯⋯⋯⋯⋯⋯⋯⋯⋯⋯⋯⋯⋯⋯⋯⋯⋯

* The German tradition of "Bruderschaft trinken" as explained here:http://prawfsblawg.blogs.com/prawfsblawg/2006/07/drinking_brothe.html. Thanks to Svitlana Bednazh for pointing this out.

come friends forever!" I don't remember how I escaped that proposition. He didn't leave and then, when he finished the bananas, one of which he fed to Terry by uttering: "Learn to work with a microphone, beast!" And he showed how you need to work with a microphone. The shameful sight nearly turned me inside out.

He didn't even go when the Slovak liqueur had been drunk up to the last drop. When he had swallowed the nut-flavored liqueur, he promised to embroider my socks, because this was his hobby – embroidering socks. And he insisted that I immediately got up and dragged those ones over to him that I wanted to see embroidered. "This will be, it turns out so, a little rabbit with lilies of the valley – that's what this will be!" He put my socks in the outer backside pocket of his slacks.

"And you can draw that into your nostrils!" Violoncello said, taking proper care of the package with grated chocolate. And he took it in. And he began to sneeze. Little piles of a brown-colored liquid stained the kitchen walls. Emile also took it, because it interested him, and ran to the washbasin. Gestapo grabbed me by the elbow and said that we should immediately stop this outrage and called a taxi.

Emile took Terry, Gestapo took Violoncello, and they went out onto the street. I managed to attach the rooster to Violoncello's meat-filled pastry. All the same stealing – isn't for me. I immediately began to smoke. Silence. How good this is – complete silence.

I decided not to clear things from the table. I'll do that tomorrow. So I smoked another cigarette. My guests hadn't returned and I spread out the sleeper couch. When I settled myself to go to sleep, I felt a certain discomfort in the area of my back. And I pulled out a cardboard boot. There were two black stains on the cardboard boot.

One of them was signed "Rome," next to another one, lurked a question mark, which somehow reminded me of a little chess horse. On the other side of the boot the following words were written: "What kind of city is this, ha?" I got up from the couch, found in the supermarket bag three chocolate bars of Milka (how is it that Terry didn't chew them up?) and put them in the drawer with kitchen things (hooks, adhesive hangers, broken corkscrews, a thermometer, etc). "No sweets for you, crafty Milik! Milik – is a baby moth."

CHAPTER VI

*In the least about how one can acquire a dog, when you
don't plan to. And also about work, Nona and Eva.*

I couldn't sleep. Though Milik and Gestapo comported
themselves quietly, having returned after seeing Violoncello
home. They quickly went to sleep and didn't disturb me.
They didn't run to the kitchen for water, juice, or coffee.
It's too bad, because I had already prepared several killer
phrases as a reaction to their running around. It often
happens that when someone of the representatives of our
celebrated humanity doesn't do what one-hundred percent
ruins your mood, but you're one-hundred percent expecting
it from them, your mood turns out to be utterly ruined.

Not far away Terry constantly stirred, snored, and
smacked his lips. Of course, if you're in a deep sleep, you
won't pay attention to these kind of movements and sounds.
And when you sleep poorly – you hear even the whispering
of the kitchen curtains. What in general can they talk about?
How is it, their intercurtain life? When I settled on the sofa
bed, tired from insomnia, contemplating what the heck to
do, Terry instantly woke up. "Ufuf," he said, like an eagle
owl. For certain, this meant: "Finally calm down and go to
bed, you crazy fellow." I lay down, but I didn't calm down.
Strawberry juice was overflowing through my body. Maybe,
it was turning into Tymofiy's "Sister-Strawberry" wine….

I was thinking about Violoncello. About what kind of
relations could have been between him and Sara. About

what he'll think when he sees his rooster on his hat, and not on the collar of his turtleneck. He'll think, maybe: "O, the little chick has turned into a real rooster and has learned to fly!" Well why does such idiocy eternally crawl into my head? And socks – too. If I had returned from the evening and found male socks in the pockets of my pants, I don't even know what I would have thought about. If Inna was present next to me at that moment, she would right away have pointed out my latent homosexuality. "And I've warned you," she would have noted, and her pointing finger would have squinted in my direction. I needed to reproach that finger as a phallus, because it always points out some direction. "Ururur," Terry informed us about himself. I disturbed him. "Know that I'm at home! I want to – I sleep, and I want to – and don't sleep!" And I intensified my words with my pointing finger-phallus. "Rurxxx," Terry answered me. He didn't even lift up his head. I closed my eyes and imagined several sentences of anonymous memoirs: "He always wore socks with embroidered little rabbits and lilies of the valley. His contemporaries till now don't know the answer who embroidered those socks for him and what those little rabbits symbolize. Fertility?"

My cell phone squealed. "Sara!" But it wasn't Sara, it was Violoncello. "Pavych (I forgot to inform the fact that when Violoncello seriously moved on, he began to call me 'Pavych,' and I called him 'Valiko'), one sock was embroidered. The second will be ready shortly. I can't sleep!" The telephone was showing 3AM. "Thank you, Valiko!" Send it off. If at 3AM an almost stranger is embroidering tiny rabbits for you on your socks, maybe you're not the last scumbag in the universe. I thought to myself, laughed to myself, turned off the sound on the cell phone, and fell asleep.

I woke up because the sun was burning a fire on the back of my neck, and early-morning God was harshly examining me. I don't like it when I'm being examined, and even more don't like it when I'm being looked at when I don't see it. The early morning God turned out to be Gestapo. Though he wasn't looking at me – I had already fantasized that. He rummaged through the shelves looking for something. While doing this he didn't bang anything. A spy. Terry disappeared somewhere. "Good morning," I said. Gestapo also bid welcome. "And where's the slut?" I asked not without surprise. "Excuse me?" "Where's the slut?" "I don't meddle in your personal life, young man. I told you that yesterday already. The answer will be: I don't know where your slut it, it doesn't concern me. Call everything by its own names! Do you have someone specific in mind? Maybe, Valentyn? He's not here. We sent him off yesterday in a taxi, if you haven't forgotten." "I remember. Not Valentyn. I'm talking about your slut, and not mine." "Mine?" Lord, what a bothersome bumpkin he is. I sighed and uttered: "Get up, slut! Get up, be a human being! Why are you still lying down, slut? Lift up your stinking butt and get out there , dammit!" "That is you had in mind the alarm clock? It's just interesting to me, from where did you get the habit of using foul language?"

But he got on my nerves. "Listen, it's not me using foul language. At least I don't have that kind of alarm clock. It's your, you must admit, alarm clock, that announces all those sluts, butts, and crap!" "It's mine," Gestapo answered pompously. "But what do words have to do with this? You don't need to listen attentively to them. You sense the intonation! Up, up! It's such that you itch to wake up, to do something useful for humanity, not so? Do you happen to know where the coffee is?" I was at a loss. If a person, with whom you're apparently arguing, asks about such placid things like where the coffee is, continuing to try to resolve relationships seems not so smart. My momma wouldn't have praised me for this. Tymofiy wouldn't either. Sara, maybe, would have praised me. Though – I'm not sure. In any case, where are you Sara, may the devil return you to me!

"The coffee's supposed to be there. A big black can. You can see the word 'coffee' written on it." You need to calm down, no need to start a new day being agitated. "There's no other kind?" "But why doesn't this one suit you?" "By the fact that there is none." "Why is that so?" "We gave it yesterday to Valentyn." "That's reeeeally interesting. Can you go into a little more detail?" "He said that he's going to embroider your socks for you, and that's why he needs to support the alertness of his body. That's why it was decided to give him the coffee in the black can to keep his body alert. In principle I didn't know how to react to similar things. That's why I remained silent. Gestapo continued his search. "The coffee was just there," I said sullenly. "Listen, stop mocking the ugly mug. What, did the end of the world happen? We'll buy both a can and coffee."

"And if I had taken your flask, you know what I'm talking about. I gave it to Valiko. How about that? Do you like it?" "Well, you know, you can't compare here." "Well, you know, it depends on how you look at it. From my point of view, these are all the same things." I thought that after such a not very successful conversation, Gestapo would leave the kitchen, but no. He put on the teapot and prepared everything for the tea. In principle, people who are constantly accused that they have lied about the weather yet again, have strong nerves. "Do you mind?" He inquired pointing to the teapot. "No." I looked at the telephone. Two text messages. One from Valiko. He announced that he finished embroidering the second sock, and wished me a peaceful rest of the night. I received it at 4:30. Another was from Tymofiy. He was interested in how things were with me. "Everything's okay with me, how about you?"

I am one of those people who, when someone else is next to you, gets down over pregnant silence. This kind of silence is always much more disturbing to me than shouting, indignation, quarrels, and empty chitchat. Not that I need constant chatting. No. But I need to have contact. It's difficult to explain, one needs to feel it. The contact can be silent, but consolidating, in any case, not like it is now. "Hmm. Won't you be late for work?" I asked. He came up to me, took a cigarette, and opened up the apartment. "You don't mind? This is the way I repair my lungs on the occasion of chemical warfare," I explained. He didn't dare contradict me, though I saw that he doesn't like this. "No, today I have library day. I work at home. The only thing that I would ask of you is not to smoke in the presence of Emile."

There echoed "The Sarabande for String Orchestra and Piano." In several minutes Emile and Terry appeared in the kitchen. Both of them were shaggy and sleepy. "Did you find the boot under your pillow?" Milik momentarily cheered up seeing that I'm no longer asleep. Terry, checking the bowl (empty), jumped onto the couch and lay down on my washed tee-shirt. "I found it," I confirmed. "Well?" "I don't think I should play with you." "Don't think, play! There when Heracles Petrovych… remember him? Like this, when Heracles Petrovych simply played cards (and he was a player), he was invincible, and then when he began to think about this, or whether it was worth playing cards, he frightened fate! His card-playing career ended, and he built a cooperative on these winnings. Do you understand?"

"You'll be late for school," I grumbled. You have to put all these saranskys (it'd be interesting to know what their names were when they weren't old?), hercules petrovych, uncle taras, oleska, alik, neonilka, zhorik, elka, iraida together with the illya rasvetovyches (who else did I forget?) to Gestapo's flask and never open it! "But I don't have to go to school today. Today's schedule is for unimportant subjects. I'm going to prepare myself for the academic concert all day, though true, with breaks. That's why I'll take Terry for a walk, and I also have to take out Tsunami for one. Where did you put the key?" "What key?" "Tamarantonivna's!"

"Tamarantonivna's keys, tarantino's films, tamarisk, tartlets, tarantas… Interesting. Here's why she passed them along to me. Naturally. In the living room."

I thought that to remain at home under these conditions – was suicide. "Emile, make your own breakfast, feed Terry, and I'll go to my room to work. Hang in there, boys." Gestapo poured himself a large cup of tea and started to leave. "To my room" he said – didn't you hear that?

"Have you had breakfast?" The little dude asked me. I said that I'd have breakfast in town. I immediately understood that I'd be slipping away out of here. "Eh, you poor coffee maniac, you can't allow yourself to be dependent on anything! Dependence ruins karma. I can make a drink for you from shaved chocolate, from the stuff we didn't manage to sniff into our nose yesterday! Not coffee, of course, but it'll loosen you up a bit!" "Who made those fairytale drinks? Old lady Saranska? Harry Potter?" I hmmmed. "No. Old lady Saranska can't drink coffee or eat chocolate. Her blood pressure's too high. Instead she always has black mountain ash berries, Yerba mate and chilly pepper." "What's that for, for fortune telling?" "Maybe you can even use it for fortune-telling. I don't know exactly. Old lady Saranska uses that for lowering her blood pressure. She adds chilly pepper in a cup of mate and drinks it. And her blood pressure – slam-bam – slides down! And I'm going to have blintzes with cheese!" "For lowering blood pressure?" "For increasing immunity!"

"When will you return?" "I don't know, why?" "You should at least come back for lunch, there'll be something fresh instead of consuming trash again!" "We'll see." "Don't forget about the boot! I tried!" "Ok, ok. That's it. Sit down and play." "I have to also go out with the dog. Hey, where are you going? Go to your father to say to him "see you!" "Why do that?" "Because that's the way we do that in our family. So he doesn't worry where you've disappeared." "I don't think that he's really going to worry much." "He will, he will. I know him." "Ehhh. I'm outta here. Bye." "Good luck, Pavlo! Thanks for letting me know beforehand!" Gestapo stepped out of the kitchen, went into my-his room, and turned into a different person. Unbelievable!"

On the fifth floor Wazuka and her master, noted by Milik as MM, constricted my elevator space. I decided I ought to say hello. "O," said MM. The bitch Wazuka didn't say anything. I grew still anticipating. When a person says "O" to you, in the majority of instances he doesn't limit himself to this "O". That's the way it was. "Is this your shaggy little ragamuffin with a halo on his little head?" In general I'm not used to people, whom I've never even said "hello" to before, toss similar questions at me, that's why I begged pardon. "I don't need these 'beg your pardons.' You tell him: if I hear or see him tell a lie in my direction one more time, I'll nail that halo on his head, understand?" "What's that?" "Just that." "Iwannabelovedbyyou"* whirled around in my head. We arrived. "As for Marilyn, you're an overly aggressive individual," I said to him. "You won't be respectful – that can also end badly." I won't say what my back heard from MM; the bitch Wazuka said "grrrrrr" to me.

Though I defended Milik, I was raging. It wasn't enough that the number of people in my building who were itching to dance on my grave was increasing. I decisively pulled out the phone, dialed Sara's number – there still was no connection. Diabolo, crap! Then I wrote a text message: "Call me right away! Right away!" I began to think, whether she intentionally shut off her phone to see how I was handling her crazed relatives, or whether she could rely on me in crucial moments and other such stuff? I hated this. He who

....

*   The 1928 song made famous in Marilyn Monroe's rendition in the movie *Some Like it Hot*.

his entire life has never examined anyone isn't deserving of everyone examining him at will. "School – is for Examinations, Life – is for Life." That was my motto. My schooling ended long ago and I just wanted to live. I started to smoke, and then with satisfaction tossed my cigarette butt onto Yevheniya Petrivna's balcony. For the first time in my life. That's for you – I yielded to temptation.

When I turned to go on farther, I saw Nona. It's interesting why every time that you're furious with your girlfriend, do other girls instantly turn into tempting angels? Angels with tender lips, seductive eyes and eyelashes that flutter like angel wings. Angels that carry comfort and calm to an anxious, torn heart. "If I didn't know you, I'd think you're planting a bomb! Hey there!" She addressed me. "Where are yours?" She, maybe, has in mind Emile and Terry. "Hey there, mine are at home. And you're taking a stroll?" I decided not to pay attention to the thing about the bomb. "I've already had my stroll. I'm on my way to work and saw you, so I decided to say 'hello'!" Some people have such joyful faces and intonations; it's as if they always are ready to give an enthusiastic speech and pop in an unnecessary prize for someone! Just grant them the opportunity!

I thought: might I not allow myself to invite Nona for morning coffee? After all, I had a really difficult morning; the day also doesn't promise to be any easier, and as for the evening – it's enough to hope. Nona was dressed in a jumper with a checkerboard pattern (with the same wonderful cut-out on her neckline, that I noted yesterday on her previous jumper), a black skirt of a tempting length, and black suede boots with eyelets. I never understood why sew something like that and why wear it. Inna considered such footwear for slags. However, Nona didn't look like a slag. I think that Inna would acknowledge . But I still didn't understand, why I never saw Nona earlier – she constantly whirls around with her dog in fact under my nose, several times a day! "Are you also going to work?" She asked in the meantime.

I looked at a live grasshopper that settled on her B-cup bust; it folded its knees, stirred its whiskers, but she didn't notice or feel it. But my gaze, wherever it was directed, was difficult not to notice or sense it. I suspected that right now she would begin either to feel embarrassed or get angry, and then there'd be no coffee. So I imagine her telling her friend at work: "And then he stared at my tits with the look of a maniac, as though he wants to chew them off, I nearly went crazy…" I needed to say something urgently.

"Nona, you have… ahhhh, on your sweater, at the level of E-4, if you're playing white, and I'm black, a grasshopper. You need to…" "Ha-ha," my neighbor said. "Who would think that you're such an inventive man," she squinted in the sun. "On the level of E-4, yes?" "Approximately," I confirmed. "If I'm playing white?" "Yes." "That is, I've already made my move, right?" I was at a loss. "Now make yours. Well, eat up that grasshopper, Pavlo, well?" And here he jumped! Thank God, because I simply didn't know how to conduct myself, eat it or not. My temples were burning as though someone had discharged a Colt-45 in them. Nona, completely naturally, began to scream. "Oy-Oy-Oy." "Everything's good now. He jumped off." "Lord, how awful. I need to run now. Sorry, be well, till we meet again!" The seductress ran off in short steps. When the game turns into life, it's very hard to turn it into a game again. At least Nona wasn't one of those. And Sara… enough about Sara. "Have a nice day!" I wished to Nona and went my way.

I needed to cajole myself with tasty coffee. Not far off is a very pleasant coffee shop, and I set off toward there. It just had opened up; besides me there was a guard sitting there, who was reading an article about British princes. Maybe, the article was sufficiently controversial, that's why he constantly was distracted from the letters to look at the photographs of princes and shake his head. "Can I have an omelet with ham and a double coffee?" The waitress, who was twirling a tray, gave me the hope that I could. Then she bent over to the guard. "What surprising thing has that hot guy done now?" The guard shifted his eye to the photograph of the princes. "Who?" He asked. With her eyebrows she made a "can you guess?" sign and went to the bar counter.

I often had breakfast with Inna in this place. We argued, made up, ironed out various family-house matters. Suddenly I had the urge to hear her voice. I don't know why. But I dialed the number of her cell phone. She didn't answer. Nevertheless she sent a text message: "This is Inna Dudnyk, a lawyer, you just phoned me. Who are you?" You can't pose such questions to a person who constantly has doubts. Because this person can lose what's left of his common sense. They brought me the coffee. She's asking who I am? That is, she wiped out my cell phone number from her memory, and also from the memory of her telephone. And I just switched the number of her cell from the "family" group (when she phoned, an icon appeared of three trees, because that was the notion of the designer of my phone about family) to "outside of groups," in fact just after Sara moved in with me. "He wanted to escape from his own wedding, when after his divorce he became aware of the fact that his wife erased the number of his phone from her memory. Or perhaps, she never included it there." Ab-surd-ity.

"And I could easily knock their heads off. Completely. Once, and everything's ready!" This was the local guard. "Not worth it," I said. "And of course, it's not worth it. I think that someone for sure was guarding them. Then they would soooo knock my head off. I am simply acknowledging the fact." The guard was a person from Tymofiy's card file. I asked for one more coffee and my check at the same time. In the meantime he sat closer to me. "Have you seen them?" He was talking about the princes. "Well, yes." "Don't lie! Here I saw them. With my own eyes. Like I see you. Because I worked there." "Where?" "In the London clubs; he earned money on the side as a bouncer, what sort of work is this?," the waitress added. "Yulka, envy isn't the best of your character traits!" "I'm Vova," the guard introduced himself. "I'm Pavlo." "So, Pavlo, I saw them just like I see you. There the princes unceremoniously hang around clubs." I gulped some coffee. "In general, the country, I'll tell you… In every restroom someone's shooting up or snorting cocaine." "Really? Even in the London National Gallery?" "I already told you that I worked there, and didn't hang out like a tourist. Listen, what the hell do I need your gallery for?" I thought: what the hell, Volodya boy, do you need the restrooms for? But I reconsidered going into more detail. I settled the bill and took off. That's it, I'm outta here.

I made my way toward Talliy's office. It's always pleasant to chat with him about whales, dolphins and other pleasant things. Too bad there are fewer and fewer pleasant things. But a surprise was waiting for me there: no one was in. Everyone had gone to the front. Even the old timers. Neither the secretary Maryna Longstockings,* whom I slept with after an alcoholic indiscretion, after which I was afraid to phone the office and come in until I figured out she didn't remember it had happened. And later she acted like she categorically needed to drag me to bed (as if that didn't happen, that's a chick for you!), but I didn't lose my vigilance. Why was it necessary for me not to stay with her one on one, and just when I did need to stay with her – not to drink.

Neither the guard Kindratych, whom everyone called Kant Son-of-Socrates Nietsche for his philosophical look at life. Kant Sokratych was not an average person. For example,

....

* *Dovhopanchokhy* in the Ukrainian. We've opted for the literal meaning of her name in English.

     LARYSA DENYSENKO

he loved to ask: "Well, what's new?" And when you began to answer him, for example, that you're having your teeth treated and don't see the wide world, he rebuffed: "Is that something new? People have suffered so much over their teeth as long as humanity has existed. And they've been getting treated for just as long. But I ask you: what's new? Earlier there weren't any singers who sang with their gills, but they're showing up now. Whether it's a lie or not, no one knows, but that's new!" Or he might ask: "Who would Voltaire correspond with right now, eh? Well, I have in mind someone he wouldn't be embarrassed by. Not with anyone. Maybe with Castro, though... to study Spanish. Maybe he'd learn it. Voltaire is a high-spirited guy. Because if he didn't correspond with anyone – he'd croak from grief. No way for an intelligent person to be without correspondence. With whom do you correspond? I'm saying it's impossible without that.

There's... Mao Zedong – that was a person. He lived by intuition, plus they have Feng Shui. Then there's Fidel Castro – I'm not thrilled with him at all. He ruled for fifty years, with the USA next door, and nothing happens to him! It's because he used his intuition correctly, ours don't know how to do that. There's something to that Feng Shui. There's a mirror at our place, you see it? In the southeast corner. There it has a negative effect on financial matters. I've already been telling Talliy, telling him, but he doesn't care! Our Talliy isn't Castro. He won't stir until you place him in a casket. But I already checked: he dragged the mirror to a different corner, and what do you think? Money appeared!

And why did you hang that funeral wreath on the door for the boss? You could have at least decorated it with ribbons, but you sit here, look at it, horror overcomes you. Who thought up those wreaths? Not the office, rather a funeral parlor. Maybe the Americans, they've frittered away all their intuition... Very recently I saw a certain well-known actress on the Internet. Well, of a respected age. So, she says, she can barely drag her footie; she wants to film her last clip, and that's it. Go. And here's what I want to say: you need to go diving with some guys in a diving suit, look for sunken ships, go on snowboards from up high and – boom. Here's Castro – he ruled for so many years, you – the last reel and already you're giving up?"

Besides, that Kindratych taught the entire office to drink tea exclusively at 12 noon and 5PM, and when he saw someone with an electric teapot or a cup at an unallotted time, he became extremely dissatisfied and made a memo in his notebook.

And then after a month he said to the most undisciplined tea-maker, the system administrator Serhiy, that according to his calculations, he will have cancer of the stomach in ten years. In a word, the old man also wasn't in the office. And it was too bad, sometimes I felt like listening to his chattering. And I understood right away that I should absolutely invite him to my place and sit him down with Emile at the same table. It would have been interesting to listen to their conversation. The old Saranskys going against Voltaire and Fidel Castro.

"Talliy, hello, where are you all?" "What, you haven't crawled over to the post office today?" "No." "Here devil. Listen, it'll be interesting for you to find out we're going on a picnic right now. Together with the office of Roma Avramovych" (in our circles they called Roma Avramovych "the victim of a single letter." In every agreement with new clients or partners, Roma scrupulously corrected the "b" with a "v": people love to believe in miracles). I also worked for Roma's agency. "What are you doing?" "You won't believe it. We're on an island. Whooaa, who knows what the name of this is? Damn, and there are tour operators, geographers, topographers. They don't know, can you imagine? I would call this island of Overgrown Inflexible People and Flexible Willows.

It's small, about ten kilometers. Or maybe less. Somewhere near the pancreas of the Dnipro River. Do you know where the heart of the Dnipro is? That's the orientation. Our tour program is – fishing, vodka, singing bards. And I, as you surely know, don't eat fish, don't drink vodka, and haven't listened to bards since my school days. And here – it's an entire three-piece suit. A little fish was caught on a triple hook. I would have never believed that there could be such an unsuccessful combination, and here – you have it. I sit here, chewing on a cheese sandwich with a Fanta." "Have a nice vacation," I muttered. I wasn't happy. I'm also not a big fan of bards, but this was better than the Sarabande for String Orchestra and Piano by G. F. Handel.

I realized: I didn't have anywhere to go. Numskull. The metro swallowed me. I decided that I'd get on in the direction where there'd be less of a crowd. There really weren't very many people. I even found a seat. A dude who was hiding his face in a white parcel settled down opposite me. Green shafts of onions that stuck out were so similar to the tail of Ara the parrot that it gave the impression that the dude was devouring it. You imagine something like that, ugh! I shut my eyes. "Here if someone appears wearing poppies on their clothing, I'll step out after her or him and go to the McDonald's closest to the metro station," I thought.

A young couple was standing next to me. "And I've already cooked up what I'll give you for your birthday! Guess!" "Expensive?" "Expensive." "A Porsche?" "No, you guessed wrong. Try again." "Is it big?" "Very big." "Ha-ha, a soccer team?" "Oh no! It's tied to something material, but it's not material." I was surprised at how he maintained his enthusiasm to play that game. My head was already aching. There was no one wearing poppies. "How is this not material? Am I able to touch it?" "You can't!" "Love? A star?" "No-oo." I'm going to kill her this very second. I saw a woman with tiny poppies on her skirt. Finally! I knew it, I knew it! "I'm kinda getting tired of it . Well what is this – that's expensive, big, not material? An island or something?" The poppy woman came closer to the doors, and I moved after her. "You think better!" "You, in general, understand yourself what immaterial means? Give me an example." "I'm not going to point to anything, think yourself." "Metro station Postal Square." "What are you going to give him, tell me quickly, because I have to get off!" I didn't expect that from myself. "English language classes," she reported. "What the frig is that! " Why are you saying this and to whom? Who is he to you?" I heard as I slipped out.

She was sitting and rummaging in a Happy Meal box. Eva. There was no toy close by, I recalled, that she collects. Maybe she already has put it away in her bottomless hand-bag. "And what do Ternopil terriers wear – wide-brimmed hats or caps?" Eva reminded me of a variety show dancer. Long legs, short slacks (maybe even short pants), bustier tops, high heels; milky chocolate hair, so straight and shiny that you're surprised how till now she hasn't cut her neck; bright red lips. "How are things, diva? Wake up, it's me!" Suddenly I felt that I was truly happy to see her. I always liked her and I didn't understand why she and Tymofiy sep-arated.

"Unexpectedly," Eva uttered. "Will you join me?" I said I'd join her, and right now. "You're not ordering anything?" She took an interest. "I should look after you. I'm just going to an open cashier – and you to the free city of Ternopil." "Stop that, I'm not going anywhere, go on." I ordered wings, fries, two coffee Americanos and a cherry pie. She ate in silence. I said I was happy to see her. "Me too," she said. "I almost got married." "But me – no." I thought I was too happy at Eva's appearance too soon. "Listen, once we used to get on fine, so what is going on now?" "I don't know. You understand, I have a feeling that I've stolen something from you and ran away with it, and now you've found me and are thinking whether to drag me to the police station or not. And sometimes it seems to me that you've stolen something from me." "One time Tim wanted to declare you dead, but I didn't let him do that." "Dead?" "Uhuh." "And if he did declare that, then what?" "I don't know. Maybe your bank cards would be canceled. Or: you come to glue on a new picture in your passport, and the passport office woman loses consciousness." "Dead. Yes, yes. You needed to continually write him letters and then look what he'd do. Why would he need that?" "He wanted to get married." "But he didn't get married?" "No. She went to Ternopil." "And yours didn't go, that's why you nearly got married?" "Yes. Her name is Sara." "Is that the Sara who went to school with you? The big titty one? She used to make jokes about your butt." "That's the one." "What, fate united you? Or the tits?" "Maybe. If fate dresses like a drunken sailor." "I didn't know that you like big tits." "I also didn't know that and right now I'm not sure if that consoles you."

"She went to Mexico. For her job." "So you're here alone, despairing?" "Not by myself." "Naturally. Does she also have big ones?" "What?" "Tits." "Who?" "Her. The one you're not alone with." "No, it's not like that. Sara's relatives are living with me. They don't have very big tits, if that interests you, because they're a boy and his father. True, there's also a spaniel, but he also is without big tits. A male dog." "You're sad somehow. Why did they dump themselves on you out of the blue?" "Remodeling at their place. At least that's the way they explain it. Do you want a bit of truth? I've really gotten tired. I'm not used to have so many people living with me all the time." "Not counting the dog." "You don't have to count him, but you're forced to deal with him." "And are you angry with her that she didn't warn you in advance about this? At Big-Tittied Sara?" "I'm angry, you hit the mark. Very." "And she doesn't want to communicate?" "Maybe she doesn't, or maybe she isn't able to. The phone is constantly outside the network, a wild country. You know, I've already begun to assume that this is normal for her. Well, I have in mind, normal, when someone comes without advanced notice and remains for several weeks? She has a hyper-communicative family. Though she knows that I and my family aren't very sociable. That is they – are family – a dormitory, and we, my family, a little house of a recluse. From another perspective, she doesn't control her own openness. I've gotten entirely confused. Here, have you told Tymofiy a lot about yourself?" "In general not very much. In any case, not so much so as to declare me dead." "Did you tell him about your first time?" "No, I didn't. He didn't ask." "But I asked. Several times." "And what of it?" "Sara says that she didn't give any notice – she already doesn't remember who she did it with the first time." "And you told her about that?" "I told her. In general I consider this a quite pleasant memory." "That is, was it during the day?" "Eva!" "And why are you indignant? You started it yourself. With Inka?" "No. Back off." "How can I back off if I'm curious. How is it not with Inka? You were with her from the first grade!" "Well, what of it? This doesn't mean anything." "How does this not mean anything? I remember: she acted like a she-Cerberus with you, like your first teacher. And she let that slip? The initiation into men of Pavlyk Dudnyk without her participation? Wow. How did she just forgive you? You didn't later justify yourself by saying that you were raped?"

"There was no 'wow'." It happened by accident. While we were riding to help the collective farmers reap the corn, and Inka then was ill." "So you did it in the corn?" "Well, yes. Why are you laughing?" "That's nothing. I simply thought if you were a girl, I would have asked: in the corn with a corn stalk?" "Ugh." "Well, what did they call her, your corn girl, you remember?" "Natalka Sobko." "From your grade?" "No, she was even from a different school." "And how do you know that she's a Sobko? She what, said to you: Natalka

Sobko. And you are – Pavlo Dudnyk. You greeted each other and began to do THAT?" "No, what's with you – are you sick? Her teacher called her: where are you, Sobko? Sobko, Natalka, immediately come here. And she got up quickly, put on her pants and ran off."

"Yes, of course. She older than you?" "To this day I don't know if she was older or younger. I don't even know if it was the first time for her, because I was thinking only about the fact that it was the first time for me. Though I didn't even manage to get frightened. We suddenly came together, did that, and that's it." "Hmm-hmm. That is you got glued together and immediately ran from each other?" "Not entirely right away. She also pulled out a splinter for me. A corn stalk …" "And where did you get it stuck?" "Not into…" "Eva! Into my hand. And I want to tell you it was really painful. And that's it. Now you tell me how it was for you the first time. Comfort a friend." "It would be interesting to listen to what that Natalka Sobko says about her first time. I can swear that she doesn't even remember your name!" "Why is that?" "Aha! You don't want to know that, right? You think she dreams about that first time and your name her entire natalkasobkovian life? And at night she whispers: "Pavlo, o Pavlo… Well, of course." "As regards others, you're very talkative. And what about yourself? How was your first time?"

"Why do you need to know that?" "So we can be honest. I told you, so now – your turn." "Oh, that's my communist upbringing. To be honest. To be fair. In a comradely way. Good. It was very exotic; you won't guess for anything how it happened!" "Just try without any guessing. I had enough of that on the metro." "The metro?" "That's unimportant. Tell me!" "I had a girlfriend. At the moment she's turned into something else, that is, she's not a girlfriend for me anymore. And her mother's a gypsy. And her name traditionally – was Rada. She loved to tell fortunes for us. And she foretold my first time. As though it will happen before

I'm seventeen, on a plane with a foreigner." "I would say – cool!" "And how. She read my fortune at fourteen and at that time I never had flown anywhere. And at fifteen I flew off with my parents to the Crimea. You can't imagine how things were for me the day before. I was afraid I wouldn't have my period at that time, and it ended a day before the flight! I thought it was a sign. I put on my Sunday underwear. Do you have fancy underwear?" "It's like I don't. Any kind of clean underwear I have is fancy."

"I thought so. And why do you need Sunday underwear when you go to harvest corn? I had one pair of Sunday underwear at that time: Polish ones, they were white, with a strawberry and an inscription 'Sunday' – from a set that was called 'a weekly'. Do you know anything about such a thing?" "I'm not sure." "Well, they had sets of seven panties: Monday, Tuesday, Wednesday… and so on to Sunday! The entire wrapping was an impossible luxury. My mother was able just to buy me one of them. The Sunday ones." "And you put them on." "Yes, and I would constantly sniff them to see whether they didn't have a scent. And just in case I sprayed my mom's Jasmine deodorant there. I sprayed it so enthusiastically that it was hell for me down there. I turned it into a jasmine bush. I looked impeccable. Believe me! Long legs, shiny hair, along a short-short skirt – a clasp zipper. It seemed to me that for THAT I'd definitely need to take off my skirt to make the process easier: just snap the zipper – that's it. The skirt is on the floor." "Some kind of crazy crap. But what happened then?" "Nothing happened then, because there wasn't a single foreigner to be found in the entire plane. At least the kind about whom you might say without question: he's a foreigner. A Latvian sat next to my father. But back then, unfortunately, Latvians weren't foreigners. Though we exchanged looks, nothing came of it then. Neither on the return flight. I didn't fly anywhere else – so a year was lost." "The prophecy didn't come true,

God came to your, a pagan's, defense, amen!" "You know, the most interesting thing is that I believed that. Just that first time. So over the course of the next year I didn't give myself away to anyone as a matter of principle. And they asked for it, and how. They got in line as though for goods in low supply. In the summer we again planned to fly to the Crimea." "So did the prophecy come true or not?"

"I'll tell you. I decided not to rely on the whims of fate, that's why I got myself a vibrator. It was called a Norelco Massager, ok, made in 1970. I don't know who manufactured it, but it was definitely made by a foreigner. My mother maybe to this day thinks it was a hair drier. She even tried to use it, and then declared it didn't work. The Norelco Massager was bright yellow. You could plug it in, and it also worked on batteries. It was hard to get. 'Invented by a woman who knows a woman's needs,' hee-hee-hee!" "So you?..." "Yes, this time I managed without Sunday underwear. I took it to the plane and did it." "And the foreigners? Were there foreigners in the plane?" "I didn't look. I had my own. You know, I'm one of those people who likes tomtits. There are more tomtits as opposed to cranes, and they won't, I expect, get into the Red Book of endangered species. At least it was enough for me at my age."

Stunned, I kept silent. I've never met a woman whose first man was a Norelco Massager or any other brand. And it turns out just such a woman was right at that moment sitting next to me. The wife of my best friend, my God… Lord, I hope, Sara isn't one of them too. "Listen, any way you want, but I can't call it my first man. In my view, this is unnatural in general. Where are the hands, the lips, and finally the tongue, where is everything? Can you compare this? It's castrated satisfaction – to sleep with a vibrator, phooey." "It depends with whom you compare it. Once I lived with a Norwegian. He was a fisherman. When we were making love I had to keep an eye on him and warn him just when he was getting ready to come, in a word "Yank it!" "What-say?" "Here's what-say for you. Right at "yank it!" he pulled his member out of me. Like a fishing rod being jerked. And he came in the air. It was a show! It was like beating egg-white cream with a mixer, pulling out a nozzle, and not shut it off! And prrrrrr – all over the walls." "Yank it?" "Yank it. And just 'yank it.' Otherwise – hello motherhood! I told you he was a fisherman. He hated condoms, maybe they reminded him of a fish's bladder, I don't know. So with the Norelco Massager it was a lot calmer."

"And with Tymofiy?" "Everything was good with Tymofiy. Don't worry." "Listen, if everything was good, then why did you take off? Why'd you run away?" "I left. How can I explain it to you… Good. Have you ever lived in banana-lemony Singapore?" "Sometimes I imagined, though you know that, in principle, there are no lemons there. Tim, it seems to me, was born there." "Ehe. The place of birth is banana-lemony Singapore. Did you know that he wanted that printed in his passport? And in our refrigerator there are no bananas, not a single lemon. A mouse would commit suicide in it. And it doesn't even need a dress for a funeral that I could sew and sell." "Listen, he always worked and never talked about the fact he didn't have enough money." "But he had enough of it. Because he always lived in banana-lemony Singapore; there's a strange attitude toward money there. Weird. He could give away money to a swindler or to an unlucky wretch because he was downtrodden. He could buy you an expensive gift. Yes, I know, you didn't think about that, but he spent money smiling like a saint: you felt like hitting him – but it would have been shameful. And for what?"

"You know, you get terribly angry with yourself because you're really itching to thrash the saint. He smiled, and I looked out for dog owners. "Excuse me, does your doggie need a winter coat?" "Do you know how some owners looked at me?" "I didn't know… that is, I didn't think that…" "All of this is sad, because I loved him, but as it turned out, in my case it wasn't enough. He often used to sing (in Russian):

    'And, tenderly recalling a different May sky,
    My words, and caresses, and me,
    You cry, Yvetta, that our song has been sung,
    And the heart not warmed
    Without the fire of love'"

"Listen, I've long wanted to ask you, where do dog clothing seamstresses get trained?" "Well, how to explain it to you. At the Engineering-Math Department of the university." "???" "That's the way it is. The head is filled with numbers, not a single number in the wallet, and a person is capable of studying anything. Hunger is a stimulus, better than any kind of ambitions." "Eve-Evita. You've really helped me today. Really, don't laugh. I've understood how stupid I was. About everything." "Don't punish yourself. We all live this way. There's not enough time to yourself. Is there enough time for others under such conditions? We have too little of an ability to sacrifice, otherwise we wouldn't survive. On the other hand, if there weren't people sacrificing, we also wouldn't survive. That's the way it is. Do you love her?" "A lot. But now I've been thinking if that will be enough? For me personal space is really important." "I understand. But doesn't she respect that?" "In general – she respects it. But those relatives of hers… They aren't bad people. They're not without quirks, of course, especially Milik, though the father there… he keeps the spirit of Jerusalem in a flask, can you imagine? One word – not faultless people. But I myself am not a paragon of sanity." "Like the majority of us. Amen." "Amen."

"Listen, believe me, if a girl doesn't want to talk to you about the first time, then she herself hasn't discussed this with herself lo-o-ong ago, forget it. That's not the main thing." "I'm trying to come to some understanding. But then she also won't talk long about her former husband too. I have an aversion to military guys. I can't stand them. So then why, first woman, tell me, would you marry soldiers?" Eva crawled into her handbag and pulled out a passport. "For example, for this," she said. With great interest I looked at her passport, but didn't understand anything. "What's this for?" "Place of birth – Potsdam, GDR. My father was a military man, a colonel. His brother, a major, named him after that city "the puss from Potsdam." Military jokes. "The puss is walking in shoulder straps, that's colonel PPO."

"Sorry. In talking about military guys I meant not in the sense of your father." "Though if only in the sense. Till the age of six I lived in Potsdam, then we were "asked" to leave from there. White socks, lacquer shoes and a "kangaroo" hoodie. Not far from Berlin, and sometimes they allowed us to come now and then. In Berlin mother laughed with a special Berlin laughter, or that simply was my childhood perception of mother and Berlin. Sanssouci Park, o that Sanssouci Park.

I played a stylish young lady there. And the Belvedere, on the wall of which I scribbled (how much of that scribbling was there): "Eva was here." They teased me calling me Eva Braun. In fact, when the authorities found out that my parents had called me that, they were really eager to force my father to go back to his homeland, but something there didn't work out with them. And my mother named me not out of religious considerations or Nazi fanaticism, but for the sake of beauty. They just liked the name. My mother called me a child of 'the parks, romances, and vile officer's swearing.' It was like that. And I still know how to walk like an honor guard. If you behave yourself well – I'll show you. The school serviceman was enraptured. Though, maybe, he liked my legs, who knows what more he had inside himself – a serviceman or a man."

I wanted to find my passport, but I never dragged it around in my wallet. Something else lay there instead of it, and I pulled out that "something." It was Milik's little Italian boot. "Well, you're just a Prince Charming. Looking for Cinderella? Check the size on me? What's this?" "How should I say it to you. It's a task. I need to guess how the city is marked there." "That's your new job?" "No, that's my new co-habitant. Emile. Happy children's games! He's checking the quality of my education." "His name is Emile and he loves to delegate tasks. Interesting. Have you guessed already?" "No. I need an atlas, and in general I'm not sure if it's worth bother with this. One time I already figured out his rebus. 2515 – what's that?" "Seducing a minor when you're 25 and he's 15." "This is a parasolka, a little umbrella." "Why?" " 2 (para) is a pair, the fifth note (sol) – G, 'k' is the fifteenth letter in the alphabet. What do you think?" "Nothing. I feel like 45." "What's this?" "Kva-solya-Beans. Kva – that's some kind of number four, and 5 – is G (sol')."

"Kva – that's a frog.* It's very strange that you're not Emile's mother. Eva, did you go to Ternopil at all?" "I'm there right now. Listen, it seems to me that while Sara's gone, you need to have something of your own. Well, while the strangers are at home. The little guy, who rapes you with geo-games, and an old guy with a holy flask." "What, for example of my own?" "A dog." "I have a dog, thank you, that's enough for me." "But it's someone else's dog, you need your own. You bring home a puppy and prove you're the master of the house. Is that bad? Besides that, a puppy is a creature that'll always be on your side. Agree to it! I have friends. They can give us a fantastic puppy." "You need to take care of it, have time for that. "You have a lot

....

*   *Kva* comes from the verb *kvakaty* (to croak like a frog).

of time, don't lie. It's as if I don't know what your schedule is like. Has it changed?" "It hasn't." You're not living alone, looking after an animal is guaranteed. You'll be doggified with Sara. Let's go."

So we went, and after half an hour I was holding it in my hands. "You just take a look what a fabulous angel!" I took a look. The "fabulous angel" was about the size of my palm and looked like a glove. It was white with black spots, didn't know how to bark, couldn't walk, and couldn't see very well. Additionally he had eyelashes – really funny ones, short and black. "Take a look what a fabulous nose he has!" I looked. The nose was teeny weeny, if you could consider it a nose at all. "According to the standards, just the upper phalange of your thumb could fit on its tiny nose. Let's check! Well, put it on, put it on! Your puppy is your phalange! Fabulous!" Eva informed me that I had become the owner of a "fabulous" French bulldog puppy.

"O, this is like at Nona's," I said. "Nona's? And where do you live?" I informed her of the address. "We know that, we know! Odil Fernanda Manioza Duflet! A fabulous little girl, she has an impeccable mask." I agreed that the little girl was fabulous, if you have in mind Nona. She doesn't apparently wear masks, but it was worth taking a closer look. Then I noted that they had mixed it up, because Nona's dog's name was Pancake.

They burst out laughing. "And of course, Nonochka calls her as she wishes, but according to the documents her dog is named just as we said." "And do they also call this one according to his documents?" "Of course. Hold him." "Ziegfried Daniel Guillaume Lord Fauntleroy de Chateau." "Eh." "Don't eh me. You can call him anything you want. This is for the documentation."

Eva went with me. I needed support to introduce to Milik and Gestapo Ziegfried Daniel Guillaume Lord Fauntleroy de Chateau. "Good, I'll accompany you with the lord.

Maybe I'll get a new order. Maybe your spaniel will need a raincoat? I have all the samples with me, and it's soon going to rain as heavily as it can." Eva said to me in answer to my hospitality.

CHAPTER VII

In the least about a different point of view on dolphins and whales. A different point of view on Gestapo. Numerous points of view on Eva.

"Who is this so adroitly firing away?" "Emile." "Certainly something German," Eva listened closer. There, thank you. "That's the Sarabande for String Orchestra and Piano by G. F. Handel," I informed Eva, passing along to her the Fabulous Angel. It was napping with me, but when it ended up in Eva's arms, it grabbed her finger, then recoiled from it and began to look about. I tried to find my keys. And thought about what if G. F. Handel had used not notes, but letters and words, I already would be about to quote him word for word and acquire the reputation of an intellectual in certain circles. I think that such a person as G. F. Handel didn't write sheer stupidity. Talliy would have certainly been impressed.

"Hello," I said loudly. For I'm a polite person, I'm preparing others for my appearance, the more so to the sudden appearance of others. And I tickled Butterfly behind the ear. He came up to sniff me, then took a look at Eva. "Terry, this is Eva with Angel. Eva, this is Butterfly, Terry," I announced. The spaniel was intrigued. "Tell him not to even think about jumping. I'm wearing expensive stockings!" "Terry, no! They're friends," I uttered the arsenal, in my view, of an experienced dog keeper. Eva said that Angel might get frightened, it's too dark here, there's a strange fully grown dog, you need to let him go onto the floor where he'll be living, and it should be bright. We dragged our feet to the kitchen. Terry yelped and scraped his claws.

Emile stopped playing and stood up. It was evident that Eva had produced a certain impression on him. "Soon the name of the Goddess of Spermatorrhea will change," I gloated. "Emile, this is Eva, Eva – this is Emile." My mood was fantastic. I felt like a queen from behind Caroll's *Through the Looking Glass*. "Pudding, this is Alice, Alice – this is Pudding." "Oy," the little dude shrieked. "What a fabulous little thing it is!!!" And slowly snatched the Fabulous Angel from the arms of the potential goddess of potential spermatorrhea, Terry practically drew the entire scent of the tiny guy to his nose. But he didn't bark and he didn't insult him. Whew. I was a little bit afraid of that, though all these self-assured canine seamstresses, canine doctors and producers of champions would try to convince you that such an acquaintance would occur without problems. And, what if suddenly Butterfly, imbued with hunting instincts, meets us? "No, this is Pavlo's," Eva smiled. "Woohoo!" The little dude beamed.

In the meantime, Gennadiy Stanislavovych dropped by in the kitchen with his own imposing persona. Whether he was dressed like that all day, or had heard a woman's voice and changed his clothes, it was not clear, but he looked nearly as fabulous as Angel. A white sweater, soft slacks, tanned brunette, pulled back wavy hair. Elegant macho. I sensed that Eva took an interest in him. In general, it was the first time I took a look at Gestapo not like at an impudent, kind of wild professor and father of an offspring from hell (read Milik here), but just a man. With the eyes of a detached person. It's more often better to look at him with the eyes of a detached person, because your attitude can drastically change.

"Good evening," he roared amiably. "Gennadiy, father of Emile, uncle of Sara. You see, we were forced to ask for temporary shelter at the husband of my niece's place." "Eva." "Oh," Gestapo uttered. It wasn't just a simple "oh," it was great veneration for Eva's name. Species – Gestapo, sub-species – Gestapo Sexualis. If it wasn't enough, were they planning on flirting or not?

"Father, look!" Milik! Glory be to him! "Yes, what's this going on? Terry, don't get in the way, don't be jealous, old man, don't be jealous! It's a French bulldog puppy."

People who were gathered around me could guess the dog's breed – as easy as ABC. Gestapo took a look at Eva. And here's a surprise waiting for you. "It's mine, Gennadiy Stanislavovych." "Eh." Gestapo wrang out of himself. I really didn't expect to receive the same kind of "oh" as Eva did, but he could have had a burst of generosity with a sound other than "eh."

"Eh… I didn't know, Pavlo, that you intended to get yourself a dog." "If I had known, if I had known, we wouldn't have gone to the Carpathians, "I chuckled." This was my subconscious dream that slept and slept like a wintry sea, and here finally broke the shores today, and boom – I have Fabulous Angel." "I always said to Pavlo that he really needs a dog," Eva took note and began to look all around. This was a special look. For example, I immediately comprehended that she was looking for a place to sit down. Gestapo, who's also not a dunderhead in such things, understood this and stood up quickly, an adroit lad.* "There's no reason for us to stand, I think we can turn to an aperitif to toast our acquaintance! Emile, arrange for an hour-long break for yourself and find something to go with coffee! Eva, which libation do you give preference to?" Gestapo smiled so hard that if he had smiled that way to me, I would have looked

....

* The description of Aeneas in the first lines of Ivan Kotlyarevsky's famous Ukrainian mock epic poem *Eneida* (1798).

for something to defend the honor of my own ass. Eva also smiled at him, more reservedly, but…

To avoid all kinds of suspicions coming into my head, I thrust myself to look for something to drink. What amazement I had when I saw three bottles of Baradero Anejo on the shelf, Chianti, Martini Extra-Dry, and several bottles of dry white French wine for the formation of a nostalgic mood. "Eureka!" I shouted and approvingly looked at Gestapo. However, he didn't look at me. He and Eva were setting the table. The young dude, as they say, was shuffling around the apartment. He cut up apples (green apples, which is appealing, one more point for Gennadiy Stanislavovych, the old Lovelace. It turns out all these legends about wool-gathering professor mental cases was a lie); he cut kiwis in half, and stuck a little teaspoon into each half so that it would be easy to scrape out the soft part. A lemon, bananas (where could you get away from the banana-lemony Singapore in our times?), and nuts, dry biscuits…? Small snacking sandwiches with anchovies, almonds, and dill. I want to make a note that I wasn't emboldened to taste them, and I also don't advise you to do so, though no one who ate them got food poisoning.

After we had sat down and the glasses were filled, I decided to explain Eva's status. Strictly speaking, Gestapo could have thought up whatever he pleased, he knows how to do that. "To our acquaintance!" He proclaimed. "This, as I said, is Eva, she's the wife of my best friend Tymofiy! Maybe Sara's told you about him." "A brown-haired guy in girls' sweaters, who answers letters from psychos and sings like Vertynsky?" Emile responded. Eva began to laugh loudly. Gestapo looked at her as if, maybe he already knew she had her tonsils removed. When she had calmed down (this didn't happen very quickly: Fabulous Angel, for example, in that time had managed to wake up and make a puddle), she said: "I'm practically a dead spouse." "In what sense?"

Gestapo collected himself after a lost silence. "In the sense of my husband," she answered. The old man liked that. Milik too. He said that that can be very convenient. Eva turned her head to him, her hair glided along her neck and I was again surprised that it didn't cut her skin. "That is to say?" She asked.

"Take Zhorik for example. Pavlo, do you remember, I told you I saw him getting burnt?" I shook my head in a doomed way. It started. "It was like this. He constantly was cheating on Neonilka, that's his wife," he explained to Eva. "Old lady Saranska warned her before Nila married him that he doesn't have a member between his legs but a toll gate: when a woman just approaches – welcome, it promptly raises up!" To see the expression on Eva's face was total satisfaction; let her realize with whom in a Christian way I'm forced to share my home. Gestapo poured out the drinks. "Zhorik told all his babes on the side that Neonilka had died. True, he was afraid that she really would die after he so often buried her, that's why he called her different names. Halyna, Katrusya, Lora, Kleopatra. And one time he got into a mess! He got to know one woman whose name was Margo. He fell in love with her, but she didn't give him everything because she was a respectable girl." "Emile!" The father warned Emile. It was the first time I heard the old man reacting somehow to Emile's tall tales.

"Father, what's so bad that I said? This is life's truth!" The young dude took exception and continued. "And Zhorik, in order to lure her, began to complain about how difficult the life of a widower was, and she began to cry. And he saw that the girl was impressionable, there everything was working, and he began to weep. Zhorik could begin crying under any circumstance. So he begins crying, repeating: "My poor Lyudmylka, how can I live without you, tell me?!" And here (not Lyudmylka, but Margo) says to him: "How? What Lyudmyla? Your wife's name, Heorhiy, is Neonila!" Zhorik began to lie, to completely lie, and said that he really once had a wife named Neonila, and later – Lyudmyla, but right now he's a free bird because they all had dumped him. It turns out that that Margo was the daughter of one of Neonila's co-workers, and had somehow seen Zhorik in childhood. He didn't pay any attention to her. Zhorik pays attention to the ladies only then when… you know…" The young dude uncertainly took a look at Eva. "What?" She asked. "Well, 'when it pours between the legs, a girl laughs, thank the heavens above I'm not pregnant.' Do you understand?"

Even I felt Gestapo's gaze. Emile too, that's why he began to extricate himself. "This is such a funny saying, just a funny saying! It's not me who made it up! Sara taught me!" Gestapo looks at me as if I'm guilty of the fact that Sara taught vulgar funny sayings to his child. Maybe he thinks that I taught her. But he isn't talking to me. "Emile, first you either apologize before Eva, and second, end that story in a decent way. Or you'll go to your room. I'm waiting." A father's anger.

Subdued Emile mumbles something unintelligible, then continues in a normal voice: "That evening Zhorik didn't luck out with getting any. Margo told her mother about whom she had run into. "Can you imagine that Zhora's, Neonila's Zhora's new wife died. Her name is Lyudmyla!" And her mother tells her: "Margo, be smart, don't talk bunkum!: Then for a long time she explained which one of them was talking bunkum, and then her mother Margo gave a call to Neonila. Zhorik then ran away to spend the night at our place, whining that all his vexations were because of the ladies; he grumbled to mother how he got burnt. He burned himself a few times, and here just recently Neonila set him on fire. Finally." I waited to see what Eva would say to this. She said that it was time to feed the Fabulous Angel. "By the way, Pavlo, have you given him a name?" Gestapo asked. "Right now," I said and stepped out. "Where are you going?" Voices could be heard. Eva was feeding the puppy dog. I brought the pedigree papers and read out: "Ziegfried Daniel Guillaume Lord Fauntleroy de Chateau."

"Have you thought about how you're going to shorten it? That is not him, but his name," Gestapo took an interest. I've not thought about it, that's why I said the first thing that came into my head: "Zig!" "Heil!" Eva shouted out. Silence met our individual voices. "This, of course, is a joke?" Gestapo asked. "Why a joke? That's a normal shortening," I sank into explanations. "Pavlo! Sorry, Eva, that I'm forced to talk about this in Your presence. Pavlo, you, maybe, have noticed that our family, how should I say it to you, well… is a tad Jewishy, isn't that so?" Emile expressed it more simply: "You'd call him Adolph!" I remained silent, because I hadn't thought about anything like that. "Pavlo, in as much as you're a part of our family, at least for the time being, and in the nearest future I don't see any changes in your status, it seems to me, it would be worthwhile to refrain from similar actions." "Sorry. It's just a shortening." My look at that moment was the very same as during Emile's justifications regarding his "simply funny sayings." "I'm convinced that Pavlo didn't have anything bad in mind," Eva confidently intervened. She was holding the little fur ball in her hands. It ate up everything and kept winking its eyes.

"Let's call him Zizi!" "Zizi? That's the name of a French whore. He is not going to be any Zizi! Zizi, Zuzu, Frufru, Zhuzhu. Phooey! Emile, you yourself are Zizi." Eva touched her temple with her hand. Her gesture meant: "Lads!" Of course that gesture didn't concern Gestapo because with great satisfaction he had made her a cocktail with vermouth. "And what about Zi?" She suggested. "What kind of name is Zi?" "A normal name." I said it's my dog, and I'll give him a name myself, whether anybody likes that or not. We drank for a certain amount of time in silence. It's true that Gestapo from time to time muttered something into Eva's ear.

"Listen," she said, "does Terry need little overalls or a rain coat? I know how to sew comfortable clothing for dogs!" He definitely needs it!" Gestapo's a quick guy. "Then hold the angel, and while Pavlo is thinking, we'll take measurements on Terry." And she began to take measurements. When she had squatted, she almost knocked her forehead with her knees; Eva's legs were really long. The Polonskys didn't believe their own eyes.

Then Eva said that she had to go. And she thanked everyone for their hospitality. Then the Polonskys said "how'saboutcoffee?" And she stayed for coffee, which I made. "His name is Ziggy. Does that offend you?" Polonsky, who was telling Eva about the changes in climate in the countries of Western Europe and the effect of this process on the skin, didn't react. And Emile said that the name Ziggy is similar to the name of a dog, who never gives up. The question was settled. I carefully took Ziggy from Gennadiy Stanislavovych's knees, not without satisfaction noticing the buckwheat-milky spot on his stylish little pants. Emile pulled over a pillow from a padded stool and we made the little guy a bed. Here I noticed that Emile also didn't like the fact that Gestapo was wrapping around the little flower Eva. "Excuse me," he loudly announced. "I need to practice!" "Sonny boy, today you can alter your schedule a bit, I'll let you," the magnanimous Gestapo pronounced. "No!" And the Sarabande for String Orchestra and Piano by G. F. Handel began to echo.

"Even from outside the door I recognized the Germanness in that music," Eva uttered quietly. It was as if she were bewitched by the music, and from that so threw herself back in the armchair that her shoulders nearly touched Gestapo. This "nearly" was sufficient enough for him to start floating. And I, little by little, became enraged. That's why I took my cell phone (they equally prattled about Handel and the Germanness of his music, and also about how important it is to perceive music, for some it's given, for other's – no), and I calmly typed out a text message to Talliy. A short. "G. F. Handel." I expected Talliy to turn out to be not so much tired of the bards that he wouldn't give a damn about everything and get drunk. Bababoom. And here is Talliy, the little ones. "When you talk about Handel, then the first thing that's worth recalling: he started to play music at age of seven, and at nine, he already was a composer. At twenty he wrote his first opera Amelia, after which he travelled to Italy to study. As strange as it seems, the composer lived nearly his entire life in England, there he was buried with great esteem. The legacy of Handel – fifty operas, twenty-three oratorios, countless chorales, organ concerts, and entertaining pieces. As you, surely, understand, dry numbers can't convey the greatness of his accomplishments. P.S. G. F. Handel doesn't have any relation to whales and dolphins. I also expect that you don't put him in the same category as them. Talliy reminded me of the terms of my job, very much in a Talliyan way; he's matchless.

I'll finish writing about whales this evening or tomorrow morning, but right now I have to do everything so that a tasty sandwich doesn't come of Gestapo and Eva. "Germanness?" I expressively uttered that word. I can't say that they responded in a lively way to my line, that's why I gathered in some air into my lungs and began: "I don't know about what kind of Germanness you can speak if, in reality, Handel was a Brit. He didn't show his face in Germany, and was buried like a grand bigwig in Westminster Abbey." This produced an impression. No doubt! Gestapo didn't expect that I was as well versed in music. Though yesterday, using the example of Violoncello, I strove to bring to him information that I'm not really that kind of zeromusician. Does everyone know about the existence of Yo-Yo Ma? I doubt it. "So what of it?" This is Eva. "Eva, well, think a bit yourself. Here you were born and for several years lived in Germany, acquiring for your entire life satiation with the German spirit. The same thing happened with Handel. Britishness, here's what you can hear in his music." "Hear? Maybe. And here to sense the Germanness. You don't think that my stay in Germany made of me a German woman?" Emile kept playing on. He's got strong nerves.

I said that in my view Eva has a bit of a German woman in her. Even a lot! Gestapo began to raise objections. Then I chose better what German women might have (of course, according to my view), and ascribed those features and habits to Eva. How practical she is, tidy, how regular her facial features are, an innate sense of style, how nice her legs are, and how adroitly she runs. And the main thing – her back. What a firm expression of her back! Let's look. "What are you getting at?" She asked. It was not the best of questions. I was getting at the fact that she should be getting home. But she wasn't getting ready to go there, and people like me can't openly point to the door to any-one. Even more so, to the wives of your best friends. Even nearly dead wives from Ternopil. The conversation was losing a given direction and sense, and so not to create a pause, I asked Gestapo if they hadn't proclaimed him Emile in honor of Handel's opera Amelia. Emile had the opportunity, without stopping his playing, to twirl his fin-ger by the crown of his head and squeak in my direction the word "cretin."

I managed to achieve something with that question. I can't say that I managed to distract Gestapo from Eva, but he mentioned his wife. He said that neither he nor Mila (that's Emile's mother's name, I didn't know that before) were not fans of Handel, though he considers it high qual-ity music. It seemed that Eva didn't like how this subject meekly uttered the name of his wife. Darling Mila. "So that you know, I was named in honor of my mother,"

I heard Emile say.

"Because mom's full name is Emilia." In my view, to name children after your own name is nearly perversion. People who do that have a gigantic ego. Usually it's characteristic for men, and usually, they name their boys after themselves. Though it's entirely likely, that as a result of male egotism, names such as Yevhenia, Valeria, Valentyna, Viktoria, Oleksandra, Slava, Ivanna, Bohdana have appeared… And this is far from a complete list! Our "I" is stronger than the "I" of a statistically average woman. But the mother of Emile isn't among those (though I'm one hundred per cent sure: she was named in honor of some grandfather named Emile). The business partner of Inna was not one of those – the similartoEmile'smother Larysa, who named her son Illarion. A crafty action regarding the boy. I thought whether I was capable of naming my own daughter after me? Pavlyna Dudnyk. Oh, Lord, my God. No way. If I think like this right now, and later I'll begin to insist foaming at the mouth – only PAVLYNA! I'm blowing my top.

"Eva, are you Jewish? I'm just asking because your first name is Jewish!" The young dude cheerfully asked. You have to give her her due, she didn't start to beat him up. She informed him – hardly. In as much as her father was a military man, a not very popular profession among Jewish people. They let him go abroad to work, which was entirely impossible for Jews at the end of the 1960s. Out of her entire family only she had a hypothetically Jewish first name, Eva, the others had hypothetically Ukrainian ones. "What are they?" Too curious little dude. "Mykola, Ivan, Ulyana, Kyrylo, Oksana, Vasyl. Is that enough for you? "A normal sampling." For the young dude it was enough. It turned out this was enough for Eva too, that's why she said good-bye the second time. She promised to call and left. This time the young dude didn't try to convince her to remain, though the elder Polonsky had no desire to yield his position.

Just after I closed the door after Eva, Gennadiy Stanislavovych rose up. "Well, gentlemen. I'll take Terry for a walk." Gestapo began to get ready.

And I thought that he and Eva were conspiring to meet up right away. Eh, no. "I'll walk with you. Ziggy also needs to take a stroll." "What are you saying? You can't take him for a walk yet. You haven't given him his shots, haven't you consulted with veterinarians?" "I consulted with them, really. They gave me a booklet." "So sit down and read it. A dog is responsibility." I recognized Gestapo, the old bore. "Then I'll go out with you for a smoke," I wouldn't give in. So I don't smoke up the young dude." I didn't want to remind him of the fact that they allowed Eva to smoke here, despite Milik's mug. "What, you already don't smoke on the staircase platform?" "No. I got used to doing it either at home or on the street." "Well, then let's go."

And we left. Unfriendly Gestapo, who changed into his jeans. They suited him. Joyful Terry. Bewildered me. I couldn't formulate at all why it irritated me that Eva wanted to seduce Polonsky, and Polonsky wanted to seduce Eva. In the end, it didn't concern me. It didn't bother Tymofiy either, that is, I didn't need to stand up to defend the honor of my friend, but I intervened and got angry. Gestapo released Terry from his leash on the street. I walked alongside him. "Okay if I light up?" "They're your lungs." I didn't see Eva anywhere, but this didn't mean I could relax.

I started to smoke. "It seems to me that you really don't like me much?" Gestapo was astonished. "I haven't thought about whether I like you or not. In any case I'm grateful to you for letting Emile play, and I have somewhere to work, sleep, have visitors. Sara's happy with you. I don't think that I dislike you. We simply belong to various age groups and tastes, that's why at times something irritates me, and sometimes even you, isn't that so?" "With Eva you're also of a different age group. And I don't think that your tastes match." "She is – a woman. They don't have age groups. And, as regards, the same tastes – in the given instance that's also not the main thing." "She's attractive, isn't that so?" "Attractive, though she dresses strangely." I recalled Eva's bustier top and mini-shorts. "She was flirting with you." "Attractive women need to flirt; it suits them." "And you?" "What about me?" "You also flirted with her." "Of course, otherwise her flirting wouldn't have been of full value, the mood would have been ruined. As much as possible, every man should worship a woman like a Goddess. It seems like that to me. Besides that, it's nice. Personally for me, flirtation adds a lightness. Lightness is a very important component of my personality. I don't have it. And you, Pavlo, no. You're lacking in confidence, if you want it." "I want it. Who doesn't want confidence." "I understand you're being ironic, but I never succeed in finding something witty in that kind of irony, word play is not for me. Sorry."

"That's nothing. In fact, you can switch to the informal you with me." "Thank you for the offer. I'll try, though that doesn't inspire me. Terry boy, what are you doing? Come to me!" I really wanted him to address me with the informal you. Then our relations would be more natural in my view. "It seems to me that life is a stretched out rope over an abyss. And confidence is a safety line. It's as if everyone has it, but some constantly tug at it: to check if it's there or not, or if it's too weak? That's confidence. Some never tug at it at all. They don't need a safety line, that's self-confidence. I'm one of those who will tug at it, but it's all the same – it works. And You? "And I… I choose firm ground. A rope over an abyss is for romantics, Pavlo. Those romantics are with the safety ropes or without them. So You are a romantic, Mr. Dudnyk."

During the time of our walk Emile managed to clean up the kitchen. Effectively. "Have you guessed?" He asked, and I mentioned the Italian boot. "No. Right now I'm sitting down to work. When I have time left – I'll try to guess."

"Do you work with killer whales? Yes, with killer whales.
"Pavlo, have you read the instructions for taking care of the
puppy?" I said that I took a look at it. "Then you're ready
for your first puppy night," Gestapo laughed. "I just suggest
that you make a mixture of milk in advance because it can
wake up unexpectedly and demand food." "He's making
tomfoolery for you!" Emile says. "What's that?" "You don't
know what tomfoolery is? Tomfoolery is this: he's going to
try and subdue you. For example, whether you take him to
your bed or not, you'll be playing with him at three in the
morning, and what an effect his squealing will produce on
you." "Play with what?" "You're really worried what you'll
use to play with him? He'll find something, don't worry."
Emile was making fun of me.

Ziggy, in the meantime, was examining Terry's bowl.
Terry was growling cautiously. "Oho, he'll swallow him right
now. He needs to…," I run to help. "You don't need to do
anything, calm down! They'll work it out between themselves. Terry is smart, he's aware of what's in front of him – a
puppy! This isn't a Yashka the Bottle. When he plays…" "Yes.
I don't want to hear about Yashka, I don't. Why is he a bottle? He's a drunk like Uncle Alik, how are things with him
there?" "If you don't want to hear it – then you won't hear
it, but the story, by the way, is interesting." Emile showed
his unhappiness. "Good night," Gestapo uttered. He pours
himself a glass of mineral water and adds a bit of honey.

"Good," I say. "Tell me about your Yashka. You'll drop a
word about him sometime all the same, I know you." The
little guy hmmmed. Ziggy tries to understand why he's itching to do more: to make a puddle or to go to sleep. Listen,
Hamlet. He settled down to sleep. "So it's like this, when
Yashka the Bottle plays cards with children…" "With his
own children?"

"He doesn't have his own." "And who lets him play with
other people's children?" "That doesn't bother anyone.

When he plays and loses, it's as if he's raging. He covers everyone with curses, says that he'd smack you around – 'and you simply had good luck, you little boob,' 'and I've taken completely ill today, my eyes hurt.' And when he wins – he calls himself a king. And when you tell him that he won because he's a grownup, then he screams that's it, he doesn't want to hear it and won't play with anyone else, and forget where he lives!"

"Well, yes. How old is he?" "Fifty two." "Naturally. And who is he to you?" "He's the nephew of old lady Saransky. By the way, he's a skillful veterinarian. I'll tape his phone numbers on your refrigerator, just in case!" "And the old Saranskys, who are they?" "What do you mean? That's my grand-mère and granddad from my mother's side, didn't you know?" "Then why then, you little prattler, do you call them the old Saranskys and not granddad and grand-mère?" "Because I have another Polonsky granddad and grannie. And they're younger than the Saranskys; that's why they're not old. We call them the Poles.

"Listen, I've already gotten tired and I need to work, go to sleep, take care!" "Good night," Emile Polite said. I made myself some coffee at last – my house coffee, my coffeemaker! – and opened up my laptop. There were several emails in my inbox, though unimportant ones. They'll wait. I thought for a bit and decided to write a letter. To Romko Avramovych. Sara set off for Mexico on business for him. "Hey, Romko! Listen, what's up with the people, who, by your prayers, have been dispatched to Mexico? Nobody's cell phone is working there." I really had only checked the connectability of Sara's cell phone, not having a clue if anyone else of Romko's group had gone with Sara. In as much as Romko didn't know about me and Sara, I was forced to maneuver.

Then I wrote a letter to Tymofiy. I expect that his female colleague doesn't read his mail. I wrote that I had seen Eva, that she looks great, that she doesn't say anything awful about him, she's collecting Happy Meal toys just as before, and will be sewing a raincoat for Sara's relatives' spaniel. Then I thought for a bit and added that I now have a dog. Tymofiy once also had a dog, a Fox Terrier named Charlie. He was distinguished for the fact that when he was riding in the elevator he would jump at the doors, bark as if he were mad and chatter his teeth; that's why, while Tymofiy was riding with him no one called the elevator. And when it happened that someone didn't hear him and called it, he would fly to the side so that Charlie wouldn't latch on to some piece of clothing. Men were especially careful because Charlie practiced jumping so well that his jowls would nearly touch their groin. It was appalling. I scratched myself. There was something in the pocket of my jeans – Eva's business card. "Personal sewing of clothing for your pets." Well, since the mail is working… "Hey, Eva. I wrote a few words to Tymofiy about you. I didn't tell him you were trying to latch onto old man Polonsky, but I want to tell you that it looked disgusting. Besides that, he doesn't like the style of your clothing. But, all in all, I was happy to see you. Thank you for the Fabulous Angel."

The clock was hinting at approaching midnight. And I received an email. From Eva. The witch. She wrote: "Sweatrobber1. All in all I'm also happy." "What's sweatrobber1?" "*Pit* (sweat in Ukrainian) is *pot* (sweat in Russian), *kradiy* (a robber in Ukrainian) is *vor* (a robber in Russian), 1 is a. MONSTER, he-he." I decided that I should have the last word, so I answered that I didn't know how sensitive she was and crazy to fall under the influence of the dodger and simpleton Milik, he-he.

Romko and Tymofiy were either sleeping or busy with something more interesting than emailing. That's nothing, they'll receive this sometime. "3.1415926535gift. Kisses." There, Sweatrobber1, I can't compete with her in similar rebuses, that's beyond my powers. But all the same, the last word was mine, because I sent her "kisses," to which she didn't react. No guts. And I was coping with that. Now let's open the file "Orcinus orca." Let's look how things are with Ziggy? He's moving his little nose, like he's sleeping.

"A sensation: WHALES and DOLPHINS = Pedophiles. A Camouflaged Known Swims to the Surface!"

That's how my article for Talliy began.

"Everyone knows that whales and dolphins love to play with children. Contact with them is used in many rehabilitation programs. Repeatedly we can see dolphins swimming up to the shore and playing with children. It's interesting that no one till now has asked a simple question: why do dolphins need this? Children love everything new and incomprehensible, but why children for the dolphins? Why do the dolphins allow unknown creatures (that's how they should perceive children) play with them?

It's worth saying that cinematographers and animators approach this issue indifferently. The whale Willy in the movie *Free Willy* and *Free Willy 2* was painted as a friend of children. They poetically sing the praises of the friendship of a little girl with a dolphin in the animated movie *A Girl and a Dolphin*. Hasn't anyone ever seen this as suspect? The same is true of the movies *Lake at the Bottom of the Sea** and *Underwater Berets***, and also the most well-known animated film about the adventures of the baby whale Moby Dick. It's worth noting that all these movies are either American or Soviet made. Does this not attest to the fact that large countries have taken advantage of the gravitation of whales and dolphins to children with

....

* Released in 1989 in the USSR as part of series of animated films about dolphins.

** Released in 1991 as a continuation in the dolphin series of animated movies and based on the prose tale of Eduard Uspensky.

a certain aim? Perhaps, this is one of the projects given birth to by the cold war.

It's interesting that a well-known expert on the animal world as well as the world of children, the old man Kipling, gave a human child Mowgli to be raised by a pack of wolves because he knew that if they don't gobble him up, he will grow up like a regular wolf cub; that is, it will not be imprinted catastrophically on his psyche. If everything were good with whales and dolphins — as pseudoscholars constantly assure us – wouldn't a classic writer understand that to give Mowgli to be brought up by whales is considerably more natural and safer? No, he was convinced that nothing good would come of a childhood trauma like rape, and it couldn't be camouflaged by various little lies. Mowgli becomes doomed.

New times are here, and all of us need to think about the strange presence of the attraction of the giants of the sea to our progeny. And finally proclaim the truth!

I wanted to jump to my feet, run to my bedroom and make a second bed cover out of Milik. A patchwork one. But I wasn't able to because I couldn't feel my bones. For a minute I imagined the expression on Talliy's face taking in the meaning of this whale masterpiece. Talliy's face, which treats the appropriateness and quality of the presented material with the very same elevated piety as the sheen of his own hair and shoes. I might not be able to work there anymore: Talliy might have even thought up the idea of me sleeping with his secretary. On the other hand, I don't think my secretarial transgression could change our relationship, but in combination with pedophile whales it might explode.

I sat and reread the last paragraph of my file. I made the cursor run along the screen and then I saw that "Orcinus Orca1" exists. Mechanically, not expecting anything, I opened the clone file and noticed my old file. Ooops. In small green letters at the end was written: "And isn't it shameful for you to honor perverted monsters? For all these fascinating verbal layers? You'll receive an instructive lesson for your flippancy. Respectfully yours, a victim of whale group sex. PAIX." I burst out laughing. Very quietly, just through my nose. Terry heard the oscillations and glared at me from the armchair. Then he decided he wouldn't see anything interesting anymore and went back to sleep, touching the armchair with his wet nose.

The little monster. Sweatrobber1! Sweatrobber… A quite interesting being steals sweat. Maybe, they make deodorant from just that unlucky little beast… Or maybe this is the sweat of a robber? That surely is it! There's an abomination. The sweat of a robber is Milik. In any case, I saved my file under a different name and sent it to two email addresses. And suddenly this disgusting child being sneaks up at night to my computer and does his next perfidious act? Yes. We'll change the password. "Sweatrobber1." Then I came up to the ventilation window and lit up a smoke. I thought for a bit: I need to do something to this rascal. How does he start his abominable day? I'm not going to ruin my digestion. In the end, Mrs. Emilia is not at fault. Though in her place I would have thought long and hard before I conceived and before I gave birth to Milik. But did she know, poor woman, that she would jump into such a predicament? Poor women: they are given the good fortune to give birth (in my male reasoning this is good fortune all the same), but they can always be asked harshly: is it you who gave birth to such riffraff, a murderer, a rapist? And they don't have a single opportunity to jab their husband with their finger. "No, it's not me, it's all him!. Nothing will turn out. You gave birth to him – and you'll answer for it ….

I found it! Sarabande for String Orchestra and Piano by G. F. Handel. I tiptoed over to the "R. Yors & Kallmann" family crypt. Lord how it reminded me of a coffin! I need to check who had invented the piano, maybe some unknown coffin maker? I carefully pushed up the top and saw the little hammers, in which the guerilla fighting hamster of the old Saranskys used to hide. "So that's what you're like," he thought. From three napkins I made a gag. This will be a gag for the "R. Yors & Kallmann" family crypt; this will be a gag for the Sarabande for String Orchestra and Piano by G.F. Handel. This will be a supergag! Just now I should really think well where to put it. Here or there? Too bad that I don't read music. We'll put it in the center of the crypt. The little hands of nasty Milik will pass through the center one hundred per cent; it can't be that they wouldn't. Let him run, get anxious, shout out to his rasvetovyches, having heard the crestfallen sound or even two. A mangled chord – ho-ho! It was impossible to carry out a check: two dogs nearby, Gestapo and Milik on the other side of the walls – monstrous overseers.

I smoked one more cigarette and understood that it was time to go to bed. Tomorrow, as strange as it seems, I needed to go to work. I need to bring, like a decent guy, the material I prepared. And for an honorarium. That's tomorrow, and right now – to bed!

I woke up because someone was scraping a hole in my neck.

It was Terry. "Oooo. What do you want, you wicked canine warlock?" I tried to push him away with my hands. Nothing seemed to work. Something else was playing on the floor. I turned on the sconce light. It was Ziggy. Next to him was a puddle and a little pile deposited by him. His paws kept sliding apart, but he stubbornly kept crawling toward Terry's empty bowl. Oh, Lord, why, for what reason did I listen to Eva? Adam must have thought like this once too. But it was too late to think, as in my case.

I got up to make a kasha mix. I thought I'd have a lot of trouble, but I handled it marvelously quickly. Ziggy rapidly munched, and Terry peacefully slept in the easy chair. Maybe the kasha for the puppy didn't interest the old hunter. "That's all, friend. Eat your fill – and sleep." And I went to bed again. But Ziggy didn't want to sleep. He found one of Terry's rubber abominations and pushed it along the floor. He couldn't get to me – it was too high. Though he tried. Then he crawled over to Terry, but he started to snarl at him. Quietly, though convincingly. Ziggy yelped. "Gestapo will come in a moment," I said to him. "And you, little yelper, you're going to get it. What's it called with you dogs? Sleep!" Again he came closer to my couch and dragged himself on his short disobedient paws and whined so pitifully that I took him to my bed. How nice he is to the touch, a velvet creature. He licked my face, yawned, and then settled down on my neck near my ear. With his laid out paws he looked like a little piece of a puzzle. And he began to snore. Me too. The clock gave notice that it was 5:30 in the morning. Screw you! I cursed it in my thoughts. It struck my side with single sword. 5:31. My Lord…

CHAPTER VIII

In the least about the name of a fantastic footballer, mistakes in the perception of phenomena and things, female geography teachers, and also about the rules of letter writing to strangers.

"Hey," Terry noisily greeted me. I also greeted him and asked him to move over a bit because he practically had lain on top of me. Terry wouldn't stir from his spot. An impudent spanielina. I elbowed him. "Why are you doing that?" Terry began to scream in a voice very similar to Milik's. I opened my eyes. "Is that you?" "Who did you think, that the Lordy started talking to you? You need to get up. I've already been playing with your little one for half an hour, and it's time for me to have breakfast! And study!"

Ziggy crawled from Milik's knees to my chest, spreading out in the pose of a sea star. "To have breakfast – first of all." Lord, this little dude wakes you up his entire life according to his feeding schedule, and additionally has recorded himself among the Nobel laureates, an insatiable lazybones. I didn't want to rise up. My body ached, my heart was being pricked, my head was splitting. Harmony and unity! "Listen, what time is it?" "Almost nine!" Right there I rose quickly, because I needed to bring in the article about whales at 10AM.

"What's wrong with you?" "I need to run to work. Where's your father?" "I think he's already at work, what's he to you? Did he put on your favorite shirt?" "Why didn't anyone wind the alarm clock?" "Everybody wound everything. What, are we supposed to know when you need to get up? You didn't tell us anything like that. To wake up a person out of the blue – thank you, let someone else do that. One time I woke up Edik. Have I told you about him" Look at my left ear. And now at the right. Do you see the difference? The left one is sticking out a bit – Edik socked it." "Well, why did he do that to you?" I took an interest. I understood Edik well and instantly justified him. The Polonskys have completely normal relatives.

"You understand, he loves small women. Short and slender ones. When they are with him in one bed – you just don't notice them; they differ little from Edik's single leg because he's stocky. Here. Edik crossed two legs like one, but how did I know about this? I see – two legs. Here I fell on one of his legs. It turned out that it wasn't a leg, but his wife. She started to scream. Edik woke up and grabbed me by the ear." "Naturally. Better tell me where did you get the habit of crawling into bed with practically strange men? Do you consider that normal? Who is Edik to you?" "A relative. I'd happily crawl into bed with women. But mother reared me properly, and in general this is even more dangerous. Anyway, It's not my fault that I wake up early and I'm bored, and all you grownups sleep too much."

"Then Gestapo is already at work. What, he didn't even have breakfast?" The serious attitude of the Polonskys to breakfasts – that's a family mantra. It'd be interesting to know what they thought about Sara with her unsystematic nutrition and diets? "Why wouldn't he have had breakfast? Father woke up, had breakfast, even watched your TV and scratched your bulldog puppy, and you just kept on sleeping." "And the Sarabande?" What about the Sarabande?" "Was there a Sarabande?" "By Handel?" "G.F." "There was, you see that I'm already puttering around the kitchen. For half an hour already. Besides, I managed to take Terry out,

                    LARYSA DENYSENKO

feed him, and you didn't even react to me in any way. This crawled to you in bed, and you kept sleeping!" "And where is Terry?" "Snoozing under the table. Are you feeling okay, hey?" I didn't feel very okay. I was putting things in a satchel, pulled on a sweatshirt and jeans. "Can you make coffee for me?" The little dude, amazingly, agreed. And it's worth saying his coffee turned out to be not too bad. He even slipped me a bun. Buns are an integral component of the Jewish breakfast tradition.

"That's it, I'm off, thanks for the coffee. I need to turn in my article."

Here I hit the brakes because I remembered the damn whales, more precisely – damned Milik and my unjustly accused whales and dolphins. "Ah! Whales and dolphins, right?" The little dude winked at me. I got ready to relax for a quarter of an hour of explanations that what he did with my file is called treachery, but then I recalled the little hammers of the "R. Yors & Kallmann" family crypt and remained silent. People who don't hide an ax behind their back have a right to moralizing. If you've already sharpened your tooth on your neighbor – why look closely at his jowls? Instead I presented Emile Gennadiyovych Polonsky a heavy, even condemning look. Milik, judging from the playful expression of his kisser, easily elicited similar looks by just raising his pinky . He wanted to say to hell with them. "When will you come back?" He took an interest. I said I'll be home soon, maybe for supper. "I ask you please watch after Ziggy." He promised he would. I expect that the tortured notes of the "R. Yors & Kallmann" family crypt won't serve as a hindrance to Milik's nice attitude to my puppy dog.

Talliy, as always, silently read the text. I hated such moments. You stand there like a blockhead and don't know whether he likes it or not. You have to be so unemotional. "Talliy…" "Mnnn. Don't get in the way." Listen, may I work a bit at the computer while you're reading?" "Do I look like I'm standing in your way? Go and work. But you'll be interested to know that working with a laptop on your knees is considered to be ineffective and could cause impotency according to the American Psychological Association." "Talliy once again plunged into my text. To the whales and dolphins. I expressively saw him swimming in a well-practiced stroke. His hair was glistening, flippers too.

All the same I crawled into the laptop. Potency! At the moment my lively potency is hindering me right now. But in any case, I set up my laptop practically on my knee caps. An email from two clients. And what's that? An email from some nasty Volodymyr, who writes that my destructive attitude to taiga bears witnesses the fact that I am a "vile bohunk Ukrainian nationalist"; "strange that your name isn't Taras Shevchenko or Petlura Makhno, you bendera-like plague.*" I love reactions to my work. I even collect them in a special storage folder. Sara makes fun of me for that. I'll save this response without fail. Maybe it's worth pinning to the wall; how can I be any worse than Milik? I answered him that Makhno's name is Nestor, Petlyura's is Simon. Unfortunately, a person by the name of Petlyura Makhno doesn't exist. If such a clever person existed, he would stretch out his well armed hands to you. And instead of bendera-like you should write bandera-like, if you have in mind not Ostap

....

* The 19th century Ukrainian national bard Taras Shevchenko (1814-1861), the head of the short-lived Ukrainian state in 1918-1920 Symon Petlyura (1879-1926), the anarchist guerilla commander Nestor Makhno (1888-1934), who fought against the Bolsheviks among others; and the leader of the Organization of Ukrainian Nationalists Stepan Bandera (1909-1959). These Ukrainian figures are all reviled by Russian nationalists. Petlyura and Bandera, in fact, were assassinated abroad in Europe by Soviet agents. Shevchenko, Petlyura, Bandera, and to a lesser extent Makhno are Ukrainian national heroes.

Bender,* but Stepan Bandera. And if he doesn't believe me regarding the endangerment of the taiga forest bears – let him rub himself all over with goat fat, bedeck himself with open cans "tourist breakfast a tourist" and "embassy ham" and go visit the taiga. Then I'll have something to talk about with his inconsolable relatives.

While I enthusiastically scribbled my missive, an answer came from Avramovych. "Hey, Piggy! Avramovych really loves to make up sweet names. With this he reminds me of Tymofiy's mother. In former lives they, for sure, were relatives or consorted closely. "My (Sarusya, Virusya and Denyusya) are really in Mexico without any communication connection. I especially asked them to behave themselves there so that their perception of reality wouldn't spoil out-side civilizations. It's important for me for these itineraries to be built through immersion in the traditions and customs of the local population. They need to stuff their faces only in the local eateries. They need to eliminate themselves, excuse me, just in the local shithouses. And to use just local tele-phones. To live and breathe Mexico exclusively. I'm waiting patiently for their return. And why are you flinching? Have you ordered an amulet from them? Some kind of leather owl?"

"Nice work! It's comforting that there are profession-als like you." I heard Talliy say. "Thank you. I'm just hap-py that I at least exist to comfort. Listen, haven't you ever thought about dolphins being pedophiles?" "No," the candid Talliy answered. "It's clear. And right now if you thought I had ordered a protective amulet for myself, you thought it would need to be an owl?" I didn't calm down. "No." Talliy answered one more time. "You don't need to pose a third

....

* The hero of the Ilya Ilf and Evgeny Petrov comic novel *Twelve Chairs.*

question to me, if you please. Swallow it. You seem to have problems with your head." He forewarned me. "This isn't a question. This is an announcement. I have a puppy now." "I don't understand how you can keep dogs in the house. They destroy your shoes!" "There are closets for shoes." "There are cages and doghouses for dogs." Here we've had our little talk. It's good that the joke is cheering him up, that I'm a professional. "Maybe we'll step out to a tavern, Mac? For a coffee n' cognac?" When Talliy begins to talk in rhymed couplets – it's impossible to say no to him. And we coffee'n'cognaced several times over.

Yes-yes. Silence behind the door. The little dude is sitting at the kitchen table and is copying something in a column. "Hey." "Hey." "What are you doing?" "Researching a topic." "Which one?" "The bedrock for a Nobel Prize." Milik isn't very talkative today. I moved closer and read the following:
Valery Lobanovsky
Viktor Chanov
Mykhailo Mykhailov
Volodymyr Bezsonov
Andriy Ball
Serhiy Baltacha
Oleh Kuznetsov
Anatoly Demyanenko
Ivan Yaremchuk
Pavlo Yakovenko
Oleksandr Zavarov
Vasyl Yevseyev
Oleksiy Mykhailychenko
Volodymy Horily
Vasyl Rats
Ihor Belanov
Oleh Blokhin
Vadym Yevtushenko
Gennady Lytovchenko

Serhiy Yuran
Viktor Leonenko
Anatoly Byshovets
Andriy Shevchenko.

Next to them were separate piles of letters. Very similar to something like: 15 – "v"; 7 – "b"; 21 – "o"; 3 – "sh"; 14 – "e"; 6 – "ch"; 10 – "l"; 4 – "sh" 16 "n"; 13 – "a"; 3 – "ya"; 10 – "k"; 5 – "r"; 1 – "d."

"What's that? You're copying a paper 'The Pride of Ukrainian Soccer?'" "Remember this day!" Emile Polonsky said to me. "You're a witness to the beginning of genuine scholarly research that without fail will have an influence on the development of Ukrainian, European and world soccer!" "I really beg you not to get on my nerves with your insanity." "Wait, you mean you're not interested?" I hmmmed. "So I see those names are familiar to you." What a little impudent bastard. "A little," I said, and hmmed again." It's like this! I want to analyze the names of all the prominent Ukrainian footballers. And as a result come up with the name of a soccer whiz!" In as much as I remained silent, Emile continued. "Do you do crosswords?" "Very rarely." "Have you figured out crossword jumbles in which you get letters first, from which you need to make a word? Well, how else can I explain this to you? You figure out the entire crossword. And gather all the necessary letters. And it comes out for you, well, say, GRINSEY!" Milik repeated "GRINSEY!" "And you walk around with this in your head, you analyze the letters, and suddenly – click, you've solved the puzzle, and you understand that this isn't the name of a Georgian prince or a mythological being, but SYRINGE!" Very interesting," I said. "And I'll also have it. Without fail there will be that 'click'!" "And you get syringe? How could a word like that come into the head of a person of your age and gender at all?"

"And what, is it a secret? Syringe? Maybe you became ill at ease after this, so sorry! Listen, well you can't be the way you are. You write such articles. You're not so dim at all! Don't pretend. I've also chosen a means of defense for myself… Here, in fact, our geography teacher, Enserpniya Serhiyivna, admires you. She collects clippings of your articles and quotes you in class. And right now what are you demonstrating to me? Oy, regarding the geography teacher. I nearly forgot!" "What did you not forget?" "Stop by to see her today, please." "Whom?" "The geography teacher!" "And tell her that I'm your father? What a mess have you already made? What did you do to her? Have you drawn an extra continent on the globe or erased Australia?" "I haven't done anything to her, or to the globe either. I'm not a pervert. And in general I'm a good student. In a certain sense you've done something to her." "?" "You are her idol. A luminary of geography, a projector of tourist itineraries, a master of geographic opuses. She dreams of meeting you personally." "What have you yapped to her about me?" "Nothing special." "Special. But what?" "I said you're nice, that you're my uncle and you'd be happy to chat with her. Everything else she's read in those magazines that publish you. Well… maybe, she's fantasized something there, you know, a fifty-three year old woman is capable of fantasizing sooomething at which you can be pleasantly surprised!"

"That's it! Enough!" "You're such a psycho…" "Wait with your Harpiya Serhiyivna. I'll think a bit whether I should meet her or not. Explain your damned SYRINGE to me!" The little dude hung his head. "Well, I'm trying to explain it to you, but you don't understand anything!!! And you seem to be completely drunk." "That's slander." "So why is the coordination of your movements so uncertain? You're jabbing me with your head." "I've gotten food poisoning. You know how that happens when you have dinner out?" "What did you eat?" "Nothing special. Japanese food. Rice. Snails.

Eel." "Just that?" "Of course. I wouldn't have been able to forget so quickly what I ate an hour ago." "I'm simply asking because that rice, snails and eel definitely reek of cognac."

An observant little riffraff. I decided to turn his attention back to the footballers with a syringe. "Better for us to talk about research. Than about the peculiarities of my daily eating habits. I don't understand? Good. Then try to explain some more. A real 'scholar' has to be persistent." "Good. I'm trying to put together the name of a whiz of a future football player. So that when a boy is born with that name, they'll snatch him up right away and take him to the soccer field, onward to victories!!" "Nonsense." "Not really! You'll see! You skeptics will all see!" "Of course there could be errors, but even right now one can see without fail which letters will be in the name, because certain letters come up a lot, certain ones a handful of times, and others are entirely absent! But "o," "n," "l," "k," "b," perhaps, and "v" will be there without fail! "Sh" and "ch" are not excluded. I'll be analyzing this constantly!"

The little dude had a surprisingly enthusiastic and fiery look! I told him that he should keep me in the know. "Is it interesting for you?" "Very." "And parallel to that I'll be working on which date and in which month that football whiz most likely will be born!" "Super, Milik! Goal. That is – bravo!" "And if you take into consideration the theory of nudging, everything will be entirely good!" "What kind of devilry is that?" "A theory. Very simple. When you conscientiously work on something, you stimulate the appearance of things that are linked to your activity or even to your thoughts. Here I'll cipher the name of the whiz footballer, and he'll be born!" "Children aren't born that way, dear Emile!"

"Very witty. But you know what happened with Harik?" "I can't even imagine. Either who the heck Harik is, or what happened to him." "Harik… well, it's unimportant. It takes a long time to explain." "Really? It's not linked at all to the old Saranskys, to Zhorik, Elka, or Yasha?" "Not at all." "And it's not Violoncello's nephew? I can't imagine." "Not often, but it happens. And so that you know, irony is a disease of the feeble! There! This is not the point. The point is that once at New Year's, and according to the Chinese zodiac it was the Year of the Boar, Harik's girlfriend gave him a stuffed piggy! No one other than Harik liked it. Harik's mother named it a muddy thing, because it was, in her view, dirty. But Harik really liked the gift because it was covered in mud stains. A unique piggy, camouflaged, and Harik named it that. Harik's girlfriend also considered the piggy unique and wished that the year for Harik would be distinguished in the very same unique way. And his granny said to him: Harik, child, get rid of that creature because if you don't you'll end up going to the army this year. Harik laughed that it was, so to speak, superstitious, that it was stupidity. But in the spring he was taken into the army." "Insanity." I said. "Of course it's insanity. The university where he was studying lost its accreditation; they cleaned out the military department, and poor Harik – was snatched; he was camouflaged. And for what? Everything in the Universe is interrelated."

"How much trash is in your head – it's awful. But all the same bravo to you. I didn't expect that you'd be so… creative!" You thought that I just know how to bang on the piano keys?" I decided not to stay on the topic of banging on piano keys. "I was mistaken, old man. Everyone has the right to make a mistake." "You're telling me about this? Don't you remember, I told you about Zhorik and Neonilka?" "It began. Listen, maybe you can stop accosting Zhora, let him sleep peacefully already." "That story isn't about him." "Then why did you mention him?" "So that you'd remember him. Because that story is about his son Lyonya." "So he has a son?" "He does. He has a son." "And what of it?"

"One time a friend of Lyonya's (well, his name doesn't mean anything to you) gave Lyonya a little box with something metallic in it for his birthday. And Neonlila thought it was an earring. There were even two of them. And she also thought if a boy gives another boy an earring for his birthday (even two of them!) in a nice box with a golden ribbon, what does that mean?" I guessed roughly what it might mean. "It means Lyonya is gay. You should have heard how that news hit her. She phoned mother three times a day and at night too. She really was crying, we all felt sorry for her. She loved Lyonya, but she didn't like homosexuals. When she saw them on screen or in the newspaper, she would spit. It turns out she was spitting at her own blood. Though my mother was surprised at Neonila's disgusting attitude toward gays. Having a man like Zhorik, who was a skirt chaser, acting like a drunk going for liquor, she had to value the fact that there are other men, who are above these issues. But you, yourself, know women's logic! Neonilka couldn't believe Lyona was that way. He. She, rather." "And what of it?" Again I got interested. "Nothing. Then Zhorik found that little box; and good that it was before Neonilka got into clarifying relations with her son. And it turned out that in that box were a fishing hook and a winter fishing lure." I started to laugh out loud.

"And there's also the story about chemo and sarcoma. For some reason old lady Saranska thought that their Elka had gotten cancer." "Lord, may God show mercy. What are you talking nonsense about?" "It's true. Elka said to her girlfriend on the phone that she was going for chemical hair treatment, though her hair was falling out, but nonetheless she needed to have it done." "And what happened?" "Old lady Saranska instantly thought that Elka had cancer. And she began to call everyone in our family." "Oho." I said. "Ehe." Milik reiterated. "And when Elka returned with terribly damaged hair, the old lady got even more scared!

And it was only afterward that it became clear that Elka had gone to the hairdresser's." "Your poor Elka, something's constantly happening to her." "Do you understand there are no accidents in life? There are a bunch of things that bear information for us. It's worth it just to find the cipher. Even fairytales. Here, look: a flying rug. It attests to the fact that we'll eventually have planes. And an apple that rolls on a plate and shows the future? That's the prototype of an ultrasound!" Milik got carried away a bit.

"There won't be any more stories?" "No! But there will be geography. So will you go over to meet my geography teacher?" "Listen, why the hell should I get involved?" "What, is that hard for you?" "Well no, it's not hard, but it's a bit idiotic in my opinion." "Give her the latest issue of a magazine with your newest article, it'd be nice if there was a picture of you in it, autograph it for her – she'll be really thrilled. You need to do nice things for people, bring them presents, isn't that so?"

So I went to do something nice for someone. I took her the gift. I can't believe it. Why am I doing this? I've never hankered to be Santa Claus. I've never wanted to dress like him. But right at this moment I have a gift package, and inside it there are chocolates and a bunch of magazines with my brilliant writings. Emile's school isn't far from my building, so I was lucky in this regard – not to have to elbow my way to the other end of the city.

She was sitting at her desk. An average woman. You might even call her elegant. Her blouse was a grayish pearl color, light slacks with a classic cut, and she was wearing pumps. Short ash-colored hair. She looked fantastic for fifty-three years old. She was reading one of the magazines, in which I published my articles. When she looked at me, I felt maybe the same thing that beginner-stars must feel at first. In her gaze there was both rapture and the impossibility to believe her happiness: is this really

HIM? She kept looking at me and touched her finger on a page of the magazine. Maybe that was my name under an article title. Or a small photograph.

I imagined just such a picture. I'm sitting on a bench reading the XXL magazine (maybe, I exaggerated with "I'm reading," let's say rather – I'm perusing it, when I suddenly see – the girl of the month. She's smiling at me and asking me to take a stroll. Or Steven Spielberg. And she says to me: "Hi, Paul! How sweet to see you, hiya…."

"Pavlo, is that really you? What a joy!" Stevie would have addressed me just like that. Milik wasn't mistaken, his teacher was sincerely overjoyed at my visit. "Good day, E-eee-eee." I knew that I'd forget her name. "Yes, it's me. I've come over to you. I've brought some magazines." "Sit down please, why are you standing! I'm enrapt by the way you write. Emile said that you are his uncle, but at first you don't believe such things. You know these young boys; they love to fantasize. But later I thought: but he won't say that his uncle is Cousteau or Thor Heyerdahl. So who knows, maybe he's not lying?" I wanted to say that Milik never lies, but immediately thought better of it.

"My name is Enserpniya Serhiiyvna. You can just call me Enserpniya, very pleased to meet you. You maybe are surprised at what a nice name it is?" Though it never would have come to my mind to put that name in the category of nice, in acknowledgement of the fact that I was amazed, I nodded submissively. "Oy, it's a bit of a long story. When I was born, they gave me the name Nataliya, and my entire childhood they simply called me En, and that's what I called myself. And later I went to school, and there were two Natalkas in our class: me and one other little girl. And what's interesting, they called the other Natalka En, too, so they began to mix us up because we didn't respond to any other name. To this day I don't like any natalkacoinages. So then they decided to call me –

En Serpneva,[*] because I was born in August, and her En Lyutneva,[**] because she was born in February. Are you following after the chain of events? Belletristic fiction, isn't that so?" I kept following.

"But why didn't they call you by last name? Then no one would have confused you. Do you have a last name then?" I took an interest. "Of course I do. But we didn't like it when we were addressed by our last names, we were children! Did you like it when people called you Dudnyk when you were a kid? I wouldn't have liked it!" I thought about it a little and decided I wouldn't have liked it either if they called her Dudnyk. "So then. My mother never addressed me by last name!" "Naturally." "We went to school, grew up, and when we received our passports, then En Lyutneva registered herself as Enlyuta, and I became Enserpniya. No one else has those names!" "She added joyfully.

"Very interesting! Thank you for that story. You have a really cozy office, but it's time for me to go. Things to do, many things to do." However Enserpniya thought differently. She began to boil water for tea. "What are you saying, Pavlyk, wait a bit. We haven't had the chance to talk about your writings, your journeys. I'd be interested to know about your thoughts on the teaching of geography in schools! We'll eat your wonderful chocolates now! Good-bye perfect figure!" She conspiratorially winked at me.

That's all I needed! I had no idea about teaching geography in schools. Little interested me about the teaching of geography in higher educational institutions. I was far beyond that. You can call me a writer. Recently I've been enticed by the approach of remaining at home, wandering about the Internet, and writing fantastic articles. And

....

[*]   Meaning "August."
[**]   Meaning "February."

sometimes I felt like seeing something with my own eyes. Besides that, I adored discovering new alcoholic drinks for myself, and discovering new alcoholic drinks is theoretically a sad and thankless business. "If not for wine, the devil take you all, and not a work memo." That's the way I roughly thought. But I didn't dare say that. No, not in this life. "Strictly speaking, I've never thought about the methods of teaching geography to be honest." I informed her. "Too bad. That's really too bad! In my firm conviction, you need to think about that. Every day! In as much as people such as you share your recipes for fascination with a subject, we would be able to educate a healthy, geographically active generation. What do you say?" I looked at her. "What do you say?" She repeated. "Definitely?" I tried to guess.

"That's good! Just don't forget to share your thoughts with me!" With "definitely" I hit the nail on the head. "Here's some tea." I took the cup. "You, surely, are surprised, Pavlyk, how it is I'm not asking which kind of tea you like?" "I laughed, just in case. But I was careful not to repeat the trick with "definitely." "But this is because I'm a very careful reader! I read your article about the proper brewing of tea! And here. Well?" "I guessed that I have to taste it. "Oh, wonderful, thank you!" "You see! If you've convinced such an old and stubborn woman as me about this, that she doesn't know how to brew tea, and then re-teach her – and this just with the aid of your word – then with young, supple minds, you're capable of creating miracles, Pavlyk, just miracles!"

And I thought what could I say so as not to insult her and have the chance to disappear from here? That would be a real miracle. She told me about her way of seeing the teaching process, about my articles, about how incredible Florence is, where she was this past summer (her sister lives there), about current information technologies, and about the fact that the subtropics are advancing. "Enserpniya Serhiyivna," I finally was emboldened to say. "Yes?" It seems I interrupted her thought about tomato phytophthorosis that has an effect on consciousness of a human being nearly in the same way as LSD. From where does she know about the effect of LSD? I don't even mention why to regale on phytophthora? "I'm sure you'll understand, I have a very important meeting. With experts on the diseases of tomatoes." I was already angry from goodness knows what. I was rambling on, but I wasn't able to stop. "That's why I'm very thankful to you for these thoughts. They will help me during my discussion. But I must leave you. They're waiting for me." Can this work? "Well?" A subsequent well. "Undeniably!" I said confidently. "Good, then till next week!" "Till next!" "Of course I'll still remind you, and we'll talk about the topic of your lecture during the weekend, but I'll start preparing the children for a meeting with you tomorrow!"

I couldn't understand, how did I agree to give a lesson to Emile Polonsky's classmates? He's going to pay dearly for this.

CHAPTER IX

In the least about former husbands of our women and former military guys, and also about the church.

"Good evening!" It would be interesting to know if they teach these investigators to speak in a kind of tone so that even simple words sound like accusations? Let the strength be found to endure her after Enserpniya. "Good evening. Eee… Tamara Antonivna." "Take this." With those words Tamara the cop put a stiff piece of paper in my hands. "Thank you." I said it just in case. The stiff paper turned out to be an honorary decree, signed by the Minister of Internal Affairs. "Is this expressly for me?" "To a certain extent yes." "For what?" "What's for what?" "What's this for me for?" I couldn't control myself. "This is an honorary decree for your little guy." "For Milik?" For what?" "An incredibly inquisitive person. You. You should work for the agencies. Your little guy asked if we have any honorary decrees. I said, of course, there are. Then he asked me to bring it. I brought it. I can't imagine for what reason he needs this. Maybe he wants to give you an award? Just don't ask for what. For today that's enough of this asking for what." We rode along further in silence. Tamara the cop and me with an Honorary Decree from the Minister of Internal Affairs.

The apartment again met me with silence. It would be interesting to know, to where did the Sarabande for String Orchestra and Piano by G.F. Handel disappear? Did my plan for stuffing up the little hammers work so well that the little dude has been unable to cope with the problem so far? Though… Maybe he's fidgeting till now with the ciphering of the name of the brilliant footballer? "Hey! Is anybody home? Terry ran out to greet me, said hello, and disappeared again to the kitchen. Is he feeding, or not? Ziggy didn't come out to greet me, it's hard for him: by the time he coordinates his paws – he's already tired.

In the kitchen where I made my way, besides the dogs and Milik, who occupied my couch, sat a man at the table in a long black raincoat. His gray hair was gathered into a thin ponytail, and on the floor, closer to the cabinets, lay a wide mattress. In my view, people who bring sad news home have just that kind of look. But I couldn't know if these people come with their own mattresses. It seems to me that this is too much – to simultaneously bring bad news and mattresses. It needs to be determined what to drag with you. On the other hand, maybe, this is "Rasvetovych," the one who repairs pianos? "Good day, Pavlo," in the meantime the Man in Black uttered to me in a deep penetrating voice. In just such a voice someone in the metro once tried to persuade me to give money for improving the conditions of Kyiv's children's playgrounds. I didn't give anything then, because our children's playgrounds still look like ratty little sheds.

"You, maybe, are a little surprised by my presence in your home. I'm Father Makariy." With his smile the unfamiliar Father Makariy offered me to rejoice over his presence in my dwelling. To be joyful that he called on me! By the time I collected my thoughts, the little dude grabbed the honorary decree. "That's for me!" "That is, you Father want to bless the piano?" For some reason that appeared to me to be natural. The piano was refusing to play – Rasvetovych couldn't help it because if the problem was an unclean spirit, Gestapo summoned the Father. "The piano? I don't see a need for that. Emile, child, do you need to bless the piano?" "He doesn't want to bless the piano! This is conscience tormenting you, you've stuffed your papers there!" Aha. So this scoundrel found the papers there and pulled them out without any assistance. Well of course, the future Nobel laureate. Sweatrobber1.

"And you don't know anything about me, yes?" I shook my head. Should I be embarrassed or not? What me, should I know something about him? Is he a well-known saint or something? Father Makariy. That's not a raincoat, but a cassock. Once Talliy's secretary said that a cassock would really suit her. I thought long, does she want to seclude herself in a monastery until it was explained to me that she had in mind a sari. If I were Milik, I would have told this wonderful story without fail. I avoided priests. I can't say that I was afraid of them or felt guilty before them. Nothing of the sort. But I never wanted to communicate with them. I don't know whether it happens to somebody else in the same way as it does to me.

I didn't even know how to address them. To be polite and to the point. I had a similar problem with military people. I'm not versed in military ranks, but at least they have little stars that you need to count (one star – this is one thing, two – something else, three – something else), and those have just a cross. One. For everyone. For them, for us. That's it. How do you tell them apart? "Your grace?" I tried. Father Makariy made a sign of the cross. Just in case – just in the way I thanked (just in case) the representative of the law enforcement organs, Tamara the cop for the decree for Milik. "It's entirely sufficient if you will address me simply as Father Makariy." For some reason I was anxious to ask whether they drink to "priestly ranks" and if they pour vodka on icons of the Mother of God on crosses.

"Why have you bugged your eyes out at him like at an ultra-right nationalist to the monument to granddad Lenin? Did my school influence you? This is Sara's husband. Valyerka!" Milik entered his corrections. "Take care of yourself, child! Behave yourself!" 'Valyerka' called down to Milik. I didn't like something. Is it not through old man Lenin that he pricked him? How could I keep from staring? Sara's husband? In my building? Dear Lord, he's a former military guy and now a priest. I couldn't have made up anything worse. I'm angry over this combination of personalities. As for me, it would have been enough for him to be either Sara's husband or a priest, or a military guy. No, he's managed to combine all this! Plus a beard and a gray ponytail. I won't be able to bear this too.

"Sara's former husband." I grumbled nevertheless, accentuating the word "former." "You're a military guy!" Indignation seized me. Though what kind of masquerade ball is this? A military man – okay be one. No, they had to discharge him in a cassock. Buffoons. "I once was, you're right. Beyond doubt." "That is, how is this once? You're an officer. I even remember your silhouette by our university next to a red car. What the heck is this?" "What does it matter to you? Here, what does it matter to you, what is he, Valyerka, occupying himself with? What's the difference whose orders he's following – the Minister of Defense or the Lord?" Milik took an interest. I ignored him. "Calm down. Haven't you or anyone of your friends ever felt the calling? Haven't you changed your destiny?" "I've changed it. But not this much. This is already too much." "How is this not too much? Your friend Tymofiy used to poison people with vodka and pills, but right now helps them with advice. This in fact is the same thing! The voice of the calling and a change in destiny!" Milik again said. "I'm going to kill you right now." I gave notice to the little dude. "My dear brothers, calm down. Think a bit about how important it is to maintain peace according to the conditions of war – by gender, age, the city and village…."

I didn't have a clue how to talk to him. Sara's former husband. Valyerka. The military guy. Father Makariy. I didn't know how to talk to priests. At least when I saw someone from religious orders, I felt like talking to them in whispers, but I didn't want to whisper the entire time in my own building. So, it was like someone had died here. As regards military guys, one question circled in my brain: "In what regiment did they serve?" I realized it was idiotic. And I sensed that without fail the conversation will later develop in the direction of: "A man who hasn't served in the army isn't a man. He's a woman. A woman who hasn't given birth isn't a woman." I hadn't served. I avoided it and would never recommend someone go to the army. But this werewolf Valyera won't be able to understand me. This military obligated rat isn't obligated to understand a civilian, he-he-he. Though, maybe, he would have understood right now that he is God's emissary. I didn't serve, that is, I wasn't a man, and didn't give birth, that is to say, I wasn't a woman, I was it – a being that the male and female worlds didn't accept.

For a change from the military guy and Father Makariy, to Valyerka, as to Sara's former husband, I had a lot of questions. In no way could I understand how she could have married him, how they lived together, why they got divorced, not to speak about the sad known first time of Sara, which gives me no peace. But how can I ask about all this when he's now in a cassock, damn him? (Forgive me, Lord! I expect you sense the difference between sincere believers and insincere servants of yours.)

"Have you had supper?" Again Milik asked. Finally I was grateful to him for this suggestion. Though more than anything I was itching to become furious at him. Valyerka's cassock restrained my becoming furious. Am I really so pious? Probably. But my piety didn't spread to Emile, that's why I went on the assault at the little Sarabandit. "You! Now with you. Why do you need a decree from the Minister of Internal Affairs? What's that to you, children's toys? You want to hang it on your wall to lay the foundation for a heroic image?" "Why not! Have you seen what kind of a family we have? A bunch of inadequate personalities, and now you've been added. And if suddenly there's something? And here — a blank! Just write down the last name — and everything's ready! You can show it to any judge. "A conveeeencing thingie" Konrad Karlovych would say. He then could rise up at the first stage of the lawsuit or, for effect, even a little later, announcing: "Respected court, respected parties of the lawsuit. I ask you to examine the petitions about the additions to the materials of the evidence of the defense No. 2 – an Honorary Decree from the Ministry of the Interior that was awarded to the defendant!"

"What Konrad Karlovych? What court?" "At first the regional court," Milik explained. "Konrad Karlovych Polonsky is a well - known lawyer from Zhytomyr, the actual head of the Zhytomyr clan of the Polonskys." Father Makariy kindly informed me about "State Harmony and the Law of the Polonskys." "You should have taken several decrees! But a little later about that." Father Makariy touched his cross, and I took Ziggy into my arms. Every person has something that calms them down.

"Let's have supper!" Milik the peacemaker began to get some food ready. And here I noticed this. I don't understand how I didn't notice this earlier.

One of my bowls filled with potatoes was centered on the table. Nothing extraordinary at first glance. Though I don't put out bowls with unpeeled potatoes on the table, but that's unimportant. The fact of the matter was in something else. A cross was depicted on all the potatoes. "What's this?" "Potatoes!" "I understand. Father... eh... What have you done with them, christened them?" Father Makariy's face filled with streaming goodness. Maybe he finally realized I'm a psychopath. And felt it with his skin: you have to conduct yourself carefully with me. Like with doves — suddenly one of them impregnated the Virgin Mary? Who knows what I'm yapping….

"In what sense?" Nonetheless he asked. "In the Ortho-dox, father, exclusively in the Orthodox." I answered. Father Makariy slowly blinked his eyes. Maybe he's not Orthodox? "Was he consecrated? Maybe you have that kind of program in the patriarchate: to transform every fruit in embryo form, that can turn out to be an insidious Buddhist, into an ardent Christian."

"What fruit? What Buddhists? What are you talking about?" Father Makariy demandingly looked at Emile, who, in his turn, cheerfully kept looking at me. "Emile, what is this about?" "About the potatoes," the little dude and I answered. Father Makariy put the bowl closer to his face. And crossed himself. "Dear Lord, what's this?" "That's what I'm asking you, what is it?" "Emile, what's happening with the potatoes?" If this is a joke, then I have to convince you: it hasn't succeeded, and I definitely will have a talk with your father this evening. Did Pavlo teach you this, child?" "I'm not his teacher, so that you know. I'm the lover of your former wife." I was on fire. "I see, this is what you mean." Emile responded, managing to put a pan and a crock on the stove. "At first I didn't under-stand. Mother marked the potatoes that are best for baking! She always does it like that. Let's eat!"

And we started to eat. "Listen," I still couldn't calm myself down, "But how did you, well that is, how did it happen that you…" It was difficult for me, oy it was difficult. "Come to God?" "Yes!" "Well what's so strange here in your view?" "It's complicated for me to fathom how a military guy can turn into a father. Well, not in the sense of a father, as a father, but in the sense of a Holy Father… In the Orthodox sense!" "You know, it seems to me that there is much that unites us besides God. For me, a military man, the statute then was my sacred thing, but for me now — it's the Bible. Rules, order, respect for higher ranks."

I remained silent and thought if it would be okay for me to suggest we have a drink. "Are you a believer?" I heard suddenly. "No, I'm an agnostic." I got up and crawled over to the wooden bottle stand for wine. An agnostic is allowed to do that. "Agnostic" is just a name for some disgusting subcutaneous parasite. You needed to call a person with a sober view of life that way. "Is it Lent now?" I took an interest. "No." "And nothing other than that?" "I don't know what you have in mind by other. Today, in particular, is a federal holiday of the Czech Republic." "We need to celebrate it. Do you celebrate this kind of thing, Father?" "I'm invited to the embassy." The disgraced one responded. "I definitely have to have a drink to that! Sara and I ultimately got together as the result of a real fake sailor, whom we treated to beer in Prague! And you, by the way, how did you get acquainted with her?" Suddenly my mood became better. I remembered the rose wine Rulandske Modre Rose of 2006 vintage, from the Moravian Bzenec winery!

"They got to know each other in Yiddish class. I didn't know you were interested in that, otherwise I would have told you earlier! You just needed to ask me, and I would have laid out everything like in a novel! Logically. Everyone praises me for that. I know how to tell stories logically." This was the first thing I heard when I arrived with the bottle. "Are you Jewish?" I asked Father?" "No, but he really wanted to be Jewish. Though my father always notes that everyone who believes in God isn't against being Jewish." "Emile! Be careful!" "And what of this? You yourself then said that there are no opportunities in the Ukrainian army, but in the Israeli one there is, and why wouldn't you leave to go to Haifa? He chose Sara because he thought that she would take him there!" Overall, I didn't know how to react."I didn't choose her for that reason." It was unclear why I said that. No one was interested in my thought. "But he – for that reason, yes! He wanted to dash off from his homeland!" In Father

Makariy's shoes I would at least say something because
Emile doesn't like silent pauses, unspoken futility. He fills
up everything instantly with words. There where your words
needed to be, he places his. Your three to his ten. You need
to be vigilant, Father Makariy! "But he was mistaken, because Sara is not one hundred per cent Jewish! Sara's mother
is a goy! This name of hers led him to a fallacy."

"How is that?" I asked again. "Yes! He thought that a
girl with a name like Sara can't be anything else than Jewish. And Sara obtained her name thanks to a compromise."
And here an insightful guess entered my brain. "So was Sara
named in honor of the old Saranskys?" "No, though they
often joked on that topic. Don't think that you're the first
kind of wit. They called her that because her mother wanted
to call her Sasha, and her father Radmyla. They pulled their
hair for a while, but then decided to call her either Rasa
or Sara to combine the two names. Sara won. Because the
name Rasa to everyone seemed to be extremely aggressive.
Though in my view, Rasa is vintage! Rasa Polonska   – wow!
And Valyerka didn't know about this!"

"Let's better drink to the Czechs!" I proposed, because I
began to feel sorry for Valeriy. I imagined that Inna's parents
could convey the reasons for us getting married. Though
from another point of view, if I had the possibility of listening to their reflections regarding a given subject, I would
do that. It would be interesting to know, like being present
at your own funeral. But I forgot that Milik doesn't drink,
therefore he won't become distracted by my proposition,
because for him it's not better at all.

With regard to father, he felt like drinking, but he didn't
know how to talk about this so as not to damage his own
reputation. "All of us in the family were against marriage!
Even Sara! But then she did this on purpose so that she
wouldn't be pressured. She demonstrated her maturity.
This is like smoking, screwing near a fence, spitting, drink-

ing cheap port wine. She didn't do any of that. Instead she agreed to marry Valyerka. Well, and she also was puffy, and it seemed to her that men weren't interested in her, except those who were distributing weight-loss pills." "Valeriy, that is, Fadda, er Father… eeeh…" "You can address me as Valeriy, what will that change?" "Thank you. While you were a military man, what did you do? " "He was an 'operator' in the Committee for State Security. He was busy with us, Jews, he-he-he. That's who he was. A reincarnation of the inquisitor." Milik was merry.

"Do you actually not believe in God?" Father couldn't think up anything other than that besides asking me just that. He ought to have asked an executioner too: "Are you really in favor of the death penalty?" "Once I was reciting the "Our Father" just before bedtime. And afterward I thought that was the same thing as the sayings in the Young Pioneer camp: you need to read them, everyone is expecting that from you, and you repeat to everyone: "To all, to all a good day, we greet all, all, all with a good day – we wrestle with the wind." I'm hearing that kind of comparison for the first time. But you can recite a prayer sincerely, isn't that so?" "Generally– yes. But you understand, I don't like lawyers and insurance agents who represent the interests of people. But in truth they just pump out money from them. Even more so, I don't really love the people of the Church, who represent the interest of God, in fact for those very same reasons, as the lawyers with insurance agents; they just have larger scales." "You know, I would not start accusing everyone as a group…" "And sorceresses? You accused them of witchcraft and accused them specifically as a group. Both the white and the black! And add the learned and the rebels!" Children of today read a real lot. I saw those thoughts on Father Makariy's face.

"Then I don't like that I can address God informally, and you just formally. Why is that so? In the end, my relations with God, these are my relations with God, what kind of relationship do you have to them? Do you hold a candle? You know how to do that, they've even made a cult of that. I don't need any mediators." "The Church unites people, it strengthens God's goodness, God's word; why can't you comprehend that?" "I don't need to reinforce anything. I hear well. And will it be interesting for you to find out about the fact that (here it was, as if Talliy has entered me) the Google search system for the word "party" gives 1,350,000 sites, and the word "church" – 965,000, but if you add the search results for the word "religion" (690,000), then a sad picture emerges. In fact, the party and the church even out with one another. And that makes me feel sick. Sites, hosting Internet pages: "order a prayer with us," "write a note to a bishop." You consider that normal?" "Education, the desire to master various sciences – have always been dear to the Lord."

Yes, it's clear, I need to drop my conversation with him. I was thinking so, but nevertheless I continued to rattle on: "Do you know, perhaps, what your young padres call the church? Shops! More precisely, like wheeler-dealers. Whose shop is the wealthiest, which is the poorest, which one is set up the best, which is the largest. And after all this you want me to go to church? With a pure heart? To bring my doubts, sins, and thoughts there?" "Maybe one such scoundrel can be found there for all of our brotherhood, but that is an exception!" for all of our brotherhood, but that is an exception!" "Really? One time when I was checking a new tourist itinerary, I was at a reception with the mayor; well, and of course, your church hierarchy was there. Without you not a single reception takes place. And then, one elder tells another lower in rank. "Therefore it's like this. If in the nearest time something exudes miracles, you can prepare yourself for work in the national economy!" From all this you're ready to make money. Even from a miracle. Like David Copperfield.* But he – unlike you – doesn't involve God in his matters."

"I see that you, Pavlo, are aggressively disposed. That's why I don't think we can have a dialogue. You know, when I was younger, I didn't skip a single discussion, but those times have changed. "But do you know, Valyerka, yours really are acting like bandits." Milik made himself be known. It was as if I didn't give a "pass" to him; I didn't scream "attack," but he came in. "Emile, you can of course, behave as you wish. As well as calling me "valyerka," but at least with guests in your own home you must conduct yourself with dignity." How touching.

By the way, about "the guest" and about the "house." "Father, be so kind as to tell me, I noticed a mattress here. Is it yours?" "Yes." Father Makariy answered respectfully, after meekly taking a look at it. "That is, if I understand correctly, you want to spend the night in my apartment?" "That's completely fair." As regards fairness and completeness, I have certain doubts. With regard to these things I have my own point of view. However I want to ask something else: why is this so suddenly?" "What?" "Pavlo is interested in knowing why you've intruded on him!" "Ah, about this. You have a point. We have a two-day gathering declared. In the Monastery of the Caves. As a rule I usually stay at Emile and Gennadiy's place, since they live close to the shrine, but as you know, they are remodeling their home." "Aha. They're remodeling, so you've come to my place?" "Absolutely. However, don't worry – tomorrow I'm already going to my rectory. The shops." He added and cut loose a smirk that wandered along his beard. Watch out, don't get scratched!

"What, for example, do your confessional disputes lead people to? The wife of my friend was getting ready to give

....

* The famous American illusionist (born 1956).

birth. She was already at the birthing center. Labor pains began. She was in awful pain, barely managing it. She walks around, hunches over, whispers for it all to end quicker, for the baby to be born quicker. And here among all the future mothers a padre appeared. And he began to offer to bless them so their labor pains would be easier. And what do you guess that nearly all the women asked? "What is your confession? A normal one or not?" Because everyone knows that you continually define where the true church is, and where it's not. You're always accusing someone and disenfranchising them of their status. So what can they talk to you about?" Father Makariy sighed. It's interesting to know if they have a black list? Well, where they enter the names of people, for whom under any conditions they don't absolve them of their sins. You come – the soul seeks atonement. Father recognizes himself as a composite picture. You try, you make a clean breast of everything. You believe in the forgiveness of sins. At the same times he twirls his middle finger under his cassock and meekly smiles at you: I forgive you for everything, and God forgives. But he himself… ruins your karma.

"May I smoke? That won't be too taxing for you?" "Me. Not at all. Cancer might tax you later. But your cancer doesn't tax me, if I may be candid. And, of course, I'll pray for you." You're a provocative priest, you see. And not a lover of children at all. A bearded billy goat.

"You'll give me the evil eye – I'll issue a grievance against you. Over your website. I'll inform them that you're a black magician." "A wizard!" Milik corrected me. "Emile, isn't it time for you to take a walk with Terry?" "You want to get rid of me? To talk about Sara? Good. You have fifteen minutes." I poured out some more wine. "Would you like some?" He took the bottle in his hands. "Despite the fact that Catholics made this wine, and Jews the bottle, the wine doesn't infringe upon Orthodox canons. As much as I've been talking to him – I haven't heard of a single rebellion. Father took a look at me in a way as if he were striving to understand what the words uttered by me tasted like. He remained silent.

"Do you really want to talk about Sara?" "Yes. She's a person not a stranger to me. How is everything with you?" "She's in Mexico at the moment. A work assignment. I'm feeling lonesome. I have the impression that she's been gone for a really long time. Though just several days have passed. But I constantly have guests here, new impressions, and I…" "I understand. Sorry for the intrusion, but you've saved me. I hate hotels. Even church-run ones. Gennadiy assured me that I won't get in your way." "Good that he didn't say that I'd be uncontrollably happy to see you. Though he could have warned me about it in advance. About the fact that you may drop by. Or at least about the fact that you're a man of the cloth." "Do you have any disagreements with the church?" "No. No disagreements with the holy synod either. But you understand, the realization of the fact that the husband of your wife was a military guy at the start of the relationship, then they got divorced, and then you see him in a cassock – gives rise to certain questions. You feel like rereading some tear-jerker novel of some Englishwomen."

"Are you reading novels by Englishwomen?" "Not every day. Just when my feelings get heightened, they steal my faith in humanity from me, or on St. Patrick's Day.

It's true, on St. Patrick's Day I exclusively read books in green covers." "Naturally. As regards Sara, my choice and our divorce. This all absolutely happened not because of Sara. Emile was right. We didn't love each other. Though we tried to live in the right way. There was one basic mistake in this – you can't live the right way just for the sake of living the right way. Do you understand? We were young and stubborn, though I can't comprehend why we worked on what was not there. Maybe we didn't fulfill our fantasy in childhood." "Did you really want to emigrate?" "Yes, I'm not one of those patriots." I grew pensive. I was one of those patriots. From which camp was Christ?

"And afterward when you didn't get support, you decided that it was enough of marriage for you?" "If you simplify everything (or complicate it) – yes it was like that. It was hard for me to live with Sara. She doesn't know how to sympathize, but knows how to feel life as a celebration. To live life as a celebration. But I need to sympathize, to quietly walk side-by-side, to be set at ease, and not to be drawn into the whirlwind of actions and laughter. I don't like celebrations. I don't know and don't want to celebrate anything. Just through the Church, right now, I came to the realization of the celebration of certain events, but as regards worldly solemnities – my thought remained unchanged. A celebration is an exception. Tiny bright sprinklings on the peacefully gray background of a carpet. I don't want to live with constant bright sprinklings that become larger each time. I need an ordinary life: gray, deep blue, white – without sprinklings, well, just with a few." I used to be jealous of people who understood what life they need.

"Often when I returned at night from being on duty, I saw her sleeping, squeezed from one side by Mueller, and from the other by Noiger. From them, she had bruises appearing here and there; her skin was really thin, and they're too hard. I came to the realization that there's no room for me next to her. How can I compete with them?" I flinched. No, I understand that it had passed, but listening to that is equally uncomfortable. The same thing as washing someone else's sperm-covered sheets. "At times one of them lay next to the bed. And then I put him in place." "Noiger?" "Or Mueller. More often – Mueller." All the same, military people are a particular breed. To find some Noiger or Mueller under the bed of your wife at night, yet still have the strength to put him back in place.

O Lord, a chosen profession. And what about a chosen people? More precisely, one of his daughters.

They say that Chinese wise men put really young Chinese girls in bed with them so they remain with their intellect. And what does a Jewish girl do? She sleeps in the presence of her living husband with Noiger and Mueller, in order to become wiser? Finally Father Makariy turned to me and saw the expression on my face. "Oh, I see that you're not…" He began to extricate himself. "How could you think that… These are – dictionaries! Mueller and Noiger. Dictionaries. That is, the compilers of dictionaries." He confused his own evidence. "What?" "Well, I have in mind that that's what the dictionaries are called. By the names of the compilers. English-Russian is by Mueller, and Spanish-Russian is by Noiger. Sara had a serious attitude to the study of foreign languages, do you understand? And you already managed to think God knows what." I understood and I managed.

I didn't begin to ask about Sara's first time. Or either about their first time together, even if those times coincide. Noiger with Mueller was enough. I felt like having a few drinks, but to get drunk in the presence of a priest was awkward. I didn't have enough daring, and because of that I got angry with myself. Milik fidgeted in his room and Terry destroyed his food. They returned from their stroll. We needed to talk about something, but I didn't know about what. "For some reason Gestapo's not here." "He has a meeting." "Can you find me some kind of blanket?" "Of course." Suddenly the cell phone could be heard. Father Makariy moved his hand under his cassock. It had the look of being on the border of propriety. Demis Rusos' "From Souvenirs to Souvenirs" was screaming from under his cassock. Why not with a psalm? On the other hand – Demis Rusos is Orthodox, that's for sure. It's not Tarkan beseeching from under his cassock!

And I'll be spending this night with that person. "Pavlo Dudnyk presents. The blockbuster *People in Cassocks*. The joint project of Stephen King and J.K. Rowling." "The great wanderer and the discoverer of the new-European continent, and suddenly a producer, Pavlo Dudnyk told us in an interview about how he slept with a priest, who in Soviet times was the husband of his wife. It is just this touchingly disgusting story that became the basis of a cycle of novels by the English writer J.K. Rowling about the alter ego of Harry Potter. Stephen King agreed to become the author of the dialogues." If I were to be honest with myself, I haven't moved far away from Milik. I need to stop making up stupid stories, otherwise you won't manage to come to your senses when you hang fake diplomas on the walls.

In the meantime, Father Makariy talked about "building objects": someone turned in building objects, and someone didn't accept them. If I had heard this conversation elsewhere, I would have thought that supervisors (true, believer supervisors , because the conduct of those who didn't accept secret objects, Father Makariy called not pleasing to God). "I need to play!" Here he is, my salvation. Sometimes he comes in the form of the Sarabande for String Orchestra and Piano by G.F. Handel. "I beg you, Milik!" Milik distrustfully glanced at me. But he didn't sit himself down next to the crypt immediately. At first this charming elfin child jumped up to the bottle with Moravian wine, filled a glass, and offered it to me together with an egg stuffed with chanterelles. I nearly started to cry, honest. "Here it's like the last glass of water that comes from the hands of a thankful child to the hands of its ill parents!" "You have to taste it. This way it's harder to get drunk."

Someone rang the doorbell. I was about to get up, but Father forestalled me. "Have dinner," he said indulgently and went to open it. And I continued to have wine for dinner. "Gestapo," I decided. But it wasn't Gestapo because Terry squabbled with the visitor. Besides Terry I couldn't hear anyone, so I got up to take a look what was happening there. My neighbor from below was looking at Father Makariy in silence. I didn't know what his name was. But I figured out why he had come. The neighbor was looking at Father spellbound, with the look of a lost child. For sure! Not often does a holy father open the door for you. Especially when you've come with the firm intent to argue!

I sought to help lost children, for which one time I was smacked by a hot-under-the-collar mother who gave me a good kick with her splendid Turkish shoe and made me into a pedophile. I didn't know my neighbor's name below, but I often saw him on the balcony. He smoked there. And I knew that he was an adherent of silence. All sources of a din – planes, children, street cleaners, cars, dogs, balls – he called the same, "sukanakh."* It sounds like a nice Arab name. And he threatened all "sukanakhs" that he would tear off their balls. He said the same to me, that is, to Milik, in fact, after the first performance through the last of the Sarabande for String Orchestra and Piano by G.F, Handel. And today from my mailbox I pulled out a small letter, on which was noted, who I was and what he would do to me if I didn't stop playing.

And right now the neighbor was looking at Father Makariy and didn't understand what to do with all this. If a person in a cassock turns out to be a "sukanakh," it is a lot harder to believe in that than one can imagine. Finally he uttered "Zxrrrggg." The face of Father Makariy shone with goodness. But even he, so mindful and generous in the light of feelings, couldn't understand what he wanted from him. "Sukanakh!" The neighbor said to Terry, made a sign of the cross and left. I want to add that a week later Sara

....

*   A composite bad word meaning something like "effing SOB."

          LARYSA DENYSENKO

and I took an hour to wash off the inscription: "A werewolf in a cassock – cross-sucker," which appeared on our door.

But this was to happen a week later, but today at night, my mother called to tell me my father had died.

CHAPTER X

The last. In the least about loss and discoveries.

"Pavlo, this is your mother, I'm sorry, it's late, but your father just died." Something kept thumping outside. I'm sorry it's late. I'm sorry, everyone. Mother was telling me about it, how it happened, and I was listening and nodding, though she didn't see it. I can't understand why I was nodding, and why I kept saying "yes" to everything. She was saying how "he got an attack, took his Corvalol*, it seemed as if it had eased." Then he got another attack, and they called for an ambulance. Father was then given an injection. They took his blood pressure and informed mother they couldn't see any problems. In fact, they neither got nor encountered any more problems from father. Because he died.

Something kept thumping outside. There were celebrations. The reality of my childhood in the twentieth century was thumping outside the window: housewives were thrashing rugs. The reality of my maturity in the twenty-first century is also thumping: the daily thumping of fireworks. The essence of what we have gotten used to is gradually turning into something else. From warm, comfortable and homey to distant, celebratory and from the street, remaining, at first glance, as the same: thump-thump-thump…

....

* Corvalol is heart medication and a mild tranquilizer, popular in Eastern Europe and the former Soviet Union. It is a transparent liquid with a characteristically strong aroma.

In winter, when I was a pupil in school, mother sent us together with my father to clean rugs on the snow. The snow had to be compressed a little with frost. You had to check whether it stuck together or not. If it was sticky – you couldn't clean the rugs. An interesting picture: a white backdrop with scattered rugs on it. Families were coming out into the courtyard. Thump-thump-thump, thrash-thrash-thrash. And then, meticulously examining which rug left the blackest imprints. It was a relief when that kind of imprint was left from the neighbor's rug and not yours. We care for our home well, our rug leaves a little gray, but after "thosefromapartmentfiftysix" – Mother of Jesus, it can't be any blacker. "And aren't they ashamed? What did they do with it?" "Don't mention it, I'd be embarrassed to take it outside." That was us. Those from apartment fifty-six. And we were ashamed a little, especially mother.

"Pavlo, we ought to... I mean – a funeral. Hello, hello, Pavlo, do you hear me?" "Hello, good evening. No, this is Father Makariy. Pavlo seems to be doing okay, but he is keeping quiet. Now, I'm sorry. Gena, Emile!" I was silent. Why didn't he call out Terry and Ziggy? A funeral. Such a stupid word. A thumping one. I'm sorry it's so late. "Fill up his glass... anything..." "Yes, I'm listening to you. I'm sorry, what's your name? Larysa Heorhiyivna, very pleased to make your acquaintance. And I am Father Makariy. No, this isn't a joke, no. How can you? I'm sorry? Who kind of sensed it? Pavlo? Well, we'll sort it out later. I've just come to a conference and am staying at Pavlo's place." "On tourism," I added, "Tours to hell and Eden are being organized. An all inclusive system. Discounts – for regular customers, he-he-he-eee." "Good evening, Larysa Heorhiyivna, this is Gennadiy Stanislavovych, the uncle of Pavlo's fiancée. That is, he has a fiancée? They live together, yes. What happened? No, she isn't with him now. It happens my son and I are with him now. No, my son isn't Father Makariy. Yes,

Father Makariy is also here. I swear I'm not Tymofiy, and we aren't consuming anything. It's a long story to explain, Larysa Heorhiyivna, I'm very sorry... Okay. Our apartment is being remodelled, and, well... Larysa Heorhiyivna, I'll gladly explain everything to you later. Still, what happened? Right. I understand. Allow me to express my condolences. Larysa Heorhiyivna, I understand how difficult it is for you, but perhaps we can try and talk about what we ought to do in the next few days."

Svitka called father "beach Jesus." Because he would tan just standing up. For this, father was leaning against a wooden lounger, laying it against a concrete beach wall. Father threw his arms around it, bent his head, pale and thin on the background of the wooden lounger-cross. I didn't like Svitka calling him that. From time to time I itched to fight with her, but I couldn't crack it, because I was no longer of that age when you fight with girls, and hadn't yet reached the age when you sleep with them. The line was thin, nobody explained anything to me, but when I wanted to hit Svitka – my own groin pressed against me and disturbed my concentration. I got nervous and left her in peace until next time, which quickly followed. And again my arms drew close to her, but stopped again. Svitka, the daughter of father's colleague, was older than me, wore short khaki-colored slacks and a large ("American," that's how mother called it) hat with an image of orange-colored eastern cucumbers. She was even invited to play cards and offered sweet wine. They could only play me like a fool – the prize for having eaten a bowl of soup in the sanatorium canteen, without playing any tricks. Not even a word was mentioned about wine. Father liked the fact that Svitka called him beach Jesus, and because of that, I itched even more to hit her. Father called her "fire-fly;" together they overcame long distances of water and discussed teachers from the biology department. Svitka was a student.

"Emile, what did you pour for him?" "Whiskey," Gestapo announced.

Mother was very fond of the color white, but never wore white dresses, shirts or skirts, because I've suffered from pielonefritis all my childhood, and reacted anxiously to white — it reminded me of medical personnel. But father always gave her white dresses as a gift. And once, he made her dress in white. "That's it. Enough," he said to me, when I stuck out my lower lip to pout disapprovingly. Then I left home for the first time. I ran away. How much I hated him, how much I hated him! I walked all over without thinking repeating "Ihate you hate you hate you you snake snake snake."

Once he wrote a book. About our cats. We always had cats living with us when I was small. I don't know who among us liked the cats. Maybe, they liked us (you can't know these things with cats one hundred percent), and that's why they lived with us. So, father wrote a book *My Cats* and asked me to read it. "When you have time." When I found the time to read it, I was as angry as much as I was that time when mother dressed in white. Father wrote about cats in a way that it seemed he was only concerned about cats. As though, besides cats, nothing concerned him. As though he was only looking after them, feeding them, cleaning them, scolding them for fraying the wallpaper and net curtains, running around to vets and nursing Yeremiy to health after he had jumped from the fourth floor and hurt his back. Father's heart ached when something would happen to the cats. It was he who was surprised that Inokentiy can eat pease porridge with pork. The cats and father, father and the cats. Mother and I, even when we appeared in father's cats' life, it was only to complain to him about the cats, the disorder and the messed up wallpaper.

But I was dealt a final blow by the description of how father put down Yeremiy and buried him. Father spared

no details. He told us how he found the vet, how he held
the incurably sick Yeryoma when he was euthanized. How
then he covered him with a blanket. In an hour he went
in to check: maybe Yeremiy was still alive? He touched his
frozen back, and here Yeremiy pulled his small claws in and
out. Already dead. And then he wrapped Yeremiy in a new
blanket and took him to be buried in a box. In an empty
plot of land under willow bushes. And how he cried then
and asked for forgiveness...

It was all like that, but father took and stole my memo-
ries. He didn't borrow them, but he specifically stole them.
Because, it was Tymofiy and I who looked for a vet, listened
to the hopeless verdict (Yeremiy had lung cancer), then
found another vet and yet another, but all of them said that
Yeremiy wouldn't survive and would suffer for a long time.
He was choking on blood, was often short of breath. He was
just constantly falling down onto the floor. It was dreadful.
It was then that we decided to put Yeremiy to sleep. It was
I who held the cat, when the vet made the injection. It was
I who was afraid to bury him alive, and therefore, couldn't
comprehend: had he died or not. It was I who touched his
stiff back, and with a spinal nerve reaction, Yeremiy showed
and hid his tiny claws, as though my touch had been pleasant for him... It was Tymofiy and I who looked for something to wrap him up in, figured out how to take him out of
the house, and he seemed so heavy – maybe we simply were
afraid to hold him in our arms wrapped in a blanket? It was
Tymofiy and I who found a little patch under willow bushes,
dug a hole and thought: was it deep enough or not; and then
thought: to unwrap the blanket or to place our cat on the
blanket. Finally, we placed the wrapped up Yeremiy in there,
and then sat long and reminisced about what he was like.
And it was right then that I swore not to smoke anymore.
Never. And I didn't smoke all year. Because, it seemed to me
that Yeremiy developed lung cancer because of me...

Father was justifying himself saying that it was a literary device. "Why are you raging? I remember that it was you who were taking care of Yeremiy, but it's a very powerful scene, how couldn't I have written it?" "How could you have written that it was you?" Because I was writing from the first person! It's more distinct; it's more truthful! What difference does it make, anyway, that it was important that cats were a part of our family?" Father was also suffering instead of me in the text. "Like a spider that had caught my heart in a spider-web, Yeremiy, my brother, will you forgive me?" I was almost thirty. But I was fuming like a teenager. How did he dare steal my feelings, my pain, my memories, my guilt? "How could you at all do this?" I said that I wouldn't talk to him anymore. Never. And I didn't speak to him an entire year.

"Pavlo, they say that your friend is working at the Secretariat of the Cabinet of Ministers?" "What?" "The thing is that there's an issue with the place." "With the place? At the conference?" "At the cemetery." "Do you think one of the psychos, whom Tymofiy is taking care of, is director of the cemetery?" "No. I think they have quotas." "Psychos do?" "The staff at the Secretariat." "Well... Maybe. So. Here's his number. But I never phone him so late. No need to disturb him now." "But you won't be calling him," Emile reassured me. "Valyera will phone him. Valyera is allowed to disturb anyone and whenever possible. Because the word of God has no limits." "Emile!" Gestapo shouted to the little dude.

I knew I didn't know anything about father. Nothing. Beach Jesus, who stole the life and death of my cats. I didn't know what tasted good to him, except strong tea without sugar. He joked about his habit – drinking strong tea (heavily brewed) and talked about being a thief in his previous life. In his previous life. And in this life, which now is already his past life, who was he? How can you characterize the relationship between two grown men, if they are best demonstrated by this dialogue:

"Hi. Hi. How are you? Not bad. And you? Good. Thank you." This isn't even enough to finish a cigarette. Recognizing each other in half a cigarette – of warmth and caring, nothing can be said...

Suddenly, in front of me, I saw beautiful female legs. It couldn't possibly be that Father Makariy has lifted up his cassock, he he he? No. It was not Father Makariy, who was trying to prepare a trap for us. It was Nona. "Nona?" To be on the safe side, I asked the legs. "Pavlo, hang in there, dear. God gives – God takes. My condolences. May the earth be filled with *pookh* [down] for your father." "Yes. With Winnie-the-Pookh. It's not funny, I get it. Anyway, Nona, what are you doing here?" "Here, I thought you knew about it. I'm a funeral director. I'll take care of your father." "I see. Father would have liked that. I mean, the fact that you'll take care of him. A pity, not when he was alive. The world isn't perfect, is it? So, it turns out that you're the angel of death, and not the Goddess of Nocturnal Emissions?" Nona remained silent. She didn't know how to answer that. I didn't know myself. She probably didn't quite hear what I said about Winnie-the-Pooh, but the Goddess of Nocturnal Emissions made Nona a slightly confused goddess. She didn't dare to smile. Even a sad all-forgiving smile. Damn it. How, anyway, does one react to sympathy? I could never express it, and never had to receive it, but now...

"Pavlo, ehe-hey." This is the little dude. "What?" "She really works at the funeral parlor. I thought you knew her. Haven't you talked to her?" "Little dude." "What?" "I've spoken to her, maybe, two or three times. I still have spoken to father more often..." "So what?" "That's the thing, that it's nothing. I – nothing. Not a thing. Nothing at all. I don't know about him." I was expecting that wretched Milik would now tell me something explicitly disgusting, or will re-tell me another Polonsky family story (or, maybe, a Saransky family one), but he simply placed his head on my lap.

People in black. Interesting, didn't they name an action movie like this? Mother held my hand. At the same time, she both supported me and held on to me. We became an object of permanent support. It was awkward. I haven't spoken to her lately, and, here, I found an excuse to let her lean on me: father's funeral. In short, mother had at last received it, if that's what she was waiting for. People in black were coming up, touching my jacket, that is, were hugging me, in support. Sometimes, I saw Tymofiy, but I couldn't focus on him at all, although he came up to me a few times and said something. I didn't understand who all these people were? My cell rang. "Pavlo? This is Eva. I've learned about your father. I'm sincerely sorry, hang in there, please! I can't come, because Tymofiy is there. Do you understand? I'll certainly call back later." You don't have to respond to sympathy. I couldn't make myself say thank you, it seemed crazy to me to thank? What for? For the fact that someone is saying a few words of sympathy regarding my father's death? Craziness. How crazy all this is. Father Makariy mumbled something appropriately churchy. "Mom, has father been a believer?" "Pavlo, shush." Mother is all about this "shush." If there had been less of this "Pavloshush" in my life, it's likely I would have known about my and their life a little more...

"Isn't this, Violoncello?" "Pavlo, this is Valentyn Yuri-yovych, he brought his musicians friends, Gennadiy suggested he do that." Mother, despite her daily confusion, was keeping things in order. I saw a woman alone not far from Valentyn. I saw her trying to control her own breathing. A slender woman, over fifty (though – who knows?). Instead of a black shawl, she had a black hair band on her head. It reminded me of Sara and Milik. "Who is that?" "That's Olha. Your father's ex-wife. I couldn't keep from informing her. I thought that at this kind of moment, it wasn't important who was to blame. It's not a time to weigh old debts." Mother intentionally didn't look in her direction. I didn't know anything about the fact that father had another family before us. "And where are my... brothers and sisters? Here somewhere too?" "No. Your brother died two years ago. A car accident." Interesting, is it always like this? Does a funeral always turn into a soap opera? Or is it only me who's lucky? Is it worth going up to her or not to express sympathy? Is it worth it or not to prop up her elbow, the way I'm supporting my mother now? In fact, she was also his wife. Is it worth it or not to come up and ask why no one ever tried to introduce me to my brother? What was his name, anyway? "Slavko. His name was Slavko." Mother responded, and I realized that I had uttered the last few sentences aloud. "Olha didn't want to introduce you to each other. He – too. Father. They didn't like crowds. Common dinners. Who needs it?" I kept silent. Slavko, for sure, didn't need it already. Oh, Lord.

"We got lucky – it's not raining." I flinched. Was this about work conditions and weather conditions that cemetery workers were talking about, or what do you call them?" "We got really lucky! Absolutely great! Super!" I supported them aloud. They looked at me with a totally indifferent expression on their faces: weunderstandyoursorrowbutyouareanidiot. Mother started to sway my hand. "Pavlyk, shush, calm down, I beg you, calm down. You understand nobody means anything bad." I can't say I was worried. It's late.

I couldn't eat anything at the table. "You have to eat – it's disrespectful, Pavlyk." Mother was saying. And not only she. "At least sip a little borsht, Pavlyk, you can't not so respect your father." "Disrespect." No, this isn't disrespect. Disrespect – it is, all your life, not feeling close to that person. Disrespect – is growing distant, disrespect – is not even trying to be friends. Disrespect – is only now trying to find various memories, rocking them, laughing, crying, getting angry, living together with them nearby. Precisely at this moment, living together, when he is no longer with you. This is what disrespect is. This, and not borsht. Disrespect

– is not knowing his friends. "Mom, who is that?" "Anatoly. Father's friend. They once used to work together. Don't you remember? He came to visit us." I couldn't remember. The majority of people who sat next to me now were eating, drinking, expressing their sympathy, saying appropriate words. They were people unknown to me. Still, the imposed attention of strangers is less irritating than the attention of relatives. I was a hopeless loner. Imaginary closeness through half a cigarette – this is what I could offer them.

How not funny or how not tragic this is, I was only recognizing friends or relations of the Polonskys. I nearly knew all of them. Violoncello came up and said that he remembered my socks, but didn't fetch them, because he thought it wasn't appropriate. I imagined him passing them to me in a little black plastic bag tied shut with a black ribbon. Nonsense. Good that I recognized at least somebody. Familiar faces were points of gravity for my eyes. They are like sticks for the elderly, when there's something to lean on. Familiar faces were what I could lean onto, in order not to lose sanity and not to fall down.

From time to time, somebody stood up with a glass in his hand and said a few words about what my father was like. I couldn't listen to it: it seemed as if all of them were lying. His first wife (still, who said that she was the first? Maybe, she was the second, third, nobody said anything, maybe father was a Blue Beard) didn't say anything about what he was like, as my father, her husband, the father of her deceased son. She was trying to look at all of us proudly, at my mother, at me, but her look was full of guilt. Like mine. That's why I felt an unexplained closeness to her, of which I was ashamed.

Suddenly, it occurred to me: what if father was killed? Then a detective would visit me. They always visit the closest relatives. He would have asked me, for sure, he would have asked: "What can you tell me about your father? Do you know how and what his life was like? Whom did he talk to lately? Did he borrow money from someone, or maybe, he owed it to someone? Maybe, he had enemies or problems with mistresses. Did father have mistresses? Maybe – a male lover? Was he interested in underage girls? Did he gamble at the casino? Did he drink? Have you noticed, maybe, he started suffering from depression, or was exhibiting strange behavior toward ordinary things? And what was your relationship with him? Good or bad? Did you experience arguments, conflicts, financial disputes?" And then what do I say?

I would offer him a drink. And would pour one for myself. We'd guzzle whiskey or rum – I don't know exactly what – and then I'd try to explain to a stranger how it happened that I don't know anything about my father. Not a thing. Not recently, or at all. Except... memories of childhood. "Have a look at the kaleidoscope of my memories about father," I'd offer. The detective would look through all the pictures three times. "Is that all?" "There are no other pictures in this kaleidoscope." And then he would give me an indignant look. Though... he is probably not that type of person who could be surprised at the likely state of affairs, he would have heard worse than this. But even now, when I'm simply imagining this, I feel disgust for myself...

"Pavlusha, but you mustn't be like this! If you don't want to eat – at least have a shot of vodka!" An unfamiliar woman with her hair pinned up with a black rose addressed me loudly and explosively. She has such an operatic face that I wouldn't have been surprised if she had sung to me about this drink of vodka. I can't recall when people needed to beg me to have a drink.

Milik sat next to me and was stuffing his face with chopped liver dumplings. "Tasty," He caught my look. "Why aren't you eating?" "I'm thinking." "About what?" "About funeral wreaths. There are so many of them and they're all the same." "It was me. I ordered them." "You?" "Yes, your mother asked me to." Probably, I should stop being surprised at either my mother's requests or Emile Polonsky's actions. "And what did you write on them?" "Wrote? Nothing. Who'd let me?" "I mean, what inscriptions did you request." "The standard ones. From the Internet." "What?" "What-what!" The Internet offers those kind of services: you can copy drinking toasts, cake inscriptions and inscriptions for funeral wreaths. It's a useful thing. Have you tried to invent inscriptions for funeral wreaths?" "No. Although... yes. I tried." "Well... I was burying myself. To a certain extent."

I became quiet. I didn't want to continue, because I would have had to say that, while I was burying myself, I imagined myself as Spielberg's successor. And the funeral wreath, the inscription on which I had invented, was specifically from him. Because I tragically died during the filming from a crazed cameraman's camera. The inscription from Spielberg was like this: "Overall, it's not important, whether a person feeds on a flower's nectar or is a cannibal, because at the exit everything is the same: shit. He didn't like people, but he never fed on them." Another wreath was from Bill Gates. It said: "In reality, a smart person stands out, because he uses logic to convince an idiot. He managed to do that twice." I still can't remember now what I meant especially by "twice," but I remembered the inscription perfectly. I've also invented how someone placed a wreath for me from Marilyn. It said: "Cinema kills the best." Perhaps, it was the wife of the cameraman. She got his insurance, my death helped her to get rid of her husband and obtain a significant amount of compensation for her life with this monster. I was proud of the inscriptions, but I didn't want to say anything to Milik about them.

"Are you sure you wouldn't like any memorial wake rice? It's with fruit. It's healthy. Really? That's good. And do you know you're a latent Jew?" "Don't talk nonsense, Emile."

"I'm telling you for sure. Nowhere, except in Jewish families; Larysas aren't called Lyalya Dolls. And many call your mother Lyalya the Doll. I've heard it." "Good. And do you happen to know, whether, perhaps, with us, Jews, it's not customary to commemorate nine days of a forty-day anniversary?" Emile didn't know it. But he promised that he would certainly find out.

It was quiet at home, everyone advised me to sleep a little. The chief devices for saving yourself that are used by a human being who lost another human being include: eating memorial rice from the wake with borsht and sleeping. None of the disgusting rubber things that my house was filled with squeaked. I didn't want to sleep. Strange, but I didn't even want to have a drink. I made myself tea. Like my father's. Strong with no sugar. It seemed more appropriate to me than a hundred thousand condolences and a glass of vodka covered with a slice of black bread.

"And did I tell you about Lola?" "Who is she, the Goddess of Nocturnal Emissions?" "No, it was my sister. She died when she was ten." "I'm sorry, I honestly didn't know that. I'm sorry." "In fact, her name was Lolita. Father named her that because he likes Nabokov. Have you read *Lolita*?" "What horror. Listen, forgive me for this goddess, for these nocturnal emissions, I honestly couldn't think that..." "So, have you read it?" "I've read it." "I'd never name my daughter that name, how about you?" "I don't know. I've never thought about children." "I just wanted to tell you that I don't remember her at all. Well, like you – your father. Because she never wanted to speak to me. She had her own life, friends, secrets, toys. She was very proud of the fact that the novel was named after her."

"You also have something to be proud of in this sense." "Of what?" "Have you ever read about Emil of Lönneberga?" "No." "Strange. With your inquisitiveness, I was convinced that you would have found out this information a long time ago. It was written by Astrid Lindgren." "Mother of Karlsson?" "Yes. Wait, don't disappear anywhere. I'll find the book now. I've got it. Here, listen. "Emil from Lönneberga. This was the name of the boy who lived near Lönneberga. Emil was a little prankster and very stubborn. Clearly, he wasn't as pleasant as you are. Although, by the looks of it, he was a skilful boy – what's true is true. But until he began to scream. He had round, blue eyes. His face was also round and pink; his hair was fair and curly. You look at him – a real little angel! But don't rush to be moved." Emile kept listening. "You know, if you don't take into account Emil's fair looks, then you are both very alike. Give it a read. These stories aren't that childish!" "Do you think father named me in his honor?" "I don't know. But on the other hand, you can thank him, that he didn't name you Dorian or Eddie.* In fact, he also didn't name you after Enei!"** Emile giggled. "Eddie is by Limonov, right? Yes, I've read it!" "But shall we read about Emil? At first – you, and then – I?" And we began to read about Emil. At first – I, and then – Emile. But then I fell asleep.

When I got up, everyone was still asleep. I, unhurriedly, took a stroll with Terry, who found something to do with every blade of grass and bush. I was thinking about Sara. The autumn air reminded me of her – the daughter of autumn. This was Sara. Sara was in the kitchen. There she was a disgusting rubber thing that squeaked every time I stumbled on the damn thing in the dark: two food bowls, two water bowls. There she was, the refrigerator filled with memorial food, which had been prepared by Emile. Sara was in the bathroom. There she was – gray underwear with

....

* The infamous picaresque Soviet period novel *It's Me, Eddie* (1977) by Russian writer and political dissident Eduard Limonov.
** It refers to the Cossack Enei in Ukrainian poet Ivan Kotlyarevsky's mock epic poem *Eneyida* (1798).

the face of Mickey Mouse, striped socks and the Dupont for Men cologne. Sara was Emile who slept in our bedroom. Sara was his impudent dreams filled with pictures. Sara fell silent in my study, where she was the printed schedules of the behaviors of cyclones, basic warm-up pants, elegant spectacles in a silver frame, as well as a flask in which sacred air was resting. And what of me? I was fond of this Sara, I was used to her.

And then she arrived. With leather owl amulets, with her sharp smile, with idiotic jokes, with active legs that left bruises on my back and thighs by morning; with her plans, her openness and crazy expectations. And – with her love. For me.

Once (I no longer remember which word or situation it referred to) I expressed my sympathy to Gestapo regarding his Lolita. "Pavlo, are You hinting at something in this way?" He asked me. "Hinting?" I was surprised. "Not hinting?" Gestapo was surprised. "And what do you want from me then?" I carefully looked all around me, as though – there was no one. "Listen, it was simply Emile who told me about it. At my father's funeral. I understand that it's difficult for You to think about it. About Lolita. But I wanted, please understand me correctly, to express my sympathy. Just that. Nothing else." "Sympathy?" "Sympathy." "What sympathy?" "My sincere sympathy." "Sincere. Thank you. And with regard to what, allow me to inquire, do you feel sorry for me?" "With regard to the death of your daughter. Really I don't understand, why are you reacting like this. If it's unpleasant for you, you should say that you don't want to talk about it, wouldn't I understand that?" "Whose death? Pavlo, if I asked you how you feel at this very moment, I'd be fooling you. I've long been worrying about the state of your emotional health. But, in any case, what are you permitting yourself to do? Is this a normal subject for jokes in your mind? Inventing daughters, and then expressing sympathy, because those daughters, so to speak, have died?"

My stomach was already on fire. Damn Milik. I can't believe it! It doesn't even creep into your subconscious. How can it be – inventing sisters and then burying them? I understand why he did it then, he really, thanks to this story, pulled me out of a state of contrition and fear, but at what price?! Psycho. "Gennadiy, I... got confused, I'm sorry. I've been overworked. I really didn't want to offend you. You know yourself – sometimes things come over me." "You mean, very often." I smiled. "And may I ask one more question?" "About dead children?" "Oh – no. About literature." "Hmm." "Do you like Nabokov?" Gestapo became pensive. "In principle, I respect his work. I can't say that he's my favorite writer, but – he's a master. Undoubtedly, a master. But what? "Well, nothing." I can imagine he'll be saying something about me to his wife today. And like this - almost every time. Horrors.

I've thought, should I give Milik's ears a boxing? But instead of jumping down his throat, I burst into laughter like a madman. I really am a psycho. As well as Milik, after all, as well as, to some degree, all of us.

* * *

Gennadiy Stanislavovych Polonsky still hasn't gotten used to my way of speaking, although we have dinners together rather often. In reality, we can read newspapers during dinner, exchange short remarks about food that we ordered, and drinks, which both he and I enjoy the taste of. And that's all. Sara laughs and says we're like characters from English comedies. I, sometimes, believe in this too, especially when Gestapo looks closely at me and says "Oh."

I no longer saw Father Makariy, though he came to Kyiv on business a few times. He got a new Jeep. Because of that, I couldn't restrain myself and sent him a text message: "To whom did the padre sell his soul for his Jeep?" To this he replied back to me with a liturgical psalm. At least, I called it that because I'm not really knowledgeable about the church liturgy and music. The only thing I am convinced of is the fact that the tune wasn't The Sarabande for String Orchestra and Piano by G.F. Handel. I've decided that our score is 1-1. By the way, Tymofiy is in regularly contact with him. They even held a combined event. I can't imagine what they did there, and don't want anyone to tell me about it. Though, I'm sure that Father Makariy is an elite exhibit in the collection of Tymofiy's psychos.

Once, a card with a Ternopil landscape arrived from Eva. It turns out that she's taking part in an embroidery exhibition, presenting her canine collection. I couldn't restrain myself from telling this to Gestapo. "If the 'elite' dress their house pets in national costume – not everything is as bad as we think." That was his reaction. I composed Eva a poem and sent it by text message:

"A doggie is sitting in a doghouse. In an embroidered blouse.

Evil people don't let it go to a club. To go dancing.

Handsome Sirko went there in his *zhupan*, Gennadiy Stanislavovych Polonsky

Another lady-bitch is dancing with him!

He walked along the fence – and didn't even stir his nose...

Here's the way to dress for damned male dogs!"

Eva replied that she doesn't understand, how with such talent, I don't work for the Ukrainian TV station. Mocking me, a canine fashionista. Last time, when we were visiting the old Saranskys, the old man was possessed by a new culinary project: "Bake a classic!" (or "Burn a classic!" He hasn't yet decided). Saransky was collecting recipes to be included in their works by writers, and with his own hand, he tested how they would come out if you used the recipe.

Nona fell in love with Violoncello. They met each other at my father's funeral. Everything began there. Up to now, I can't understand how it happened, but nevertheless – they are together. On the other hand, a violoncellist and a funeral manager is a harmonious union. At least they can work together. Very often this incredible couple comes to visit us. I observe them, not losing hope in understanding how such unions happen. Although, maybe, some don't understand why I'm with Sara or Sara is with me.

In spring 2008 we congratulated Emile, who had battled his way to (that is – won, pianoedout!) the first prize at the Busoni International Piano Competition. In reply to my greetings, I received a text message: "Hey, can you imagine, I've broken my wrist. A simple fracture." Ha! I didn't believe it and quickly wrote back: "You're either lying or have done it on purpose! Sweatrobber1." But he really did break his wrist. And not on purpose: he was helping his friend fix a training machine in the gym, and it didn't like the fact that he was coming toward it.

"Hey, listen, Ra!" "Hey, I'm listening, Lo!" "You know, better if our names were reversed. Ra suits me better than Lo. Lo sounds more feminine. Shall we swap?" "I don't think so. My name suits me." And how couldn't it suit her! "Listen. We need to go to Taganrog." "Oh, my Lord, Lord. Why do we need to go there? Did you do something disgusting to Talliy, and he decided enough of your "trendy" travels? "Let him sip some harsh Russian cabbage soup!" That's how he probably explained the choice of destination to himself." "Need to find a certain little boy there." "Whoa. Do you have an out-of-wedlock son there?" "Negative." "Is there an underground children's home where they give orphans away?" "Negative." "Did you stop there once at a hotel, and your Romanian sneakers were stolen, and now you've decided that you have enough strength to pay them back?" "Sara, stop it! No. We need to go to a museum there. To try

to arrange to buy one boy – for another boy." "Interesting.
We're hunting for a museum boy... aha... And if they refuse
us?" "And, if they refuse us, we'll go to the port, eat a lot of
fish, and then we'll dance the Sarabande there." "By Handel?" "Of course! By G.F.!"

To Get Ukraine

by Oleksandr Shyshko

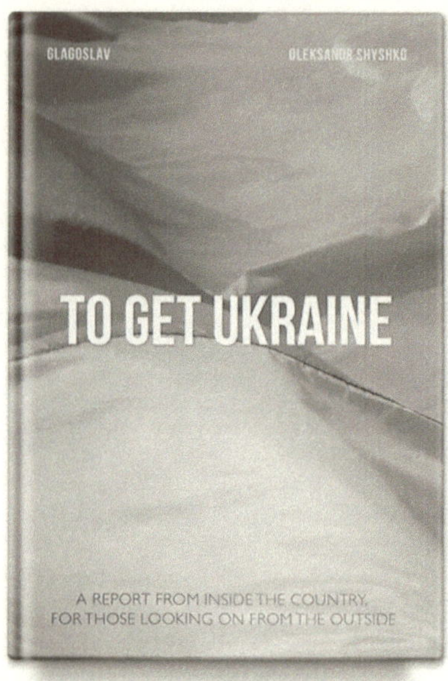

Since Maidan in Kyiv and Russian presence in the Crimea, Ukraine has never been the same. In 2014, the country is deeply divided by the conflict imposed on the Ukrainians. But since nobody actually asked the nation, author Oleksandr Shyshko decided to take matters into his own hands and look for the answer to the ultimate question – who are the Ukrainians and what do they want.

Shyshko spent his time researching the national identity of native Ukrainians, and as he went he stumbled on a discovery that led to yet another question – where is Ukraine going, the so-called Quo vadis? of the Ukrainian people. His findings and critical comments gave birth to this new book that is now for the first time being published in English. To Get Ukraine.

Buy it > www.glagoslav.com

DRAMATIC WORKS

by Cyprian Kamil Norwid

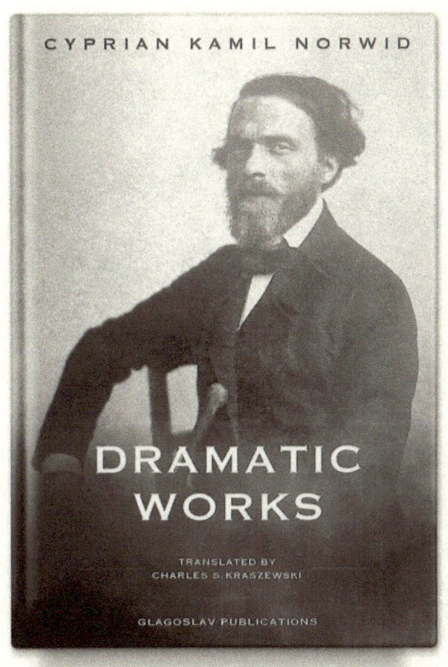

'Perhaps some day I'll disappear forever,' muses the master-builder Psymmachus in Cyprian Kamil Norwid's *Cleopatra and Caesar*, 'Becoming one with my work…' Today, exactly two hundred years from the poet's birth, it is difficult not to hear Norwid speaking through the lips of his character. The greatest poet of the second phase of Polish Romanticism, Norwid, like Gerard Manley Hopkins in England, created a new poetic idiom so ahead of his time, that he virtually 'disappeared' from the artistic consciousness of his homeland until his triumphant rediscovery in the twentieth century.

Chiefly lauded for his lyric poetry, Norwid also created a corpus of dramatic works astonishing in their breadth, from the Shakespearean *Cleopatra and Caesar* cited above, through the mystical dramas *Wanda and Krakus, the Unknown Prince…*

Buy it > www.glagoslav.com

THE SONNETS

by Adam Mickiewicz

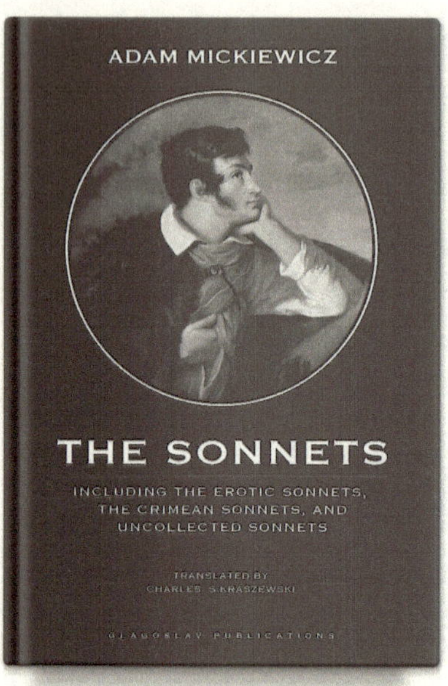

Because the poetry of Adam Mickiewicz is so closely identified with the history of the Polish nation, one often reads him as an institution, rather than a real person. In the *Crimean and Erotic Sonnets* of the national bard, we are presented with the fresh, real, and striking poetry of a living, breathing man of flesh and blood. Mickiewicz proved to be a master of Petrarchan form. His *Erotic Sonnets* chronicle the development of a love affair from its first stirrings to its disillusioning denouement, at times in a bitingly sardonic tone. *The Crimean Sonnets*, a verse account of his journeys through the beautiful Crimean Peninsula, constitute the most perfect cycle of descriptive sonnets since du Bellay. *The Sonnets* of Adam Mickiewicz are given in the original Polish, in facing-page format, with English verse translations by Charles S. Kraszewski. Along with the entirety of the Crimean and Erotic Sonnets, other "loose" sonnets by Mickiewicz are included, which provide the reader with the most comprehensive collection to date of Mickiewicz's sonneteering. Fronted with a critical introduction, *The Sonnets* of Adam Mickiewicz also contain generous textual notes by the poet and the translator.

A BURGLAR OF THE BETTER SORT

by Tytus Czyżewski

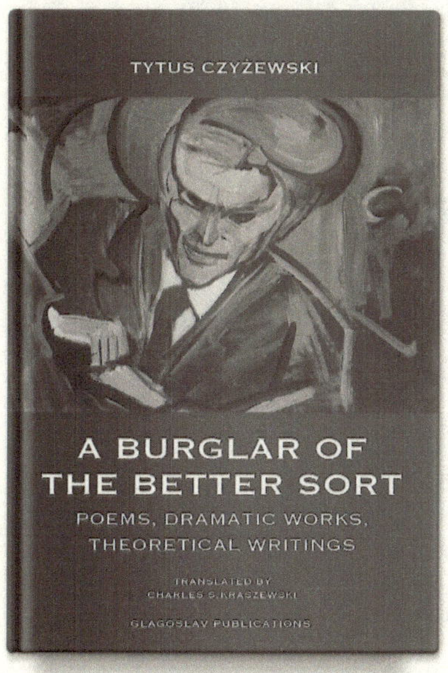

The history of Poland, since the eighteenth century, has been marked by an almost unending struggle for survival. From 1795 through 1945, she was partitioned four times by her stronger neighbours, most of whom were intent on suppressing if not eradicating Polish culture. It is not surprising, then, that much of the great literature written in modern Poland has been politically and patriotically engaged. Yet there is a second current as well, that of authors devoted above all to the craft of literary expression, creating 'art for art's sake,' and not as a didactic national service. Such a poet is Tytus Czyżewski, one of the chief, and most interesting, literary figures of the twentieth century. Growing to maturity in the benign Austrian partition of Poland, and creating most of his works in the twenty-year window of authentic Polish independence stretching between the two world wars, Czyżewski is an avant-garde poet, dramatist and painter who popularised the new approach to poetry established in France by Guillaume Apollinaire, and was to exert a marked influence on such multi-faceted artists as Tadeusz Kantor.

FOREFATHERS' EVE

by Adam Mickiewicz

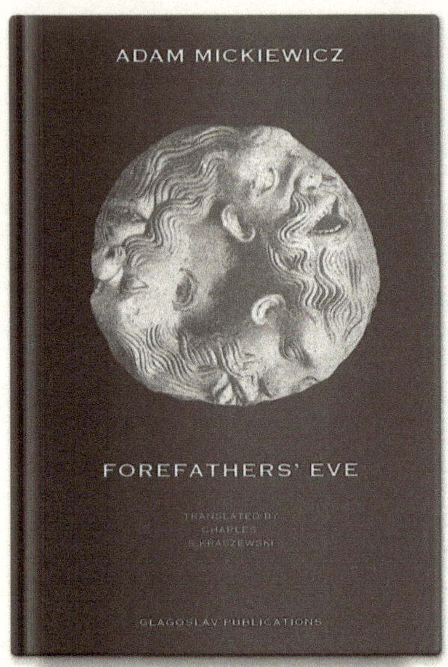

Forefathers' Eve [*Dziady*] is a four-part dramatic work begun circa 1820 and completed in 1832 – with Part I published only after the poet's death, in 1860. The drama's title refers to *Dziady*, an ancient Slavic and Lithuanian feast commemorating the dead. This is the grand work of Polish literature, and it is one that elevates Mickiewicz to a position among the "great Europeans" such as Dante and Goethe.

With its Christian background of the Communion of the Saints, revenant spirits, and the interpenetration of the worlds of time and eternity, *Forefathers' Eve* speaks to men and women of all times and places. While it is a truly Polish work – Polish actors covet the role of Gustaw/Konrad in the same way that Anglophone actors covet that of Hamlet – it is one of the most universal works of literature written during the nineteenth century. It has been compared to Goethe's Faust – and rightfully so...

Buy it > www.glagoslav.com

OLANDA

by Rafał Wojasiński

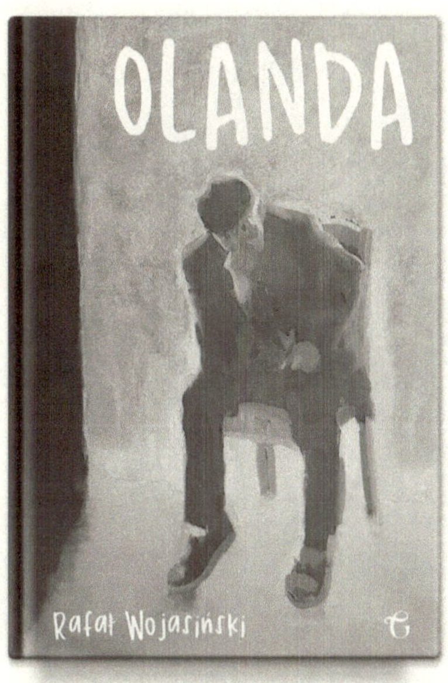

I've been happy since the morning. Delighted, even. Everything seems so splendidly transient to me. That dust, from which thou art and unto which thou shalt return — it tempts me. And that's why I wander about these roads, these woods, among the nearby houses, from which waft the aromas of fried pork chops, chicken soup, fish, diapers, steamed potatoes for the pigs; I lose my eye-sight, and regain it again. I don't know what life is, Ola, but I'm holding on to it. Thus speaks the narrator of Rafał Wojasiński's novel *Olanda*. Awarded the prestigious Marek Nowakowski Prize for 2019, *Olanda* introduces us to a world we glimpse only through the window of our train, as we hurry from one important city to another: a provincial world of dilapidated farmhouses and sagging apartment blocks, overgrown cemeteries and village drunks; a world seemingly abandoned by God — and yet full of the basic human joy of life itself.

Buy it > www.glagoslav.com

GŁOSY / VOICES
by Jan Polkowski

In December 1970, amid a harsh winter and an even harsher economic situation, the ruling communist regime in Poland chose to drastically raise prices on basic foodstuffs. Just before the Christmas holidays, for example, the price of fish, a staple of the traditional Christmas Eve meal, rose nearly 20%. Frustrated citizens took to the streets to protest, demanding the repeal of the price-hikes. Things took an especially dramatic turn in the northern regions near the Baltic shore — later, the cradle of the Solidarity movement, which would eventually spark the fall of communism in Poland and throughout Central and Eastern Europe — where the government moved against their citizens with the Militia and the Army. Forty-one Poles were murdered by their own government when militiamen and soldiers opened fire with live rounds on the crowds in Gdańsk, Gdynia, Szczecin and Elbląg.

Jan Polkowski's moving poetic cycle *Głosy* [Voices], presented here in its entirety in the English translation of C.S. Kraszewski, is a poetic monument to the dead, their families, and all who were affected by the 'December Events,' as they are sometimes euphemistically referred to.

A BILINGUAL EDITION

Buy it > www.glagoslav.com

HARDLY EVER OTHERWISE

by Maria Matios

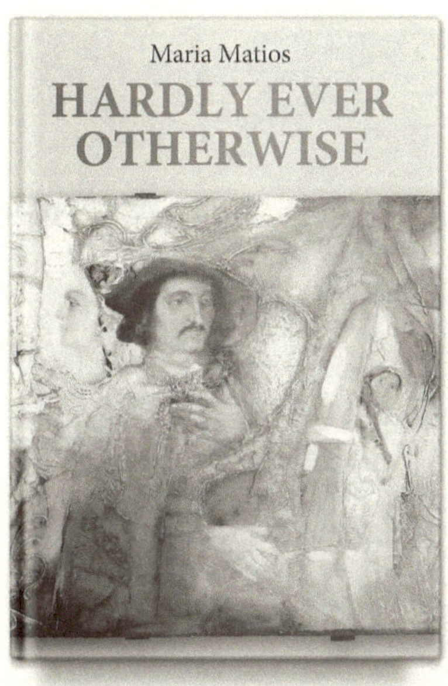

Everything eventually reaches its appointed place in time and space. Maria Matios's dramatic family saga, *Hardly Ever Otherwise*, narrates the story of several western Ukrainian families during the last decades of the Austro-Hungarian Empire, and expands upon the idea that "it isn't time that is important, but the human condition in time."

From the first page, Matios engages her reader with an impeccable style, which she employs to create a rich tapestry of cause and effect, at times depicting a logic that is both bitter and enigmatic. But nothing is ever fully revealed—it is only in the final pages of the novel that the events in the beginning are understood as a necessary part of a larger whole, and the section entitled Seasicknesspresents a compelling argument for why events almost always have to follow a particular course.

Buy it > www.glagoslav.com

The Complete
KOBZAR
by Taras Shevchenko

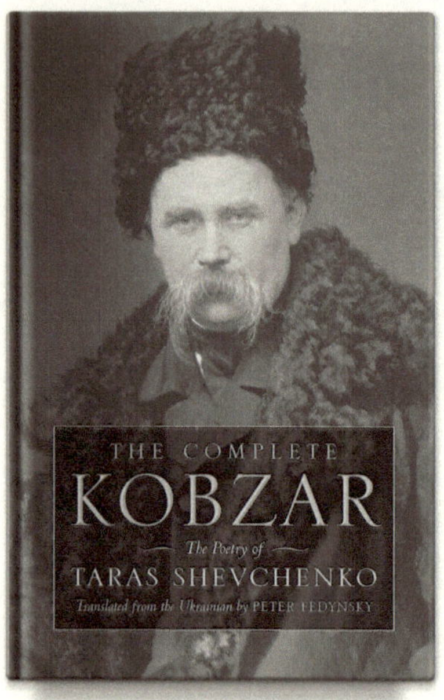

Masterfully fulfilled by Peter Fedynsky, Voice of America journalist and expert on Ukrainian studies, this first ever English translation of the complete *Kobzar* brings out Ukraine's rich cultural heritage.

As a foundational text, The *Kobzar* has played an important role in galvanizing the Ukrainian identity and in the development of Ukraine's written language and Ukrainian literature. The first editions had been censored by the Russian czar, but the book still made an enduring impact on Ukrainian culture. There is no reliable count of how many editions of the book have been published, but an official estimate made in 1976 put the figure in Ukraine at 110 during the Soviet period alone. That figure does not include Kobzars released before and after both in Ukraine and abroad. A multitude of translations of Shevchenko's verse into Slavic, Germanic and Romance languages, as well as Chinese, Japanese, Bengali, and many others attest to his impact on world culture as well.

THE VILLAGE TEACHER AND OTHER STORIES

by Theodore Odrach

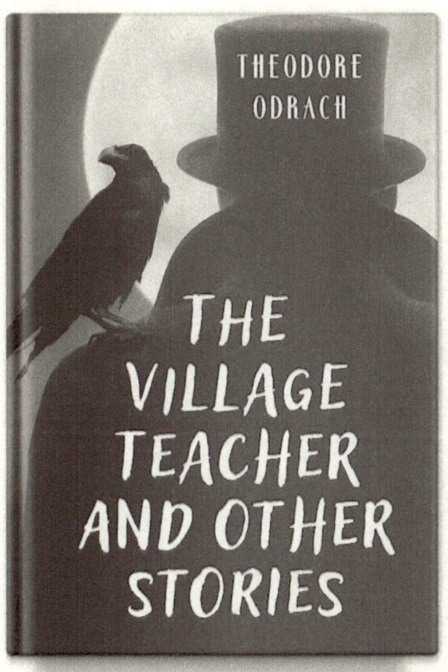

The twenty-two stories in this collection, set mostly in Eastern Europe during World War Two, depict a world fraught with conflict and chaos. Theodore Odrach is witness to the horrors that surround him, and as both an investigative journalist and a skilful storyteller, using humor and irony, he guides us through his remarkable narratives. His writing style is clean and spare, yet at the same time compelling and complex. There is no short supply of triumph and catastrophe, courage and cowardice, good and evil, as they impact the lives of ordinary people.

In "Benny's Story", a group of prisoners fight to survive despite horrific circumstances; in "Lickspittles", the absurdity of an émigré writer's life is highlighted; in "Blood", a young man travels to a distant city in search of his lost love; in "Whistle Stop", two German soldiers fight boredom in an out-of-the-way outpost, only to see their world crumble and fall.

Buy it > www.glagoslav.com

SUBTERRANEAN FIRE
The selected poetry of Natalka Bilotserkivets

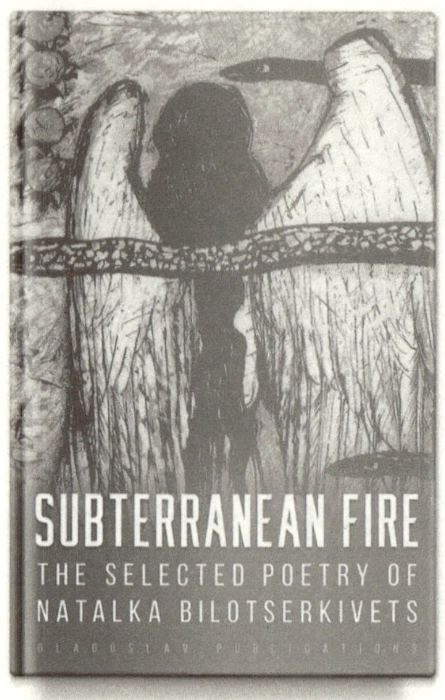

A passionate intensity moves through the subjective, intimate voice of the poems of Natalka Bilotserkivets. Through translation, Subterranean Fire continues their mysterious pilgrimage to their second lives. From one of the true inheritors – touchstones like Anna Akhmatova, Gabriela Mistral, and Louise Bogan – the poems of Bilotserkivets inhabit us as they include us in their transcendent borderland.

– American poet James Brasfield

With great depths of feeling, Natalka Bilotserkivets's poetry guides us into that uncharted territory where word meets heart. The poems, spare and often questioning, redeem that land between what is most difficult to grasp and most difficult to forget.

– Dzvinia Orlowsky, American poet and translator

Buy it > www.glagoslav.com

DUEL
by Borys Antonenko-Davydovych

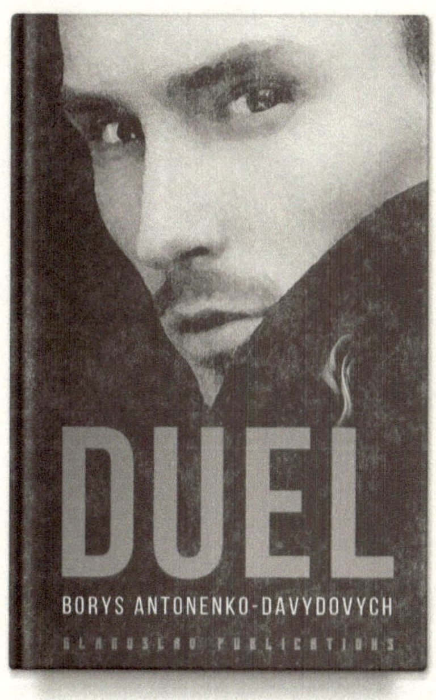

The central character in the gripping, psychological novel Duel is the Ukrainian intellectual Kost Horobenko. Set in the first years of the new Soviet Ukrainian state, the period of militant Communism, Horobenko, is forever duelling with his alter ego, the Ukrainian nationalist. This novel is one of a number of early works from the 1920s by Borys Antonenko-Davydovych, in which the writer tries to analyse the fate of intellectuals during the revolution in the Russian Empire, in particular the fate of those who were initially active in the Ukrainian national revival, and later, because of changed circumstances, were forced to switch to cooperating with the Soviet authorities. Of Antonenko-Davydovych's works devoted to this question, it is the largest and most profound, according to the literary critic Hryhoriy Kostiuk, and is psychologically complex and multifaceted. The works by Antonenko-Davydovych were welcomed for his rather sharp, satirical view of life.

THE LOST BUTTON
by Irene Rozdobudko

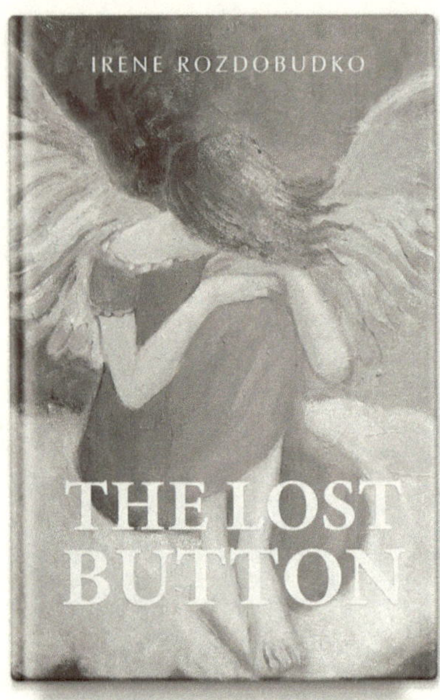

The taut psychological thriller *The Lost Button* keeps the reader transfixed. The novel encompasses an entire era from the mid-70s of the previous century till the modern day with its geography stretching over the European region including Kiev, the Ukraine's periphery, Russia and Montenegro, and at last the United States. It explores evergreen concepts of love, devotion, and betrayal and emphasizes the idea that whenever and wherever one lives, a tiny detail like a lost button has the power to set off a chain of events that would lead to either one's greatest happiness or one's greatest tragedy. It is about not looking back, but always valuing what you have – today and forever.

The Lost Button received first place in the "Coronation of the Word" competition in 2005 and subsequently was made into a feature film.

Buy it > www.glagoslav.com

- *A History of Belarus* by Lubov Bazan
- *Children's Fashion of the Russian Empire* by Alexander Vasiliev
- *Empire of Corruption: The Russian National Pastime* by Vladimir Soloviev
- *Heroes of the 90s: People and Money. The Modern History of Russian Capitalism* by Alexander Solovev, Vladislav Dorofeev and Valeria Bashkirova
- *Fifty Highlights from the Russian Literature* (Dutch Edition) by Maarten Tengbergen
- *Bajesvolk* (Dutch Edition) by Michail Chodorkovsky
- *Dagboek van Keizerin Alexandra* (Dutch Edition)
- *Myths about Russia* by Vladimir Medinskiy
- *Boris Yeltsin: The Decade that Shook the World* by Boris Minaev
- *A Man Of Change: A study of the political life of Boris Yeltsin*
- *Sberbank: The Rebirth of Russia's Financial Giant* by Evgeny Karasyuk
- *To Get Ukraine* by Oleksandr Shyshko
- *Asystole* by Oleg Pavlov
- *Gnedich* by Maria Rybakova
- *Marina Tsvetaeva: The Essential Poetry*
- *Multiple Personalities* by Tatyana Shcherbina
- *The Investigator* by Margarita Khemlin
- *The Exile* by Zinaida Tulub
- *Leo Tolstoy: Flight from Paradise* by Pavel Basinsky
- *Moscow in the 1930* by Natalia Gromova
- *Laurus* (Dutch edition) by Evgenij Vodolazkin
- *Prisoner* by Anna Nemzer
- *The Crime of Chernobyl: The Nuclear Goulag* by Wladimir Tchertkoff
- *Alpine Ballad* by Vasil Bykau
- *The Complete Correspondence of Hryhory Skovoroda*
- *The Tale of Aypi* by Ak Welsapar
- *Selected Poems* by Lydia Grigorieva
- *The Fantastic Worlds of Yuri Vynnychuk*
- *The Garden of Divine Songs and Collected Poetry of Hryhory Skovoroda*
- *Adventures in the Slavic Kitchen: A Book of Essays with Recipes* by Igor Klekh
- *Seven Signs of the Lion* by Michael M. Naydan

- *Forefathers' Eve* by Adam Mickiewicz
- *One-Two* by Igor Eliseev
- *Girls, be Good* by Bojan Babić
- *Time of the Octopus* by Anatoly Kucherena
- *The Grand Harmony* by Bohdan Ihor Antonych
- *The Selected Lyric Poetry Of Maksym Rylsky*
- *The Shining Light* by Galymkair Mutanov
- *The Frontier: 28 Contemporary Ukrainian Poets - An Anthology*
- *Acropolis: The Wawel Plays* by Stanisław Wyspiański
- *Contours of the City* by Attyla Mohylny
- *Conversations Before Silence: The Selected Poetry of Oles Ilchenko*
- *The Secret History of my Sojourn in Russia* by Jaroslav Hašek
- *Mirror Sand: An Anthology of Russian Short Poems*
- *Maybe We're Leaving* by Jan Balaban
- *Death of the Snake Catcher* by Ak Welsapar
- *A Brown Man in Russia* by Vijay Menon
- *Hard Times* by Ostap Vyshnia
- *The Flying Dutchman* by Anatoly Kudryavitsky
- *Nikolai Gumilev's Africa* by Nikolai Gumilev
- *Combustions* by Srđan Srdić
- *The Sonnets* by Adam Mickiewicz
- *Dramatic Works* by Zygmunt Krasiński
- *Four Plays* by Juliusz Słowacki
- *Little Zinnobers* by Elena Chizhova
- *We Are Building Capitalism! Moscow in Transition 1992-1997* by Robert Stephenson
- *The Nuremberg Trials* by Alexander Zvyagintsev
- *The Hemingway Game* by Evgeni Grishkovets
- *A Flame Out at Sea* by Dmitry Novikov
- *Jesus' Cat* by Grig
- *Want a Baby and Other Plays* by Sergei Tretyakov
- *Mikhail Bulgakov: The Life and Times* by Marietta Chudakova
- *Leonardo's Handwriting* by Dina Rubina
- *A Burglar of the Better Sort* by Tytus Czyżewski
- *The Mouseiad and other Mock Epics* by Ignacy Krasicki
- *Ravens before Noah* by Susanna Harutyunyan

- *An English Queen and Stalingrad* by Natalia Kulishenko
- *Point Zero* by Narek Malian
- *Absolute Zero* by Artem Chekh
- *Olanda* by Rafał Wojasiński
- *Robinsons* by Aram Pachyan
- *The Monastery* by Zakhar Prilepin
- *The Selected Poetry of Bohdan Rubchak: Songs of Love, Songs of Death, Songs of the Moon*
- *Mebet* by Alexander Grigorenko
- *The Orchestra* by Vladimir Gonik
- *Everyday Stories* by Mima Mihajlović
- *Slavdom* by Ľudovít Štúr
- *The Code of Civilization* by Vyacheslav Nikonov
- *Where Was the Angel Going?* by Jan Balaban
- *De Zwarte Kip* (Dutch Edition) by Antoni Pogorelski
- *Głosy / Voices* by Jan Polkowski
- *Sergei Tretyakov: A Revolutionary Writer in Stalin's Russia* by Robert Leach
- *Opstand* (Dutch Edition) by Władysław Reymont
- *Dramatic Works* by Cyprian Kamil Norwid
- *Children's First Book of Chess* by Natalie Shevando and Matthew McMillion
- *Precursor* by Vasyl Shevchuk
- *The Vow: A Requiem for the Fifties* by Jiří Kratochvil
- *De Bibliothecaris* (Dutch edition) by Mikhail Jelizarov
- *Subterranean Fire* by Natalka Bilotserkivets
- *Vladimir Vysotsky: Selected Works*
- *Behind the Silk Curtain* by Gulistan Khamzayeva
- *The Village Teacher and Other Stories* by Theodore Odrach
- *Duel* by Borys Antonenko-Davydovych
- *War Poems* by Alexander Korotko
- *Ballads and Romances* by Adam Mickiewicz
- *The Revolt of the Animals* by Wladyslaw Reymont
- *Liza's Waterfall: The hidden story of a Russian feminist* by Pavel Basinsky
- *Biography of Sergei Prokofiev* by Igor Vishnevetsky

  More coming . . .